also by Mordecai Richler

Notes on an Endangered Species
and Others

Notes on an Endangered Species and Others

MORDECAI RICHLER

Alfred A. Knopf   New York   1974

THIS IS A BORZOI BOOK
PUBLISHED BY ALFRED A. KNOPF, INC.

Copyright © 1962, 1965, 1966, 1968, 1969, 1970, 1971, 1972, 1973, 1974 by
Mordecai Richler

All rights reserved under International and Pan-American Copyright
Conventions. Published in the United States by Alfred A. Knopf, Inc., New
York. Distributed by Random House, Inc., New York.

These essays and reports first appeared, sometimes in a slightly different
form, in Commentary, Works in Progress, New American Review, Vogue,
Harper's, Encounter, Holiday, The New York Times Book Review, Book
Week, the Montreal Star, Macleans, Canadian Literature, the New York
Review of Books, and the New Statesman. I would like to thank the editors
for permission to reprint them here.
"Bond" and "Koufax the Incomparable," reprinted from Commentary,
copyright 1968 and 1966. "Why I Write," reprinted from Works in Progress,
copyright 1971, Literary Guild of America Inc. "A Sense of the Ridiculous,"
reprinted from New American Review, copyright 1968. "Gordon Craig,"
reprinted from Vogue, copyright 1965. "Notes on an Endangered Species,"
reprinted from Harper's, copyright 1973. "The Catskills," reprinted from
Holiday, copyright 1965. "The Great Comic Book Heroes," reprinted from
Encounter, copyright 1965. "Jews in Sport," reprinted from Book Week,
copyright 1966. "Intimate Behaviour," reprinted from The New York Times
Book Review, copyright 1972. "Following the Babylonian Talmud . . . ,"
reprinted from the Montreal Star, copyright 1970. "With the Trail Smoke
Eaters in Stockholm," reprinted from Macleans, 1962. "Going Home,"
reprinted from Canadian Literature, 1968. "Expo 67," reprinted from the
New York Review of Books, copyright 1967. " 'Êtes-vous canadien?',"
reprinted from the New Statesman, copyright 1969.

Library of Congress Cataloging in Publication Data
Richler, Mordecai, date.   Notes on an endangered species and others.
I. Title.   PZ4.R53No3   [PR9199.3.R5]   813'.5'4   73–20735
ISBN 0–394–48969–1

Manufactured in the United States of America

FIRST AMERICAN EDITION

For Bob and Audrey Weaver

and My Other Friends

in Toronto—

the Lefoliis and Fulfords,

Kildare and Mary,

J. G. McCl., and Sir Casimir's

Grandson Pete

Contents

Notes on an
Endangered Species
and Others

Bond

*C*ommander *James Bond, CMG, RNVR, springs from* a long and undoubtedly loyal line of secret service agents and clubland heroes, including William Le Queux's incomparable Duckworth Drew:

> Before I could utter aught save a muffled curse, I was flung head first into an empty piano case, the heavy lid of which was instantly closed on me . . . I had been tricked!

Sapper's Bulldog Drummond. And John Buchan's Richard Hannay:

> He began to snort now and his breath came heavily. "You infernal cad," I said in good round English. "I'm going to knock the stuffing out of you," but he didn't understand what I was saying.

There have been thirteen Bond novels in all, the first coming in 1953, the others appearing at yearly intervals until 1965, after Ian Fleming's fatal heart attack. On his initial appearance in *Casino Royale*, James Bond was thirty-five years old, an age he has more or less maintained over the years. He is some six feet tall, with a lean bronzed face vaguely reminiscent of Hoagy Carmichael, a ruthless set to his mouth, and cold grey-blue eyes with a hint of anger in them. When Bond was eleven years old, his parents, Andrew Bond of Glencoe, Scotland, and Monique Delacroiz of the canton of Vaud, Switzerland, were killed in a climbing accident; and so Bond was put in the care of his aunt, Miss Charmian Bond of Pett Bottom, Kent. At the age of twelve, he was sent off to Eton, wherefrom he was removed after two halves, as a result of some alleged trouble with one of the boys' maids. From Eton he went on to Fettes, his father's school. Here Bond flourished as a lightweight boxing champion and judo expert. In 1941, claiming to be nineteen years old, he entered the Ministry of Defence, where he soon became a lieutenant in the Special Branch of the RNVR, reaching the rank of commander by the war's end. In 1954, Bond was awarded a CMG, but nine years later he spurned a knighthood. He has been married once, in 1962, to Tracy, the Corsican countess Teresa di Vicenzo, daughter of the chief of the Union Corsa, Marc-Ange Draco. Tracy was murdered by Stavro Blofeld two hours after the wedding.

In 1955, Bond earned £1500 a year and had a thousand free of tax on his own. He had a small but comfortable flat off the King's Road, an elderly Scottish housekeeper (a treasure called May) and a 1930 4½ liter Bentley coupé, supercharged, which he kept expertly tuned. In the evenings Bond played cards at Crockford's or made love "with rather cold passion, to one of three similarly disposed married women," and on the weekends he played golf for high stakes at one of the clubs near London.

In the first Bond novel, *Casino Royale*, Bond confides to Mathis, his colleague from the Deuxième Bureau, that in the previous few years he has killed two villains, a Japanese cipher expert and a Norwegian agent who was doubling for the Germans. For these two jobs, he was awarded a double o number in the Secret Service, which prefix gave him a license to kill. Of late, however, he has begun to have qualms. This country-right-or-wrong business, he complains, is getting a little out of date. "History is moving pretty quickly these days and the heroes and villains keep changing parts." Finally, Mathis reassures Bond, explaining that there are still many villains seeking to destroy him and the England he loves. "... M will tell you about them. ... There's still plenty to do. And you'll do it. ... Surround yourself with human beings, my dear James. They are easier to fight for than principles."

Bond next agonizes over his double o prefix in the opening pages of *Goldfinger*, reacting to a dirty assignment:

> ... What in the hell was he doing, glooming about the Mexican, this capungo who had been sent to kill him? It had been kill or get killed. Anyway, people were killing other people all the time, all over the world. ... How many people, for instance, were involved in manufacturing H-bombs, from the miners who mined uranium to the shareholders who owned the mining shares?

Bond experiences another crisis (*For Your Eyes Only*) when M recruits him for an act of personal vengeance. To kill Von Hammerstein, "who had operated [sic] the law of the jungle on two defenceless old people," friends of M's. To begin with, Bond is sanguine: "I would not hesitate for a minute, sir. If foreign gangsters find they can get away with this kind of thing they'll decide the English are as soft as some other people seem to think we are. This is a case for rough justice—an eye for an eye." But once confronted with the villain in his camp,

> Bond did not like what he was going to do, and all the way from England he had to keep reminding himself . . . Von Hammerstein and his gunmen were particularly dreadful men whom many people around the world would probably be very glad to destroy . . . out of private revenge. But for Bond it was different. He had no personal motives against them. *This was*

merely his job—as it was the job of a pest control officer to kill rats. He was the public executioner appointed by M to represent the community. . . . [Emphasis mine]

Bond is not so much anti-American as condescending. Contemplating two American gangsters at the Saratoga race track, in *Diamonds Are Forever*, he wonders what these people amount to, set beside ". . . the people in his own Service— the double-firsts, the gay soldiers of fortune, the men who count life well lost for a thousand a year" (incidentally cutting his salary by a third since *Casino Royale*). Compared with such men, Bond decides, the gangsters "were just teen-age pillow-fantasies." But then, though he professes to enormously admire Allen Dulles, J. Edgar Hoover, and his CIA sidekick in many an adventure, Felix Leiter, he is not uncritical of a country where a fastidious man can't eat a boiled egg. When the villain in *The Hildebrand Rarity*, the coarse American millionaire Milton Krest, puts down England, arguing that nowadays there are only three powers—America, Russia, and China, "That was the big poker game and no other country had either the chips or the cards to come into it"—Bond replies (shatteringly, we are led to believe), "Your argument reminds me of a rather sharp aphorism I once heard about America. . . . It's to the effect that America has progressed from infancy to senility without having passed through a period of maturity."

Reflecting on the Russian psyche, in *From Russia, With Love*, Bond says,

". . . They simply don't understand the carrot. Only the stick has any effect. Basically they're masochists. They love the knout. That's why they were so happy under Stalin. He gave it to them. I'm not sure how they're going to react to the scraps of carrot they're being fed by Kruschev [sic] and Co. As for England, the trouble today is that carrots for all are the fashion.

At home and abroad. We don't show teeth any more—only gums."

While Bond risks his neck abroad, a gay soldier of fortune and pest control officer, ungrateful England continues to deteriorate.

James Bond slung his suitcase into the back of the old chocolate-brown Austin taxi and climbed into the front seat beside the foxy, pimpled young man in the black leather windcheater. The young man took a comb out of his breast pocket, ran it carefully through both sides of his duck-tail haircut, put the comb back into his pocket, then leaned forward and pressed the self-starter. The play with the comb, Bond guessed, was to assert to Bond that the driver was really only taking him and his money as a favour. It was typical of the cheap self-assertiveness of young labour since the war. This youth, thought Bond, makes about twenty pounds a week, despises his parents and would like to be Tommy Steele. It's not his fault. He was born into the buyers' market of the Welfare State and into the age of atomic bombs and space flight. For him life is empty and meaningless.

Duckworth Drew, Drummond, Hannay, carried with them on their adventures abroad an innate conviction of the British gentleman's superiority in all matters, a mystique acknowledged by wogs everywhere. Not so James Bond, who in his penultimate adventure, *You Only Live Twice*, must sit through the humiliating criticism of Tiger Tanaka, Head of the Japanese Secret Service:

"Bondo-san, I will now be blunt with you. . . . it is a sad fact that I, and many of us in positions of authority in Japan, have formed an unsatisfactory opinion about the British people since the war. You have not only lost a great Empire, you have seemed almost anxious to throw it away . . . . when you apparently sought to arrest this slide into impotence at Suez, you succeeded only in stage-managing one of the most pitiful bungles in the history of the world. . . . Furthermore, your governments have shown themselves successively incapable of ruling and have handed over effective control of the country to the trade unions, who appear to be dedicated to the principle of doing less and less work for more money. This feather-bedding, this shirking of an honest day's work, is sapping at ever-increasing speed the moral fibre of the British, a quality the world once so much admired. In its place we now see a vacuous, aimless horde of seekers after pleasure—gambling at the pools and bingo, whining at the weather and the declining fortunes of the country, and wallowing nostalgically in gossip about the doings of the Royal Family and your so-called aristocracy in the pages of the most debased newspapers in the world."

Richard Hannay, to be sure, would have knocked the stuffing out of just such a jabbering Jap. Hannay, in his thumping, roseate time, could boast that in peace and war, by God, there was nothing to beat the British Secret Service, but poor James Bond, after Commander Crabbe, after Burgess and Maclean, after Kim Philby, could not make the same claim without appearing ludicrous even to himself.

If once British commanders sailed forth to jauntily plant the flag here, there, and everywhere, or to put down infernally caddish natives, today they come with order books for Schweppes.

Duckworth Drew, Drummond, and Hannay were all Great Britons; Bond's a Little Englander.

England, England.

James Bond is a meaningless fantasy cut-out unless he is tacked to the canvas of diminishing England. After the war, Sir Harold Nicolson wrote in his diary that he feared his way of life was coming to an end; he and his wife, Victoria Sackville-West, would have to walk and live a Woolworth life. Already, in 1941, it was difficult to find sufficient gardeners to tend to Sissinghurst, and the Travellers' Club had become a battered caravanserai inhabited only by "the scum of the lower London clubs."

In 1945, Labour swept into office with the cry, "We are the masters now." Ten years later, in Fleming/Bond's time, the last and possibly the most docile of the British colonies, the indigenous lower middle and working classes, rebelled again, this time demanding not free medical care and pension schemes, already torn from the state by their elders, but a commanding voice in the arts and letters. Briefly, a new style in architecture. So we had Osborne, Amis, Sillitoe, and Wesker, among others.

The gentleman's England, where everyone knew his place in the natural order, the England John Buchan, Sir Harold Nicolson, Bobbety,[1] Chips,[2] and Boofy[3] had been educated to inherit—"Good God," Hannay says, "what a damn taskmistress duty is!"—was indeed a war victim. Come Ian Fleming, there has been a metamorphosis. We are no longer dealing with gentlemen, but with a parody-gentleman.

Look at it this way. Sir Harold Nicolson collected books because he cherished them, Ian Fleming amassed first editions because, with Britain's place unsure and the pound wobbly, he grasped their market value. Similarly, if the Buchan's Own Annual cry of God, King, and Empire was now risible, it was also, providing the packaging was sufficiently shrewd, very, very salable.

Sir Harold Nicolson was arrogantly anti-American, but after World War II a more exigent realism began to operate. Suddenly, an Englishman abroad had to mind his manners.

1 The 5th Marquess of Salisbury.
2 Sir Henry Channon.
3 The Earl of Arran.

Just as Fleming could not afford to be too overtly anti-Semitic, proffering a sanitized racism instead, so it wouldn't do for Bond to put down all things American. Ian Fleming was patronizing (Bond says of America, it's "a civilized country. More or less."), but whatever his inner convictions, there is an admixture of commercial forelock-touching. Where once Englishmen bestrode the American lecture circuit with the insolence of Malcolm X, they now came as Sir Stepin Fetchits. The Bond novels were written for profit. Without the American market, there wouldn't be enough.

Little England's increasingly humiliating status has spawned a blinkered romanticism on both the left and the right. On the left, this yielded CND (the touching assumption that it matters morally to the world whether or not England gives up the Bomb unilaterally) and anti-Americanism. On the right, there is the decidedly more expensive fantasy that this offshore island can still confront the world as Great Britain. If the brutal facts, the familiar facts, are that England has been unable to adjust to its shriveled island status, largely because of antiquated industry, economic mismanagement, a fusty civil service, and reactionary trade unions, then the comforting right-wing pot dream, a long time in the making, is that virtuous Albion is beset by disruptive communists within and foreign devils and conspirators without.

"[If you] get to the real boss," John Buchan writes in *The Thirty-nine Steps*, "ten to one you are brought up against a little white-faced Jew in a bathchair with an eye like a rattlesnake."

In Buchan's defense, his biographer, Janet Adam Smith, has observed that some of his best and richest friends were Jews. Yes, indeed. Describing a 1903 affair in Park Lane, Buchan wrote, "A true millionaire's dinner—fresh strawberries in April, plovers' eggs, hooky noses and diamonds." Elsewhere, Buchan went so far out on a limb as to write that it would be unfair to think of Johannesburg as "Judasburg": "You will see more Jews in Montreal or Aberdeen, but not more than in Paris; and any smart London restaurant will show as large a Semitic proportion as a Johannesburg club." Furthermore, like many another promising young anti-Semite, Buchan mellowed into an active supporter of Zionism, perhaps in the forlorn hope that hooky-nosed gourmets would quit Mayfair for the Negev.

Alas, they still abounded in London in Sir Henry Channon's time. On January 27, 1934, Chips wrote in his diary, "I went for a walk with Hore-Belisha, the much advertised Minister of Transport. He is an oily man, half a Jew, an opportunist, with the Semitic flare for publicity." Then, only two months later, on March 18, Chips golfed with Diana Cooper at Trent, Sir Philip Sassoon's Kent house. "Trent is a dream house, perfect, luxurious, distinguished with the exotic taste to be expected in any Sassoon Schloss. But the servants are casual, indeed, almost rude; but this, too, often happens in a rich Jew's establishment."

Sir Harold Nicolson's Jewish problem bit deeper. On June 18, 1945, he wrote in his diary, "I do not think that anybody of any Party has any clear idea of how the election will run. The Labour people seem to think the Tories will come back . . . the Tories feel that the Forces will all vote for Labour, and that there may be a land-slide towards the left. They say the *Daily Mirror* is responsible for this, having pandered to the men in the ranks and given them a general distrust of authority. The Jewish capacity for destruction is really illimitable. Although I loathe anti-Semitism, I do dislike Jews."

In a scrupulous, if embarrassed, footnote Nigel Nicolson, who edited his father's diaries, wrote, "H. N. had the idea that the Board of the *Daily Mirror* was mainly composed of Jews."

If Sir Harold Nicolson saw destructive Jews engineering Churchill's defeat, then Ian Fleming, an even coarser spirit, sniffed plotters, either colored or with Jewish blood, perpetually scheming at the undoing of the England he cherished. This, largely, is what James Bond is about.

Kingsley Amis, Bond's most reputable apologist, argues, in *The James Bond Dossier*, that in all the Bond canon ". . . there's no hint of anti-semitism, and no feeling about colour more intense than, for instance, Chinese Negroes make good sinister minor-villain material. (They do, too.)" Okay; let's take a look at the evidence.

The sketchy villain of the first Bond novel, *Casino Royale*, is one Le Chiffre, alias Herr Ziffer, first encountered as a displaced person, inmate of Dachau DP camp. Le Chiffre, a dangerous agent of the USSR, is described as probably a mixture of Mediterranean with Prussian or Polish strains and some Jewish blood. He is a flagellant with large sexual appetites. According to the Head of Station S of the British Secret Service, Le Chiffre's Jewish blood is signaled by small ears with large lobes, which is a new one on me.

The next villain Bond tackles, Mr. Big (*Live and Let Die*), is—says M, weighing his words—probably the most powerful Negro criminal in the world.

"I don't think," says Bond, "I've ever heard of great Negro criminals before."

M replies that the Negro races are just beginning to throw up geniuses in all the professions, and so it's about time they turned up a great criminal. "They've got plenty of brains. . . . And now Moscow's taught one of them the technique."

The comedy soon thickens. In New York, Lieutenant Binswager of Homicide suggests to Bond that they pull in Mr. Big for tax evasion "or parkin' in front of a hydrant or sumpn." Here Captain Dexter of the FBI intervenes. "D'you want a race riot? . . . If he wasn't sprung in half an hour by that black mouthpiece of his, those Voodoo drums would start beating from here to the Deep South. When they're full of that stuff we all know what happens. Remember '35 and '43? You'd have to call out the militia."

To be on the safe side, Sir Hugo Drax, the archvillain of *Moonraker,* is not a Jew. Instead he is cunningly endowed with all the characteristics the anti-Semite traditionally ascribes to a Jewish millionaire. He is without background, having emerged out of nowhere since the war. A bit loud-mouthed and ostentatious. Something of a card. People feel sorry for him, in spite of his gay life, although he's a multi-millionaire. He made his money on the metal market by cornering a very valuable ore called columbite. Sir Hugo's broker and constant bridge companion is a man called Meyer. ("Nice chap. A Jew.") Sir Hugo made his fortune in the City by operating out of Tangier—free port, no taxes, no currency restrictions. He throws his money about. "Best houses," Bond says, "best cars, best women. Boxes at the Opera, at Good-wood. Prize-winning Jersey herds." Alas, he has also thrust his way into exclusive clubland, Blades specifically, where, in partnership with the nice Jew, Meyer, he cheats at bridge.

If Drax is not a Jew, he comes within an earlobe of it. A bullying, boorish, loud-mouthed vulgarian, Bond decides on first meeting. *He has a powerful nose, he sweats, he's hairy,* but—but—"he had allowed his whiskers to grow down to the level of the lobes of his ears," and so, *pace* the Head of Station S, a chap couldn't tell for sure. In the end, Sir Hugo Drax is unmasked as . . . Graf Hugo von der Drache, *Sturmer-caricature-transmogrified-into-Nazi-ogre-turned-commie-agent.*

In *Diamonds Are Forever* it is a smart Jewish girl who opens the door to "The House of Diamonds," a swindle shop. On the same page, we read:

> . . . There was a click and the door opened a few inches and a voice with a thick foreign intonation expostulated volubly: "Bud Mister Grunspan, why being so hard? Vee must all make

a liffing, yes? I am tell you this vonderful stone gost me ten tousant pounts. Ten tousant! You ton't belieff me? But I svear it. On my vort of honour." There was a negative pause and the voice made its final bid. "Bedder still! I bet you fife pounts!"

Goldfinger begins to rework familiar ground. Goldfinger is clearly a Jewish name. Like Drax, he floats his gold round the world, manipulating the price, and naturally he cheats at cards. And golf.

"Nationality?" Bond asks Mr. Du Pont.

"You wouldn't believe it, but he's a Britisher. Domiciled in Nassau. You'd think he'd be a Jew from the name, but he doesn't look it. . . ."

Like Drax, Goldfinger has red hair, but, significantly, in the lengthy physical description on page 30 *there is no mention of his earlobe size.* All the same, Bond, on his first meeting with Goldfinger, muses, "What could his history be? Today he might be an Englishman. What had he been born? Not a Jew—though there might be Jewish blood in him. . . ."

Next we come to a real Jew, Sol Horowitz, one of the two hoods in *The Spy Who Loved Me.* Horowitz is described as skeletal, his skin grey, the lips thin and purplish like an unstitched wound, his teeth cheaply capped with steel. And the ears? This is ambiguous. Jewy possibly, but assimilated. "The ears lay very flat and close to the bony, rather box-shaped head. . . ."

The Fleming Ear Syndrome reaches its climax with Blofeld. Blofeld, again not Jewish in spite of the name, and easily the archetypal Fleming villain, has one hell of an ear problem. Blofeld, with old age encroaching, wishes to have a title, and so he applies to the British College of Arms, asking to be recognized as Monsieur le Comte Balthazar de Bleuville. Not so easy. According to Sable Basilisk, at the College of Arms, the Bleuvilles, through the centuries, have shared one odd characteristic. Basilisk tells Bond, "Now, when I was scratching around the crypt of the chapel at Blonville, having a look at the old Bleuville tombs, my flashlight, moving over the stone faces, picked out a curious fact that I tucked away in my mind but that your question has brought to the surface. None of the Bleuvilles, as far as I could tell, and certainly not through a hundred and fifty years, had lobes to their ears."

> "Ah," said Bond, running over in his mind the Identicast picture of Blofeld and the complete printed physiognometry of the man in Records. "So he shouldn't by right have lobes to his ears. Or at any rate it would be a strong piece of evidence for his case if he hadn't?"
> "That's right."
> "Well, he *has* got lobes," said Bond annoyed. "Rather pronounced lobes as a matter of fact. Where does that get us?"

Where does that get us? Jimmy, Jimmy, I thought, as I read this for the first time, use your loaf. Remember the Head of Station S, *Casino Royale*, Le Chiffre, LARGE LOBES, SMALL EARS. Blofeld has J——— blood!

Even more significant, Blofeld is head of an international conspiracy. Bond's most pernicious enemies head, or work for, hidden international conspiracies, usually SMERSH or SPECTRE.

SMERSH, first described in *Casino Royale*, is the conjunction of two Russian words, "Smyert Shpionam," meaning roughly "Death to Spies!" It was, in 1953, under the general direction of Beria, with headquarters in Leningrad and a substation in Moscow, and ranked above the MVD (formerly NKVD).

SPECTRE is The Special Executive for Counterintelligence, Terrorism, Revenge, and Extortion, a private enterprise for private profit, and its founder and chairman is Ernst Stavro Blofeld. SPECTRE's headquarters are in Paris, on the Boulevard

Haussmann. Not the Avenue d'Iéna, the richest street in Paris, Fleming writes, because "too many of the landlords and tenants in the Avenue d'Iéna have names ending in 'escu,' 'ovitch,' 'ski,' and 'stein,' and these are sometimes not the ending of respectable names." If you stopped at SPECTRE's headquarters, at 136 *bis* Boul. Haussmann, you would find a discreetly glittering brass plate that says "FIRCO" and, underneath, *Fraternité Internationale de la Résistance Contre l'Oppression.* FIRCO's stated aim is to keep alive the ideals that flourished during the last war among members of all resistance groups. It was most active during International Refugee Year.

Looked at another way, just as we have learned that Mr. Big may be forking out Moscow gold to pay for race riots in the United States, so a seemingly humanitarian refugee organization examined closely may be a front for an international conspiracy of evil-doers.

SMERSH and SPECTRE are both inclined to secret congresses, usually called to plot the political or financial ruin or even the physical destruction of the freedom-loving West. As secret organizations go, SMERSH is growth stuff. As described in *Casino Royale*, in 1953, it was "believed to consist of only a few hundred operatives of very high quality," but only two years later, as set out in *From Russia, With Love*, SMERSH employed a total of 40,000 men and women. Its headquarters had also moved from Leningrad to a rather posh set-up in Moscow, which I take to be a sign of favor. In *Goldfinger*, there is a SMERSH-inspired secret congress of America's leading mobsters brought together with the object of sacking Fort Knox. The initial covert meeting of SPECTRE, elaborately described in *Thunderball*, reveals a conspiracy to steal two atomic weapons from a NATO airplane and then threaten the British prime minister with the nuclear destruction of a major city unless a ransom of 100 million pounds sterling is forthcoming. SPECTRE next conspires against England in *On Her Majesty's Secret Service.* Blofeld, the organization's evil genius, has retired to a Swiss plateau and hypnotized some lovely British girls, infecting them with deadly crop and livestock diseases which they are to carry back to England, spreading pestilence.

Earlier, John Buchan, 1st Lord Tweedsmuir of Elsfield, Governor-General of Canada, and author of *The Thirty-nine Steps* and four other Richard Hannay novels, was also obsessed with vile plots against Albion, but felt no need to equivocate. We are barely into *The Thirty-nine Steps,* when we are introduced to Scudder, the brave and good spy, whom Hannay takes to be "a sharp, restless fellow, who always wanted to get down to the roots of things." Scudder tells Hannay that behind all the governments and the armies there was a big subterranean movement going on, engineered by a very dangerous people. Most of them were the sort of educated anarchists that make revolutions, but beside them there were financiers who were playing for money. It suited the books of both classes of conspirators to set Europe by the ears.

> When I asked Why, he said that the anarchist lot thought it would give them their chance . . . they looked to see a new world emerge. The capitalists would . . . make fortunes by buying up the wreckage. Capital, he said, had no conscience and no fatherland. Besides, the Jew was behind it, and the Jew hated Russia worse than hell.
> "Do you wonder?" he cried. "For three hundred years they have been persecuted, and this is the return match for the *pogroms.* The Jew is everywhere, but you have to go far down the backstairs to find him. Take any big Teutonic business concern. If you have dealings with it the first man you meet is Prince *von und zu* Something, an elegant young man who talks Eton-and-Harrow English. But he cuts no ice. If your business

is big, you get behind him and find a prognathous Westphalian with a retreating brow and the manners of a hog. . . . But if you're on the biggest kind of job and are bound to get to the real boss, ten to one you are brought up against a little white-faced Jew in a bathchair with an eye like a rattlesnake. Yes, sir, he is the man who is ruling the world just now, and he has his knife in the Empire of the Tzar, because his aunt was outraged and his father flogged in some one-horse location on the Volga."

The clear progenitor of these conspiracies against England is the notorious anti-Semitic forgery, *The Protocols of the Elders of Zion*, which first appeared in western Europe in 1920 and had, by 1930, been circulated throughout the world in millions of copies. The *Protocols* were used to incite massacres of Jews during the Russian civil war. Earlier, they were especially helpful in fomenting the pogrom at Kishinev in Bessarabia in 1903. From Russia, the *Protocols* traveled to Nazi Germany. Recently, they were serialized in a Cairo newspaper.

The history of the *Protocols*, and just how they were tortuously evolved from another forgery, *Dialogue aux Enfers entre Montesquieu et Machiavel*, by a French lawyer called Maurice Joly, in 1864, has already been definitively traced by Norman Cohn in his *Warrant for Genocide*; and so I will limit myself to brief comments here.

Editions of the *Protocols* are often preceded by an earlier invention, *The Rabbi's Speech*, that could easily serve as a model for later dissertations on the glories of power and evil as revealed to Bond by Goldfinger, Drax, and Blofeld.

Like Auric Goldfinger, the Rabbi believes gold is the strength, the recompense, the sum of everything man fears and craves. "The day," he says, "when we shall have made ourselves the sole possessors of all the gold in the world, the real power will be in our hands." Like Sir Hugo Drax, the

Rabbi understands the need for market manipulation. "The surest means of attaining [power] is to have supreme control over all industrial, financial, and commercial operations. . . ." SMERSH would envy the Rabbi's political acumen. "So far as possible we must talk to the proletariat. . . . We will drive them to upheavals, to revolutions; and each of these catastrophes marks a big step forward for our . . . sole aim—world domination."

The twenty-four protocols purport to be made up of lectures delivered to the Jewish secret government, the Elders of Zion, on how to achieve world domination. Tangled and contradictory, the main idea is that the Jews, spreading confusion and terror, will eventually take over the globe. Like SPECTRE, they will use liberalism as a front. Like Mr. Big, they will foster discontent and unrest. The common people will be directed to overthrow their rulers and then a despot will be put in power. As there are more evil than good men in the world, force—the Elders have concluded—is the only sure means of government. Underground railways (a big feature in all versions of the *Protocols*) will be constructed in major cities, so that the Elders may counter any organized rebellion by blowing capital cities to smithereens—a recurring threat in the Bond novels (*Moonraker, Thunderball*).

In fact, the more one scrutinizes the serpentine plots in Ian Fleming's novels, the more it would seem that the Elders *are* in conspiracy against England. Not only are they threatening to blow up London, but they would seize the largest store of the world's gold, back disruptive labor disputes, run dope into the country ("Risico") and infect British crops and livestock with deadly pests.

In our time, no books, no films, have enjoyed such a dazzling international success as the James Bond stories, but the impact was not instantaneous. When *Casino Royale* appeared in 1953 the reviews were good, but three American publishers rejected the book and sales were mediocre, which was a sore disappointment to Bond's unabashedly self-promoting author, Ian Fleming, then forty-three years old.

By the spring of 1966 the thirteen Bond novels had been translated into twenty-six different languages and sold more than forty-five million copies. The movie versions of *Doctor No, From Russia, With Love, Goldfinger,* and *Thunderball* had been seen by some hundred million people and were in fact among the most profitable ever produced. Bond has spawned a flock of imitators, including Matt Helm, Quiller, and Boysie Oakes. More than two hundred commercial products, ranging from men's toiletries to bubble gum, have been authorized to carry the official Bond trademark. Only recently, after a fantastic run, has the boom in Bond begun to slump.

The success of Bond is all the more intriguing because Ian Fleming was such an appalling writer. He had no sense of place that scratched deeper than Sunday supplement travel articles or route maps, a much-favored device. His celebrated use of insider's facts and O.K. brand names, especially about gunmanship and the international high life, has been faulted again and again. Eric Ambler and Graham Greene (in his entertainments) have written vastly superior spy stories, and when Fleming ventured into the American underworld, he begged comparison with Mickey Spillane rather than such original stylists as Dashiell Hammett and Raymond Chandler. He had a resoundingly tin ear, as witness a Harlem black man talking, vintage 1954 (*Live and Let Die*):

'Yuh done look okay yoself, honeychile . . . an' dat's da troof. But Ah mus' spressify dat yuh stays close up tuh me an keeps yo eyes offn dat lowdown trash'n his hot pants. 'N Ah may say

... dat ef Ah ketches yuh makin' up tah dat dope Ah'll jist nacherlly whup da hide off'n yo sweet ass.'

Or, as an example of the recurring American gangster, Sol "Horror" Horowitz (*The Spy Who Loved Me*):

'The lady's right. You didn't ought to have spilled that java, Sluggsy. But ya see, lady, that's why they call him Sluggsy, on account he's smart with the hardware.'

As Fleming was almost totally without the ability to create character through distinctive action or dialogue, he generally falls back on villains who are physically grotesque. So Mr. Big has "a great football of a head, twice the normal size and very nearly round," hairless, with no eyebrows and no eyelashes, the eyes bulging slightly and the irises golden round black pupils. Doctor No's head "was elongated and tapered from a round, completely bald skull down to a sharp chin so that the impression was of a reversed raindrop—or rather oildrop, for the skin was a deep, almost translucent yellow."

Each Bond novel, except for *The Spy Who Loved Me*, follows an unswerving formula, though the sequence of steps is sometimes shuffled through the introduction of flashbacks:

1. Bond, bored by inactivity, is summoned by M and given a mission.
2. Bond and villain confront each other tentatively.
3. A sexy woman is introduced and seduced by Bond. If she is in cahoots with the villain, she will find Bond irresistible and come over to his side.
4. The villain captures Bond and punishes him (torture, usually), then reveals his diabolical scheme. "As you will never get out of this alive . . ." or "It is rare that I have the opportunity to talk to a man of your intelligence. . . ."
5. Bond escapes, triumphs over villain, destroying his vile plot.
6. Bond and sexy woman are now allowed their long-delayed tryst.

This basic formula is usually tarted up by two devices:

1. We, the unwashed, are granted a seemingly knowledgeable, insider's peek at a glamorous industry or institution. Say, diamond or gold smuggling; the Royal College of Arms, Blades, and other elegant clubs. This makes for long chapters of all but unbroken exposition, rather like fawning magazine articles. Sometimes, as with the description of Blades (*Moonraker*), the genuflection is unintentionally comic:

> It was a sparkling scene. There were perhaps fifty men in the room, the majority in dinner-jackets, all at ease with themselves and their surroundings, all stimulated by the peerless food and drink, all animated by a common interest—the prospect of high gambling, the grand slam, the ace pot, the key throw in a 64 game at backgammon. There might be cheats amongst them, men who beat their wives, men with perverse instincts, greedy men, cowardly men, lying men; but the elegance of the room invested each with a kind of aristocracy.

2. We are taken on a Fleming guided tour of an exotic locale: Las Vegas, Japan, the West Indies. This also makes for lengthy, insufferably knowing expository exchanges, rather thinly disguised travel notes, as, for example, when Tiger Tanaka educates Bond in Japanese mores (*You Only Live Twice*).

Not surprisingly, considering Fleming's boyish frame of mind, competitive games figure prominently in the Bond mythology, as do chases in snob cars or along model railways. The deadly card game, Bond against the villain, is another repeated set piece: *Casino Royale, Moonraker, Goldfinger.*

A recurring character in the Bond adventures is the American Felix Leiter, once with the CIA, then with Pinkerton. Leiter, an impossibly stupid and hearty fellow, is cut from the same cloth as comic strip cold war heroes Buzz Sawyer and Steve Canyon. A born gee whiz, gung ho type.

If Fleming's sense of character was feeble and his powers of invention limited, the sadism and heated sex I was led to expect turned out to be tepid. But at least one torture scene is worth noting, if only because its connotations are so glaringly obvious. In *Casino Royale*, Le Chiffre pauses from beating the naked Bond with a carpet beater to say,

"My dear boy," Le Chiffre spoke like a father, "the game of Red Indians is over, quite over. You have stumbled by mischance into a game for grown-ups and you have already found it a painful experience. You are not equipped, my dear boy, to play games with adults and it was very foolish of your nanny in London to have sent you out here with your spade and bucket. Very foolish indeed and most unfortunate for you."

A roll call of Bond's girls yields Vesper Lynd, Solitaire, Gala Brand, Tiffany Case, Honeychile Rider, Pussy Galore, Domino Vitali, Kissy Syzuki, Mary Goodnight. As the perfume brand type labels indicate, the girls are clockwork objects rather than people. The composite Bond girl, as Kingsley Amis has already noted, can be distinguished by her beautiful firm breasts, each, I might add, with its pointed stigmatum of desire. The Bond girls are healthy, outdoor types, but they are not all perfectly made. Take Honeychile Rider, for instance: *Café au lait* skin, ash blonde hair, naked on first meeting except for a broad leather belt round her waist with a hunting knife in a leather sheath, she suffers from a badly broken nose, smashed crooked like a boxer's. Then there's the question of Honeychile's behind, which was "almost as firm and rounded as a boy's." A description which brought Fleming a letter from Noel Coward. "I was slightly shocked," Coward wrote, "by the lascivious announcement that Honeychile's bottom was like a boy's. I know we are all becoming progressively more broadminded nowadays but really, old chap, what *could* you have been thinking of?"

Descriptions of clad Bond girls tend to focus on undergarments. Jill Masterson, on first meeting in *Goldfinger,* is naked except for a black bra and briefs. Tatiana, in *From Russia, With Love,* is discovered "wearing nothing but the black ribbon round her neck and black silk stockings rolled above her knees." Not that I object to a word of it. After all, sexy, unfailingly available girls are a legitimate and most enjoyable convention of thrillers and spy stories. If I find Fleming's politics distasteful, his occasional flirtation with ideas embarrassing, I am happy to say I am in accord with him in admiring firm, thrusting, beautiful breasts.

Unlike Harold Robbins, Ian Fleming does not actually linger overlong on sexual description. Or perversion. He is seldom as brutalized as Mickey Spillane in page after page. If anything, he's something of a prude. The closest he comes to obscenity is "——— you" in *Dr. No.* Mind you, this fastidiousness is followed hard by a detailed description of a black man punishing a girl by squeezing her mount of Venus between his thumb and forefinger, until his knuckles go white with the pressure. "She's Love Moun' be sore long after ma face done get healed." Other, more exquisite tortures of women follow in further adventures, usually enforced when the girls are deliciously nude, but James Bond's language never degenerates beyond an uncharacteristic imprecation in *You Only Live Twice.* "Freddie Uncle Charlie Katie," he says, meaning "fuck," I take it.

The Bond novels are not so much sexy as they are boyishly smutty. James Bond's aunt, for instance, lives "in the quaintly named hamlet of Pett Bottom." There's a girl called Kissy and another named Pussy. Not one of the Bond girls, however, lubricates as sexily as does Tracy's Lancia Flaminia Zagato Spyder, "a low, white two-seater . . . [with] a sexy boom from its twin exhausts."

Ian Fleming was frightened of women. "Some," he wrote,

"respond to the whip, some to the kiss. . . ." A woman, he felt, should be an illusion; and he was deeply upset by their bodily functions. Once, in Capri, according to his biographer, John Pearson, Fleming disowned a girl he had liked the looks of after she retired for a few moments behind a rock. "He had," a former girlfriend told Pearson, "a remarkable phobia about bodily things. . . . I'm certain he would never have tied a cut finger for me. I feel he would also have preferred me not to eat and drink as well." Fleming once told Barbara Griggs of the London *Evening Standard* "that women simply are not clean—absolutely filthy, the whole lot of them. English-women simply do not wash and scrub enough." So, in complement to the image of James Bond, never traveling without an armory of electronic devices, the latest in computerized death-dealing gadgetry, one now suspects his fastidious creator also lugged an old-fashioned douche bag with him everywhere.

Bond is well worth looking at in juxtaposition to his inventor, Ian Fleming.

In *Casino Royale*, Bond, staked by British Intelligence, plays a deadly game of baccarat at Royale-les-Eaux with Le Chiffre of SMERSH, and wins a phenomenal sum, thereby depriving the USSR of its budget for subversion in France. This adventure, Fleming was fond of saying, was based on a wartime trip to Lisbon with Admiral Godfrey of Naval Intelligence. At the casino, Fleming said, he engaged in a baccarat battle with a group of Nazis, hoping to strike a blow at the German economy. Alas, he lost.

Actually, John Pearson writes, "It was a decidedly dismal evening at the casino—only a handful of Portuguese were present, the stakes were low, the croupiers were bored." Fleming whispered to the unimpressed Admiral, "Just suppose those fellows were German agents—what a coup it would be if we cleaned them out entirely."

Fleming, raised as he was on Buchan and Sapper, had other imaginative notions while serving with British Naval Intelligence during the war, among them the idea of sinking a great block of concrete with men inside it in the English Channel, just before the Dieppe raid, to keep watch on the harbor with periscopes. Or to freeze clouds, moor them along the coast of southern England, and use them as platforms for anti-aircraft guns.

Fleming's trip with Admiral Godfrey did not terminate in Lisbon, but carried on to New York. Armed, for the occasion, with a small command fighting knife and a fountain pen with a cyanide cartridge, as well as his Old Etonian tie, Fleming (and the Admiral) was supposed to slip into New York anonymously. "But as they went ashore from the flying boat," Pearson writes, "press photographers began to crowd around them. Although they soon realized that it was the elegant, sweet-smelling figure of Madame Schiaparelli who was attracting the cameras, the damage was done. That evening the chief of British Naval Intelligence was to be seen in the background of all the press photographs of the famous French couturière arriving in New York."

Fleming said he wrote his first novel, *Casino Royale*, at Goldeneye, his Jamaica home, in 1952, to "take his mind off the shock of getting married at the age of forty-three." It seems possible that the inspiration for his villain, Le Chiffre, was The Great Beast 666, necromancer Aleister Crowley, who, like Mussolini, had the whites of his eyes completely visible round the iris. Crowley, incidentally, was also the model for the first novel by Fleming's literary hero, Somerset Maugham.

M, also initially introduced in *Casino Royale*, was arguably a composite figure based on Admiral Godfrey and Sir Robert

Menzies, Eton and the Life Guards. M remains an obstinately
unsympathetic figure even to Bond admirers. ". . . it may be
obvious," Amis writes, "why M's frosty, damnably clear eyes
are damnably clear. No thought is taking place behind them";
while John Pearson writes of Bond's relationship with M
that "never has such cool ingratitude produced such utter
loyalty." If Bond's father-figure of a villain, Le Chiffre,
threatens him with castration in his first adventure, then
Bond, last time out (*The Man with the Golden Gun*), is
discovered brainwashed in the opening pages and attempts to
assassinate M. The unpermissive M. "In particular," Amis
writes, "M disapproves of Bond's 'womanizing,' though he
never says so directly, and would evidently prefer him not to
form a permanent attachment either. He barely conceals his
glee at the news that Bond is after all not going to marry
Tiffany Case. This is perhaps more the attitude of a doting
mother than a father."

A really perceptive observation, for Fleming, as a boy,
was frightened of his stern and demanding mother and did
in fact call her M.

Pearson writes in *The Life of Ian Fleming:*

Apart from Le Chiffre, M, and Vesper Lynd, the minor characters in *Casino Royale* are the merest shadows with names
attached. The only other character who matters is Ian Fleming himself. For James Bond is not really a character in this
book. He is a mouthpiece for the man who inhabits him, a
dummy for him to hang his clothes on, a zombie to perform the
dreams of violence and daring which fascinate his creator. It
is only because Fleming holds so little of himself back, because
he talks and dreams so freely through the device of James Bond,
that the book has such readability. *Casino Royale* is really an
experiment in the autobiography of dreams.

Without a doubt, Fleming's dream conception of himself
was James Bond, gay adventurer, two-fisted soldier of fortune,

and, in the Hannay tradition, ever the complete gentleman.

Bond renounces his occasionally vast gambling gains, donating his winnings to a service widows' fund; he is self-mocking about his heroics, avoids publicity, and once offered a knighthood, in *The Man with the Golden Gun*, he turns it down bashfully, because "He has never been a public figure and did not wish to become one . . . there was one thing above all he treasured. His privacy. His anonymity."

Yet even as Hannay's creator, John Buchan, was a man of prodigious drive and ambition, so Ian Fleming was a chap with his eye always resolutely on the main chance.

"Most authors, particularly when they begin," Pearson writes dryly, "leave details of publication to their agents or to the goodwill of the publisher." Not so Fleming, who instantly submitted a plan for "Advertising and Promotion" to Jonathan Cape. Copies of *Casino Royale* were ready by March 1953. Without delay, Fleming wrote a letter to the editors of all Lord Kemsley's provincial newspapers, sending it off with an autographed copy of his book. "Dr. Jekyll has written this blatant thriller in his spare time, and it may amuse you. If you don't think it too puerile for Sheffield (or Stockport, Macclesfield, Middlesborough, Blackburn, etc.) it would be wonderful if you would hand a copy with a pair of tongs to your reviewer."

This jokey little note, properly read, was an order from the bridge to the chaps on the lower deck, for Fleming was a known intimate of Lord Kemsley's, as well as foreign news manager of the *Sunday Times*, then the Kemsley flagship, so to speak.

Fleming also astutely sent a copy of his novel to Somerset Maugham, who replied, "It goes with a swing from the first page to the last and is really thrilling all through. . . . You really managed to get the tension to the highest possible pitch." If James Bond would have cherished such a private tribute from an old man, Ian Fleming immediately grasped its commercial potential, and wrote back, "Dear Willie, I have just got your letter. When I am 79 shall I waste my time reading such a book and taking the trouble to write to the author in my own hand? I pray so, but I doubt it. I am even more flattered and impressed after catching a glimpse of the empestered life you lead at Cap Ferrat, deluged with fan mail, besieged by the press, inundated with bumpf of one sort or another. . . . Is it bad literary manners to ask if my publishers may quote from your letter? Please advise me—as a 'parain' not as a favour to me and my publishers."

Maugham replied, "Please don't use what I said about your book to advertise it."

As the sales of *Casino Royale* were disappointing, Fleming turned to writing the influential Atticus gossip column in the *Sunday Times*, which provided him with a convenient platform to flatter those whose favors he sought. After Lord Kemsley refused to run a *Sunday Times* Portrait Gallery puff of Lord Beaverbrook on his seventy-sixth birthday, he did allow Fleming, following some special pleading, to celebrate Beaverbrook in his column. "History will have to decide whether he or Northcliffe was the greatest newspaperman of this half century. In the sense that he combines rare journalistic flair, the rare quality of wonder . . . with courage and vitality . . . the verdict may quite possibly go to Lord Beaverbrook. . . ."

Beaverbrook, who had an insatiable appetite for flattery, bought the serial rights to the next Bond novel and later ran a Bond comic strip in the *Daily Express*.

Once Macmillan undertook to publish *Casino Royale* in America, the Fleming self-advertisement campaign accelerated. Fleming wrote to a friend asking him to coax Walter Winchell into plugging the book. He wrote to Iva Patcevitch, saying, "If you can possibly give it a shove in *Vogue* or elsewhere, Anna and I will allow you to play Canasta against us, which should be ample reward." He also wrote to Fleur Cowles and Margaret Case: "You will soon be fed up with this book as I have sent copies around to all our friends asking them to give it a hand in America, which is a very barefaced way to go on. . . . I know Harry Luce won't be bothered with it, or Clare, but if you could somehow prevail upon *Time* to give it a review you would be an angel."

In 1955, the sales of his books still dragging, Fleming met Raymond Chandler at a dinner party. At the time, Chandler was an old and broken man, incoherent from drink. "He was very nice to me," Fleming wrote, "and said he liked my first book, *Casino Royale*, but he didn't really want to talk about anything except the loss of his wife, about which he expressed himself with a nakedness that embarrassed me while endearing him to me."

If the battered old writer, whom Fleming professed to admire, was tragically self-absorbed, he was, all the same, instantly sent a copy of Fleming's forthcoming *Live and Let Die*. "A few days later," Pearson writes, "Chandler telephoned Fleming to say how much he had enjoyed it, and went on to ask the author—vaguely, perhaps—if he would care for him to endorse the book for the benefit of his publishers—the kind of thing he was always refusing to do in the United States and a subject on which in his published letters, he displays such ferocious cynicism. . . ." "Rather unattractively," Fleming wrote later, "I took him up on his suggestion."

Chandler was as good as his word, Pearson goes on to say, "although it sounds as if it was rather a struggle. On May 25 he wrote pathetically to Fleming apologizing for taking so long—'in fact, lately I have had a very difficult time reading at all.' " But a week later he came through for Fleming, his blurb beginning, "Ian Fleming is probably the most *forceful* and *driving* writer of what I suppose still must be called thrillers in England. . . ." (Emphasis mine.) Chandler's letter of praise ended, somewhat ambiguously, "If this is any good to you, would you like me to have it engraved on a slab of gold?"

Fleming was also able to find uses for a burnt-out prime minister. In November 1956, twelve days after the Suez cease-fire, it was announced that Prime Minister Anthony Eden was ill from the effects of severe overstrain. It became necessary to find a secluded spot where Eden could recuperate, and so Alan Lennox-Boyd, then Secretary of State for Colonial Affairs and a friend of Ian Fleming, approached Fleming about Goldeneye, his home in Jamaica. Fleming, flattered by the choice, neglected to say there were only iron bedsteads at Goldeneye, there was no hot water in the shower and there was no bathroom, but there were bush rats in the roof. He did not advise Lennox-Boyd that Noel Coward's home nearby, or Sir William Stephenson's, would have been more commodious for an ailing man. He did not even say that the Prime Minister would be without a telephone at Goldeneye. "The myth of Goldeneye was about to enter history," John Pearson writes, "it was too much to expect its creator to upset it."

Sir Anthony and Lady Eden set off for Goldeneye and Fleming sat back in Kent to write to Macmillan. "I hope that the Edens' visit to Goldeneye has done something to my American sales. Here there have been full-page spreads of the property, including Violet emptying ash trays and heaven knows what-all. It has really been a splendid week and greatly increased the value of the property until Anne started talking to reporters about barracuda, the hardness of the beds, and curried goat. Now some papers treat the place as if it was a hovel and others as if it was the millionaire home of some particularly disgusting millionaire tax dodger. . . ." Two weeks later the bush rats caught up with Fleming. The

London *Evening Standard* reported that Sir Anthony, troubled by rats during the night, had organized a hunt. Fleming, distressed, wrote to a friend, "The greatly increased rental value was brought down sharply by a completely dreamed-up report to the effect that Goldeneye was over-run by rats and that the Edens and the detectives had spent the whole night chasing them. . . ."

The Prime Minister's stay at Goldeneye brought Fleming to the attention of a public far wider than his books had so far managed for him. It was now, Pearson writes, that Fleming's public began to change. "Up to then he had been 'the Peter Cheyney of the carriage trade'. . . . After Eden's visit . . . many people were interested . . . [and] began to read him. After five long years the 'best-seller stakes' had begun in earnest. . . . if Fleming with his flair for self-promotion had planned the whole thing himself it could hardly have been better done."

Fleming continued to type out his dream-life at Goldeneye, visualizing himself as gentlemanly James Bond; but the self-evident truth is he had infinitely more in common with his pushy, ill-bred foreign villains, and one is obliged to consider his sophisticated racialism as no less than a projection of his own coarse qualities.

Two final points.

It is possible to explain the initial success of the Bond novels in that they came at a time when Buchan's vicious anti-Semitism and Sapper's neo-fascist xenophobia were no longer acceptable; nevertheless a real need as well as a large audience for such reading matter still existed. It was Fleming's most brilliant stroke to present himself not as an old-fashioned, frothing wog-hater, but as an ostensibly civilized voice which offered sanitized racialism instead. The Bond novels not only satisfy Little Englanders who believe they have been undone by dastardly foreign plotters, but pander to their continuing notion of self-importance. So, when the Head of SMERSH, Colonel General Grubozaboychikov, known as "G," summons a high-level conference to announce that it has become necessary to inflict an act of terrorism aimed at the heart of the intelligence apparatus of the West, it is (on the advice of General Vozdvishensky) the British Secret Service that he chooses.

> '. . . I think we all have to respect [England's] Intelligence Service,' General Vozdvishensky looked around the table. There were grudging nods from everyone present, including General G. '. . . Their Secret Service . . . agents are good. They pay them little money. . . . They are rarely awarded a decoration until they retire. And yet these men and women continue to do this dangerous work. It is curious. It is perhaps the Public School and University tradition. The love of adventure. But it is odd they play this game so well, for they are not natural conspirators.'

Kingsley Amis argues, in *The Bond Dossier*, that "To use foreigners as villains is a convention older than literature. It's not in itself a symptom of intolerance about foreigners. . . ."

Amis's approach is so good-natured, so ostensibly reasonable, that to protest no, no, is to seem an entirely humorless left-wing nag, a Hampstead harpy. I am not, God help me, suing for that boring office. I do not object to the use of foreigners *per se* as villains. I am even willing to waive moral objections to a writer in whose fictions no Englishman ever does wrong and only Jewy or black or yellow men fill the villain's role. However, even in novels whose primary purpose is to entertain, I am entitled to ask for a modicum of plausibility. And so, while I would grudgingly agree with Amis that there is nothing wrong in choosing foreigners for villains, I must add that it is—in the context of contemporary

England—an inaccuracy. A most outrageous inaccuracy. After all, even on the narrow squalid level of Intelligence, the most sensational betrayals have come from men who, to quote General Vozdvishensky, were so admirably suited to their work by dint of their Public School and University traditions: Guy Burgess, Donald Maclean, and Kim Philby. It should be added, hastily added, that these three men, contrary to the Fleming style, were not ogres and did not sell out for gold. Rightly or wrongly, they acted on political principle. Furthermore, their real value to the KGB (the final insult, this) was not their British information, but the American secrets they were a party to.

Kingsley Amis and I, the people he drinks with, the people I drink with, are neither anti-Semitic nor color-prejudiced, however divergent our politics. We circulate in a sheltered society. Not so my children, which brings me to my primary motive for writing this essay.

The minority man, as Norman Mailer has astutely pointed out, grows up with a double-image of himself, his own and society's. My boys are crazy about the James Bond movies, they identify with 007, as yet unaware that they have been cast as the villains of the dramas. As a boy I was brought up to revere John Buchan, then Lord Tweedsmuir, Governor-General of Canada. Before he came to speak at Junior Red Cross Prize Day, we were told that he stood for the ultimate British virtues: fair play, clean living, gentlemanly conduct. We were not forewarned that he was also an ignorant, nasty-minded anti-Semite. I discovered this for myself, reading *The Thirty-nine Steps*. As badly as I wanted to identify with Richard Hannay, two-fisted soldier of fortune, I couldn't without betraying myself. My grandfather, *pace* Buchan, went in fear of being flogged in some one-horse location on the Volga, which was why we were in Canada. However, I owe to Buchan the image of my grandfather as a little white-faced Jew with an eye like a rattlesnake. It is an image I briefly responded to, alas, if only because Hannay, so obviously on the side of the good, accepted it without question. This, possibly, is why I've grown up to loathe Buchan, Fleming, and their sort.

In his preface to *The Bond Dossier*, Amis writes: ". . . quite apart from everything else, I'm a Fleming fan. Appreciation of an author ought to be *sine qua non* for writing at length about him." Well, no. It is equally valid to examine an author's work in detail if you find his books morally repugnant and the writer himself an insufferably self-satisfied boor.

Why I Write

*A*s I write, October 1970, I have just finished a novel of intimidating length, a fiction begun five years ago, on the other side of the moon, so I am, understandably enough, concerned by the state of the novel in general. Is it dead? Dead *again*. Like God or MGM. Father McLuhan says so (writing "The Age of Writing has passed") and Dylan Thomas's daughter recently pronounced stingingly from Rome, "Nobody reads novels any more."

I'm soon going to be forty. Too old to learn how to teach. Or play the guitar. Stuck, like the blacksmith, with the only craft I know. But brooding about the novel, and its present unmodishness, it's not the established practitioner I'm grieving for, it's the novice, that otherwise effervescent young man stricken with the wasting disease whose earliest symptom is the first novel. These are far from halcyon days for the fledgling novelist.

Look at it this way. Most publishers, confronted with a rectal polyp, hold on to hope, tempting the surgeon with a bigger advance. They know the score. What's truly terminal. Offered a first novel or worse news—*infamy*—a short story collection, they call for the ledgers which commemorate last season's calamities. The bright new talents nobody wanted to read. Now more to be remaindered than remembered, as *Time* once observed.

I know. Carting off my cumbersome manuscript to be Xeroxed, it was my first novel that was uppermost in my mind, *The Acrobats*, published in 1954, when I was twenty-three years old. At the time, I was living in Montreal, and my British publisher, André Deutsch, urged me to visit his Canadian distributor before sailing for England. So I caught the overnight Greyhound bus to Toronto, arriving at 7 a.m. in a city where I knew nobody and walking the sweltering summer streets until 9:30, when offices would open.

The Canadian distributor, bracingly realistic, did not detain me overlong with *recherché* chitchat about style, content, or influences. "Have you written a thick book or a thin book?" he demanded.

A thin one, I allowed.

"Thick books sell better than thin ones here."

A slow learner, I published five more before I at last surfaced with a thick one, *St. Urbain's Horseman*, which was all of 180,000 words. And retrieving my seven Xeroxed copies, I couldn't help but reflect that the £80 I forked out for them was only slightly less than the British advance against royalties I was paid for my first novel sixteen years ago. The American publisher, G. P. Putnam's Sons, was more generous; they sent me $750. But I was disheartened when I received their catalogue. Putnam's was, at the time, trying a new experiment in bookselling. If you didn't enjoy one of their books, your bookseller would return you the money, no questions asked. Only two books listed in the autumn catalogue conspicuously failed to carry this guarantee: mine, and another young writer's.

The Acrobats ultimately sold some two thousand copies in England and less than a thousand in the U.S., but it was

—as I pointed out to my aunt, on a visit to Montreal—translated into five foreign languages.

"There must," she said, smoothing out her skirt, "be a shortage of books."

My uncle, also a critic, was astonished when he computed my earnings against the time I had invested. I would have earned more mowing his lawn, and, furthermore, it would have been healthier for me.

The novel, the novel.

Write a study of the pre-Columbian butterfly, compose an account of colonial administration in Tonga, and Nigel Dennis, that most perspicacious and witty of British reviewers, might perversely enshrine it in a thousand-word essay in the *Sunday Telegraph*. Or Malcolm Muggeridge might take it as the text for a lengthy sermon, excoriating once more that generation of younger vipers who will continue to enjoy, enjoy, after he has passed on to his much-advertised rest. But novels, coming in batches of twenty weekly, seldom rate a notice of their own in England. Sixteen are instant losers. Or, looked at another way, payola from the literary editor. Badly paid reviewer's perks. The reviewer is not even expected to read them, but it is understood he can flog them for half-price to a buyer from Fleet Street. Of the four that remain, comprising the typical novel column, one is made especially for skewering in the last deadly paragraph, and two are destined for the scales of critical balance. On the one hand, somewhat promising, on the other, ho-hum. Only one makes the lead. But it must lead in four of the five influential newspapers, say, the *Sunday Times, Observer, Times,* and *Guardian,* if anybody's to take notice. Some even buying.

"Basically," a concerned New York editor told me, "the trouble is we are trying to market something nobody wants. Or needs."

The novel has had its day, we are assured, and in the Age

of Aquarius, film, man, film's the stuff that will do more than fiction can to justify God's ways to man. Given any rainy afternoon, who wants to read Doris Lessing fully clothed for forty bob when, for only ten, you can actually see Jane Fonda starkers, shaking it for you and art, and leaving you with sufficient change for a half-bottle of gin?

To be fair, everything has (and continues) to be tried. Novels like decks of playing cards. Shuffle, and read it any way it comes up. Novels like jokes or mutual funds. You cut your potential time-investment loss by inviting everybody in the office to pound out a chapter. *Naked Came the Stranger. I Knew Daisy Smutten.* Or instead-of-sex. Why weary yourself, performing badly perhaps, when, if only you lose yourself in *The Adventurers*, you can have better-hung Dax come for you? And, sooner or later, somebody's bound to turn to the cassette. No need to bruise your thumbs turning pages. You slip the thing into a machine and listen to Raquel Welch read it. "The latest Amis as read by . . ."

On a recent visit to Canadian university campuses, I found myself a creature to be pitied, still writing novels when anybody could tell you that's no longer "where it's at." But I've tried the logical alternative, screenwriting, and though I still write for the films from time to time, it's not really for me. It's too much like what Truman Capote once described as group sports.

Even so, five years in a room with a novel-in-progress can be more than grueling. If getting up to it some mornings is a pleasure, it is, just as often, a punishment. A self-inflicted punishment. There have been false starts, wrong turns, and weeks with nothing to show except sharpened pencils and bookshelves rearranged. I have rewritten chapters ten times that in the end simply didn't belong and had to be cut. Ironically, even unforgivably, it usually seems to be those passages over which I have labored most arduously, nurtured in the hothouse, as it were, that never really spring to life, and the pages that came too quickly, with utterly suspect ease, that read most felicitously.

Riding into my second year on *St. Urbain's Horseman*, disheartened by proliferating school bills, diminished savings, and only fitful progress, I finally got stuck so badly that there was nothing for it but to shove the manuscript aside. I started in on another novel, a year's heat, which yielded *Cocksure*. Anthony Burgess clapped hands in *Life*, *Time* approved, *Newsweek* cheered, and the British notices were almost uniformly fulsome. Encouraged and somewhat solvent again, I resolved to resume work on *Horseman*. After twelve years in London, I was to return to Montreal for a year with my wife and five children, to report for duty as writer-in-residence at Sir George Williams University, my *alma mater*. Or, put plainly, in return for leading a "creative writing" seminar one afternoon a week, I could get on with my novel, comparatively free of financial worry.

Ostensibly, conditions were ideal, winds couldn't be more favorable, and so I started in for the ninth time on page one of *St. Urbain's Horseman*. I didn't get much further before, my stomach crawling with fear, I began to feel I'd lost something somewhere.

I got stuck. Morning after morning, I'd switch to an article or a book review, already long overdue. Or compose self-pitying letters to friends. Or dawdle until 11 a.m., when it was too late to make a decent start on anything, and I was at last free to quit my room and stroll downtown. St. Catherine Street. Montreal's Main Stem, as the doyen of our gossip columnists has it. Pretending to browse for books by lesser novelists, I could surreptitiously check out the shops on stacks of the paperback edition of *Cocksure*.

Or take in a movie maybe.

Ego dividends. I could pick a movie that I had been

asked to write myself, but declined. Whatever the movie, it was quite likely I would know the director or the script writer, maybe even one of the stars.

So there you have it. Cat's out of the bag. In London, I skitter on the periphery of festooned circles, know plenty of inside stories. Bombshells. Like which cabinet minister is an insatiable pederast. What best-selling novel was really stitched together by a cunning editor. Which wrinkled Hollywood glamour queen is predisposed toward gang shags with hirsute Neapolitan waiters from the Mirabelle. Yes, yes, I'll own up to it. I am, after eighteen years as a writer, not utterly unconnected or unknown, as witness the entry in the indispensable *Oxford Companion to Canadian Literature:*

> **Richler, Mordecai** (1931–   ). Born in Montreal, he was educated at Sir George Williams College and spent two years abroad. Returning to Canada in 1952, he joined the staff of the Canadian Broadcasting Corporation. He now lives in England, where he writes film scripts, novels, and short stories. The key to Richler's novels is . . .

After eighteen years and six novels there is nothing I cherish so much as the first and most vulnerable book, *The Acrobats,* not only because it marked the first time my name appeared in a Canadian newspaper, a prescient Toronto columnist writing from London, "You've not heard of Mordecai Richler yet, but, look out, she's a name to watch for"; but also because it was the one book I could write as a totally private act, with the deep, inner assurance that nobody would be such a damn fool as to publish it. That any editor would boot it back to me, a condescending rejection note enclosed, enabling me to quit Paris for Montreal, an honorable failure, and get down to the serious business of looking for a job. A real job.

I did in fact return to Montreal, broke, while my manuscript made the rounds. My father, who hadn't seen me for two years, took me out for a drive.

"I hear you wrote a novel in Europe," he said.

"Yes."

"What's it called?"

"*The Acrobats.*"

"What in the hell do you know about the circus?"

I explained the title was a symbolic one.

"Is it about Jews or ordinary people?" my father asked.

To my astonishment, André Deutsch offered to publish the novel. Now, when somebody asked me what I did, I could reply, without seeming fraudulent to myself, that I was indeed a writer. If, returned to Hampstead once more, I still tended to doubt it in the early morning hours, now *The Acrobats*, in shop windows here and there, was the proof I needed. My novel on display side by side with real ones. There is no publication as agonizing or charged with elation as the first.

Gradually, you assume that what you write will be published. After the first book, composing a novel is no longer self-indulgent, a conceit. It becomes, among other things, a living. Though to this day reviews can still sting or delight, it's sales that buy you the time to get on with the next. Mind you, there are a number of critics whose esteem I prize, whose opprobrium can sear, but, for the most part, I, in common with other writers, have learned to read reviews like a market report. This one will help move the novel, that one not.

Writing a novel, as George Orwell has observed, is a horrible, exhausting struggle. "One would never undertake such a thing if one were not driven by some demon whom one can neither resist nor understand." Something else: Each novel is a failure, or there would be no compulsion to begin afresh. Critics don't help. Speaking as someone who fills that office on occasion, I must say that the critic's essential relationship is with the reader, not the writer. It is his duty to celebrate good books, eviscerate bad ones, lying ones.

When I first published, in 1954, it was commonly assumed that to commit a film script was to sell out (Daniel Fuchs, Christopher Isherwood, Irwin Shaw), and that the good and dedicated life was in academe. Now, the reverse seems to be the Canadian and, I daresay, American case. The creative young yearn to be in films, journeymen retire to the universities—*seems* to be the case, because, happily, there are exceptions.

All of us tend to romanticize the world we nearly chose. In my case, academe, where instead of having to bring home the meat, I would only be obliged to stamp it, rejecting this shoulder of beef as Hank James derivative, or that side of pork as sub-Jimmy Joyce. I saw myself no longer a perplexed free-lancer with an unpredictable income, balancing this magazine assignment, that film job, against the time it would buy me. No sir. Sipping Tio Pepe in the faculty club, snug in my leather winged-back armchair and the company of other disinterested scholars, I would not, given the assurance of a monthly check, chat about anything so coarse as money.

—Why don't you, um, write a novel yourself this summer, Professor Richler?

—Well, Dr. Lemming, like you, I have too much respect for the tradition to sully it with my own feeble scribblings.

—Quite.

—Just so.

Alas, academe, like girls, whisky, and literature, promised better than it paid. I now realize, after having ridden the academic gravy train for a season, that vaudeville hasn't disappeared or been killed by TV, but merely retired to small circuits, among them, the universities. Take the Canadian poets, for instance. Applying for Canada Council grants today, they no longer catalogue their publications (the obsolete accomplishments of linear man) but, instead, like TV actors on the make, they list their personal appearances, the campuses where they read aloud. Wowsy at Simon Fraser U., hotsy at Carleton. Working wrinkles out of the act in the sticks, with a headliner coming up in the veritable Palace of the Canadian campus circuit, the University of Toronto.

If stand-up comics now employ batteries of gag writers because national TV exposure means they can only use their material once, then professors, playing to a new house every season, can peddle the same one-liners year after year, improving only on timing and delivery. For promos, they publish. Bringing out journals necessary to no known audience, but essential to their advancement.

Put plainly, these days everybody's in show business, all trades are riddled with impurities. And so, after a most enjoyable (and salaried) year in academe—a reverse sabbatical, if you like—I returned to the uncertain world of the freelance writer, where nobody, as James Thurber once wrote, sits at anybody's feet unless he's been knocked there. I returned with my family to London, no deeper into *St. Urbain's Horseman* than when I had left.

Why do you write?

Doctors are seldom asked why they practice, shoemakers how come they cobble, or baseball players why they don't drive a coal truck instead, but again and again writers, like housebreakers, are asked why they do it.

Orwell, as might be expected, supplies the most honest answer in his essay "Why I Write":

"1. Sheer egoism. Desire to seem clever, to be talked about, to be remembered after death, to get your own back on grownups who snubbed you in childhood, etc. etc." To this I would add, egoism informed by imagination, style, and a desire to be known, yes, *but only on your own conditions.*

Nobody is more embittered than the neglected writer and, obviously, allowed a certain recognition, I am a happier and more generous man than I would otherwise be. But nothing I have done to win this recognition appals me, has gone against my nature. I fervently believe that all a writer should send into the marketplace to be judged is his own work; the rest should remain private: I deplore the writer as personality, however large and undoubted the talent, as is the case with Norman Mailer. I also do not believe in special license for so-called artistic temperament. After all, my problems, as I grudgingly come within spitting distance of middle age, are the same as anybody else's. Easier maybe. I can bend my anxieties to subversive uses. Making stories of them. When I'm not writing, I'm a husband and a father of five. Worried about pollution. The population explosion. My sons' report cards.

"2. Aesthetic enthusiasm. Perception of beauty in the external world, or, on the other hand, in words and their right arrangement." The agonies involved in creating a novel, the unsatisfying draft, the scenes you never get right, are redeemed by those rare and memorable days when, seemingly without reason, everything falls right. Bonus days. Blessed days when, drawing on resources unsuspected, you pluck ideas and prose out of your skull that you never dreamt yourself capable of.

Such, such are the real joys.

Unfortunately, I don't feel that I've ever been able to sustain such flights for a novel's length. So the passages that flow are balanced with those which were forced in the hothouse. Of all the novels I've written, it is *The Apprenticeship of Duddy Kravitz* and *Cocksure* which come closest to my intentions and, therefore, give me the most pleasure. I should add that I'm still lumbered with the characters and ideas, the social concerns I first attempted in *The Acrobats*. Every serious writer has, I think, one theme, many variations to play on it.

Like any serious writer, I want to write one novel that will last, something that will make me remembered after death, and so I'm compelled to keep trying.

"3. Historical impulse. Desire to see things as they are. . . ."

No matter how long I continue to live abroad, I do feel forever rooted in Montreal's St. Urbain Street. That was my time, my place, and I have elected myself to get it right.

"4. Political purpose—using the word 'political' in the widest possible sense. Desire to push the world in a certain direction, to alter other people's idea of the kind of society that they should strive after."

Not an overlarge consideration in my work, though I would say that any serious writer is a moralist and only incidentally an entertainer.

After a year on the academic payroll, I returned to London in August 1969, abysmally depressed, because after four years *St. Urbain's Horseman* was no nearer to completion and, once more, my savings were running down. I retired to my room each morning, ostensibly to work, but actually to prepare highly impressive schedules. Starting next Monday, without fail, I would write three pages a day. Meanwhile, I would train for this ordeal by taking a nap every afternoon, followed by trips to the movies I simply had to see, thereby steeling myself against future fatigue and distractions. Next Monday, however, nothing came. Instead, taking the sports pages of the *International Herald-Tribune* as my text, I calculated, based on present standings and won-lost ratios, where each team in both major baseball leagues would end the season. Monday, falling on the 8th of the month, was a bad date, anyway. Neither here nor there. I would seriously begin work, I decided, on the 15th of the month, writing *six* pages daily. After all, if Simenon could write a novel in a week, surely . . . When I failed to write even a paragraph on the 15th, I was not upset. Finally, I grasped the real nature of my problem: Wrong typewriter. Wrong color ribbon. Wrong texture paper. I traded in my machine for one with a new type face, bought six blue ribbons, and three boxes of heavy bond paper, but still nothing came. Absolutely nothing.

Then, suddenly, in September, I began to put in long hours in my room, writing with ease, one day's work more gratifying than the next, and within a year the novel was done, all 550 typewritten pages.

The first person to read the manuscript, my wife, was, like all writers' wives, in an invidious position. I depend on my wife's taste and honesty. It is she, unenviably, who must tell me if I've gone wrong. If she disapproved, however diplomatically, there would be angry words, some things I would have to say about her own deficiencies, say her choice of clothes, her cooking, and the mess she was making of raising our children. I would also point out that it was gratuitously cruel of her to laugh aloud in bed, reading *Portnoy's Complaint*, when I was having such a struggle with my own novel. All the same, I would not submit the manuscript. If she found it wanting, I would put it aside for six months to be considered afresh. Another year, another draft. And yet— and yet—even if she proclaimed the manuscript a masterpiece, radiating delight, I would immediately discount her praise, thinking she's only my wife, loyal and loving, and therefore dangerously prejudiced. Maybe a liar. Certainly beyond the critical pale.

After my wife had pronounced, foolishly saying *St. Urbain's Horseman* was the best novel I'd written by far (making me resentful, because this obviously meant she hadn't enjoyed my earlier work as much as she should have done), I submitted the manuscript to my editors. Another hurdle, another intricate relationship. I deal with editors who are commonly taken to be among the most prescient in publishing—Robert Gottlieb at Knopf and, in England, Tony Godwin at Weidenfeld & Nicolson—but once I had sent them my manuscript, and they had obviously not dropped everything to read it overnight, awakening me with fulsome cables, long-distance calls, champagne, and caviar, I began to arm myself with fancied resentments and the case that could be made against their much-advertised (but, as I had reason to suspect, overrated) acumen. As each morning's mail failed to yield a letter, and the telephone didn't ring, I lay seething on the living room sofa, ticking off, in my mind's eye, all the lesser novelists on their lists, those they flattered with larger ads, bigger first printings, more generous advances, more expensive lunches, than they had ever allowed me. In fact, I had all but decided it was time to move on to other, more appreciative publishers when, only a week after I had submitted the manuscript, both editors wrote me enthusiastic letters. Enthusiastic letters, that is, until you have scrutinized them for the ninth time, reading between the lines, and grasp that the compliments are forced, the praise false, and that the sour truth hidden beneath the clichés is that they don't really like the novel. Or even if they did, their taste is demonstrably fallible, and corrupted by the fact that they are personal friends, especially fond of my wife.

Put plainly, nothing helps.

A Sense of
the Ridiculous

NOTES ON PARIS 1951 AND AFTER
For Mason Hoffenberg and Joe Dughi

*I*n the summer of 1967, our very golden EXPO summer, I was drinking with an old and cherished friend at
Montreal Airport, waiting for my flight to London, when
all at once he said, "You know, I'm going to be forty soon."

At the time, I was still a smug thirty-six.

"Hell," he added, whacking his glass against the table,
outraged, "it's utterly ridiculous. Me, forty? My father's
forty!"

Though we were both Montrealers, we had first met in
Paris in 1951, and we warmed over those days now, *our*
moveable feast, until my flight was called.

A few days later, back in London, where I had been
rooted for more than ten years, I sat sipping coffee on the
King's Road, Chelsea, brooding about Paris and watching the
girls pass in their minis and high suede boots. Suddenly, hate-
fully, it struck me that there was a generation younger than
mine. Another bunch. And so we were no longer licensed to
idle at cafés, to be merely promising as we were in Paris, but

were regularly expected to deliver the goods, books and movies to be judged by others. At my age, appointments must be kept, I thought, searching for a taxi.

Time counts.

As it happened, my appointment was with a Star at the Dorchester. The Star, internationally known, obscenely over-paid, was attended in his suite by a bitch-mother private secretary, a soothing queer architect to keep everybody's glasses filled with chilled Chevalier Montrachet, and, kneeling by the hassock on which big bare feet rested, a chiropodist. The chiropodist, black leather tool box open before him, scissor-filled drawers protruding, black bowler lying alongside on the rug, was kneading the Star's feet, pausing to reverently snip a nail or caress a big toe, lingering whenever he provoked an involuntary little yelp of pleasure.

"I am ever so worried," the chiropodist said, "about your returning to Hollywood, Sir."

"Mmmnnn." This delivered with eyes squeezed ecstatically shut.

"Who will look after your feet there?"

The Star had summoned me because he wanted to do a picture about the assassination of Leon Trotsky. Trotsky, my hero. "The way I see it," he said, "Trotsky was one of the last really, really great men. Like Louis B. Mayer."

I didn't take on the screenplay. Instead, on bloody-minded impulse, I bought air tickets and announced to my wife, "We're flying to Paris tomorrow."

Back to Paris to be cleansed.

As my original Left Bank days had been decidedly impecunious, this was something like an act of vengeance. We stayed on the Right Bank, eating breakfast in bed at the Georges V, dropping into the Dior boutique, doing the galleries, stopping for a *fin de maison* here and a Perrier there, window-shopping on the rue du Rivoli, dining at Lapérouse, Le Tour d'Argent, and Le Méditerranée.

Fifteen years had not only made for changes in me.

The seedy Café Royale, on Boul. St. Germain, the terrace once spilling over with rambunctious friends until two in the morning, when the action drifted on to the Mabillion and from there to the notorious Pergola, had been displaced by the sickeningly mod, affluent Le Drugstore. In Montparnasse, the Dôme was out of favor again, everybody now gathering at the barnlike La Coupole. Strolling past the Café Le Tournot, I no longer recognized the abundantly confident *Paris Review* bunch (the loping Plimpton in his snapbrim fedora, Eugene Walter, Peter Mathiessen) either conferring on the pavement or sprawled on the terrace, dunking croissants into the morning café au lait, always and enviably surrounded by the most appetizing college girls in town. Neither was the affable Richard Wright to be seen any more, working on the pinball machine.

Others, alas, were still drifting from café to café, cruelly winded now, grubbiness no longer redeemed by youth, bald, twitchy, defensive, and embittered. To a man, they had all the faults of genius. They were alienated, of course, as well as being bad credit risks, rent-skippers, prodigious drinkers or junkies, and reprobates, and yet—and yet—they had been left behind, unlucky or not sufficiently talented. They made me exceedingly nervous, for now they appeared embarrassing, like fat bachelors of fifty tooling about in fire-engine red MG's or women in their forties flouncing their mini-skirts.

The shrill, hysterical editor of one of the little magazines of the Fifties caught up with me. "I want you to know," he said, "that I rejected all that crap Terry Southern is publishing in America now."

Gently, I let on that Terry and I were old friends.

"Jimmy Baldwin," he said, "has copied all my gestures. If you see him on TV, it's me," he shrieked. "It's me."

On balance, our weekend in Paris was more unsettling than satisfying. Seated at the Dôme, well dressed, consuming double scotches rather than nursing a solitary beer on the lookout for somebody who had just cashed his GI check on the black market, I realized I appeared just the sort of tourist who would have aroused the unfeeling scorn of the boy I had been in 1951. A scruffy boy with easy, bigoted attitudes, encouraging a beard, addicted to T-shirts, the obligatory blue jeans, and, naturally, sandals. Absorbed by the Tarot and trying to write in the manner of Céline. Given to wild pronouncements about Coca-Cola culture and late nights listening to Sydney Bechet at the Vieux Colombier. We had not yet been labeled beats, certainly not hippies. Rather, we were taken for existentialists by *Life*, if not by Jean-Paul Sartre, who had a sign posted in a jazz cellar warning that he had nothing whatsoever to do with these children and that they hardly represented his ideas.

I frequently feel I've lost something somewhere. Spontaneity maybe, or honest appetite. In Paris all I ever craved was to be accepted as a serious novelist one day, seemingly an impossible dream. Now I'm harnessed to this ritual of being a writer, shaking out the morning mail for check-size envelopes —scanning the newspapers—breakfast—then upstairs to work. To try to work.

If I get stuck, if it turns out an especially sour, unyielding morning, I will recite a lecture to myself that begins, Your father had to be out at six every morning, driving to the junkyard in the subzero dark, through Montreal blizzards. You work at home, never at your desk before nine, earning more for a day's remembered insults than your father ever made, hustling scrap, in a week.

Or I return, in my mind's eye, to Paris.

Paris, the dividing line. Before Paris, experience could be savored for its own immediate satisfactions. It was total. Afterwards, I became cunning, a writer, somebody with a use for everything, even intimacies.

I was only a callow kid of nineteen when I arrived in Paris in 1951, and so it was, in the truest sense, my university. St. Germain-des-Prés was my campus, Montparnasse my frat house, and my two years there are a sweetness I retain, as others do wistful memories of McGill or Oxford. Even now, I tend to measure my present conduct against the rules I made for myself in Paris.

The first declaration to make about Paris is that we young Americans, and this Canadian, didn't go there so much to discover Europe as to find and reassure each other, who were separated by such vast distances at home. Among the as yet unknown young writers in Paris at the time, either friends or nodding café acquaintances, there were Terry Southern, Alan Temko, Alfred Chester, Herbert Gold, David Burnett, Mavis Gallant, Alexander Trocchi, Christopher Logue, Mason Hoffenberg, James Baldwin, and the late David Stacton.

About reputations.

A few years ago, after I had spoken at one of those vast synagogue-cum-community plants that have supplanted the pokey little *shuls* of my Montreal boyhood, all-pervasive deodorant displacing the smell of pickled herring, a lady shot indignantly out of her seat to say, "I'm sure you don't remember me, but we were at school together. Even then you had filthy opinions, but who took you seriously? Nobody. *Can you please tell me,*" she demanded, "*why on earth anybody takes you seriously now?*"

Why, indeed? If only she knew how profoundly I agreed with her. For I, too, am totally unable to make that imaginative leap that would enable me to accept that anybody I grew up with—or, in this case, cracked peanuts with at the Mabillion—or puffed pot with at the Old Navy—could now be mistaken for a writer. A reputation.

In 1965, when Alexander Trocchi enjoyed a season in England as a sort of Dr. Spock of pot, pontificating about how good it was for you on one in-depth TV discussion after another, I was hard put to suppress an incredulous giggle each time his intelligent, craggy face filled the screen. I am equally unconvinced, stunned even, when I see Terry Southern's or Herb Gold's picture in *Time*.

I also find it disheartening that, in the end, writers are no less status-conscious than the middle-class they—we, I should say—excoriate with such appetite. As my high school friends, the old Sunday morning scrub team, has been split by economics, this taxi driver's boy now a fat suburban cat, that tailor's son still ducking bailiffs in a one-man basement factory, so we, who pretended to transcend such matters, have, over the demanding years, been divided by reputations. If our yardstick is more exacting, it still measures without mercy, coarsening the happy time we once shared.

Paris.

It would be nice, it would be tidy, to say with hindsight that we were a group, knit by political anger or a literary policy or even an aesthetic revulsion for all things American, but the truth was we recognized each other by no more than a shared sense of the ridiculous. And so we passed many a languorous, pot-filled afternoon on the terrace of the Dôme or the Sélecte, improvising, not unlike jazz groups, on the hot news from America, where Truman was yielding to Eisenhower. We bounced an inanity to and fro, until, magnified through bizarre extension, we had disposed of it as an absurdity. We invented obscene quiz shows for television, and adlibbed sexual outrages that could be interpolated into a John Marquand novel, a Norman Rockwell *Post* cover, or a June Allyson movie. The most original innovator and wit among us was easily the deceptively gentle Mason Hoffenberg, and one way or another we all remain indebted to him.

Oddly, I cannot recall that we ever discussed "our stuff" with each other. In fact, a stranger noting our cultivated indifference, the cool café posture, could never have guessed that when we weren't shuffling from café to café, in search of girls—a party—any diversion—we were actually laboring hard and long at typewriters in cramped, squalid hotel rooms, sending off stories to America, stories that rebounded with a sickening whack. The indifference to success was feigned, our café cool was false, for the truth is we were real Americans, hungering for recognition and its rewards, terrified of failure.

The rules of behavior, unwritten, were nevertheless, rigid. It was not considered corrupt to take a thousand dollars from Girodias to write a pornographic novel under a pseudonym for the tourist trade, but anybody who went home to commit a thesis was automatically out. We weighed one another not by our backgrounds or prospects, but by taste, the books we kept by our bedside. Above all, we cherished the unrehearsed response, the zany personality, and so we prized many a bohemian dolt or exhibitionist, the girl who dyed her hair orange or kept a monkey for a pet, the most defiant queen, or the sub-Kerouac who wouldn't read anything because it might influence his style. Looked at another way, you were sure to know somebody who would happily bring on an abortion with a hatpin or turn you on heroin or peddle your passport, but nobody at all you could count on to behave decently if you were stuck with your Uncle Irv and Aunt Sophie, who were "doing Europe" this summer.

Each group its own conventions, which is to say we were not so much nonconformists as subject to our own peculiar conformities or, if you like, anti-bourgeois inversions. And so, if you were going to read a fat Irwin Shaw, a lousy best-seller, you were safest concealing it under a Marquis de Sade jacket. What I personally found most trying was the necessity to choke enthusiasm, never to reveal elation, when the truth was I was out of my mind with joy to be living in Paris, actually living in Paris, France.

My room at the Grand Hotel Excelsior, off the Boul' Mich, was filled with rats, rats and a gratifyingly depraved past, for the hotel had once functioned as a brothel for the Wehrmacht. Before entering my room, I hollered, and whacked on the door, hoping to scatter the repulsive little beasts. Before putting on my sweater, I shook it out for rat droppings. But lying on my lumpy bed, ghetto-liberated, a real expatriate, I could read the forbidden, outspoken Henry Miller, skipping the windy cosmic passages, warming to the hot stuff. Paris in the fabled Twenties, when luscious slavering American schoolteachers came over to seek out artists like me, begging for it. Waylaying randy old Henry in public toilets, seizing him by the cock. Scratching on his hotel room door, entering to gobble him. *Wherever I travel I'm too late. The orgy has moved elsewhere.*

My father wrote, grabbing for me across the seas to remind me of my heritage. He enclosed a Jewish calendar, warning me that Rosh Hashanah came early this year, even for me who smoked hashish on the Sabbath. Scared even as I smoked it, but more terrified of being put down as chickenshit. My father wrote to say that the YMHA *Beacon* was sponsoring a short story contest and that the *Reader's*

Digest was in the market for "Unforgettable Characters." Meanwhile, *The New Yorker* wouldn't have me, neither would *Partisan Review*.

Moving among us there was the slippery, eccentric Mr. Soon. He was, he said, the first Citizen of the World. He had anticipated Gary Davis, who was much in the news then. Mussolini had deported Mr. Soon from Italy, even as he had one of our underground heroes, the necromancer Aleister Crowley, The Great Beast 666, but the Swiss had promptly shipped Mr. Soon back again. He had no papers. He had a filthy, knotted beard, a body seemingly fabricated of Meccano parts, the old clothes and cigarettes we gave him, and a passion for baclavas. The police were always nabbing him for questioning. They wanted to know about drug addiction and foreigners who had been in Paris for more than three months without a *carte d'identité*. Mr. Soon became an informer.

"And what," he'd ask, "do you think of the poetry of Mao Tse-tung?"

"Zingy."

"And how," he'd ask, "does one spell your name?"

My American friends were more agitated than I, a non-draftable Canadian, about the Korean War. We sat on the terrace of the Mabillion, drunkenly accumulating beer coasters, on the day General Ridgeway drove into Paris, replacing Eisenhower at SHAPE. Only a thin, bored crowd of the curious turned out to look over the general from Korea, yet the gendarmes were everywhere, and the boulevard was black with Gardes Mobiles, their fierce polished helmets catching the sun. All at once, the Place de l'Odéon was clotted with communist demonstrators, men, women, and boys, squirting out of the back streets, whipping out broomsticks from inside their shapeless jackets and hoisting anti-American posters on them.

"RIDGEWAY," the men hollered.

"*A la porte*," the women responded in a piercing squeal.

Instantly the gendarmes penetrated the demonstration, fanning out, swinging the capes that were weighed down with lead, cracking heads, smashing noses. The once-disciplined cry of *Ridgeway, à la porte!*, faltered, then broke. Demonstrators retreated, scattering, clutching their bleeding faces.

A German general, summoned by NATO, came to Paris, and French Jews and socialists paraded in somber silence down the Champs-Élysées, wearing striped pajamas, their former concentration camp uniforms. A Parisian Jewish couple I had befriended informed me at dinner that their newborn boy would not be circumcised, "just in case." The Algerian troubles had begun. There was a war on in what we then called Indo-China. The gendarmes began to raid Left Bank hotels one by one, looking for Arabs without papers. Six o'clock in the morning they would pound on your door, open it, and demand to see your passport. "I am a c-c-c-itizen of the world," said Greenblatt, at that time something called a non-figurative poet, now with Desilu Productions.

One night the virulently anti-communist group Paix et Liberté pasted up posters everywhere that showed a flag, the Hammer and Sickle, flying from the top of the Eiffel Tower. HOW WOULD YOU LIKE TO SEE THIS? the caption read. Early the next morning the communists went from poster to poster and pasted the Stars and Stripes over the Russian flag.

With Joe Dughi, a survivor of Normandy and the Battle of the Bulge, who was taking the course on French Civilization at the Sorbonne, I made the long trip to a flaking working-class suburb to see the Russian propaganda feature film *Meeting on the Elbe*. In the inspiring opening sequence, the Russian army is seen approaching the Elbe—orderly, joyous soldiers mounted on gleaming tanks, each tank carrying a laurel wreath and a portrait of Stalin. Suddenly, we hear the corrupt, jerky strains of "Yankee Doodle Dandy," and the camera swoops down on the opposite bank, where the unshaven behemoths who make up the American army are revealed staggering toward the river, soldiers stumbling drunkenly into the water. On the symbolically lowered bridge, the white-uniformed Russian colonel, upright as Gary Cooper, says, "It's good to see the American army—even if it's on the last day of the war." Then he passes his binoculars to his American counterpart, a tubby, pig-eyed, Lou Costello figure. The American colonel scowls, displeased to see his men fraternizing with the Russians. Suddenly, he grins slyly. "You must admit," he says, lowering the binoculars, "that the Germans made excellent optical equipment." The Russian colonel replies: "These binoculars were made in Moscow, comrade."

In the Russian zone, always seen by day, the Gary Cooper colonel has set up his headquarters in a modest farmhouse. Outside, his adorable orderly, a Ukrainian Andy Devine, cavorts with sandy-haired German kids, reciting Heine to them. But in the American zone, seen only by night, the obese, cigar-chomping American colonel has appropriated a castle. Loutish enlisted men parade enormous oil paintings before him, and the colonel chalks a big X on those he wants shipped home. All the while, I should add, he is on the long-distance line to Wall Street, asking for quotations on Bavarian forest.

Recently, I have been reading John Clellon Holmes's *Nothing More to Declare*, a memoir which makes it plain that the ideas and idiom, even some of the people, prevalent in the Village during the Fifties were interchangeable with those in Paris. The truculent Legman, once a *Neurotica* editor, of whom he writes so generously, inevitably turned up in St.

Germain-des-Prés to produce his definitive edition of filthy limericks on rag paper and, incidentally, to assure us gruffly that the novel was dead. Absolutely dead.

Even as in the Village, we were obsessed by the shared trivia and pop of our boyhood, seldom arguing about ideas, which would have made us feel self-conscious, stuffy, but instead going on and on about Fibber McGee's closet, Mandrake's enemies, Warner Brothers character actors like Elisha Cook Jr., the Andrews Sisters, and the Katzenjammer Kids. To read about such sessions now in other people's novels or essays doesn't make for recognition so much as resentment at having one's past broadcast, played back as it were, a ready-to-wear past, which in retrospect was not peculiar to Paris but a Fifties commonplace.

At times it seems to me that what my generation of novelists does best, celebrating itself, is also discrediting. Too often, I think, it is we who are the fumblers, the misfits, *but unmistakably lovable*, intellectual heroes of our very own fictions, triumphant in our vengeful imaginations as we never were in actuality. Only a few contemporaries, say Brian Moore, live up to what I once took to be the novelist's primary moral responsibility, which is to be the loser's advocate. To tell us what it's like to be Judith Hearne. Or a pinched Irish schoolteacher. The majority tend to compose paeans of disguised praise of people very much like themselves. Taken to an extreme, the fictional guise is dropped and we are revealed cheering ourselves. And so George Plimpton is the pitcher and hero of *Out of My League* by George Plimpton. Norman Podhoretz, in *Making It*, is the protagonist of his own novel. And most recently, in *The Armies of the Night*, Norman Mailer writes about himself in the third person.

This is not to plead for a retreat to social realism or novels of protest, but simply to say that, as novelists, many of us are perhaps too easily bored, too self-regarding, and not sufficiently curious about mean lives, bland people. The unglamorous.

All at once, it was spring.

One day shopkeepers were wretched, waiters surly, concierges mean about taking messages, and the next, the glass windows encasing café terraces were removed everywhere, and Parisians were transmogrified: shopkeepers, waiters, concierges actually spoke in dulcet tones.

Afternoons we took to the Jardins du Luxembourg, lying on the grass and speculating about Duke Snider's arm, the essays in *The God That Failed,* Jersey Joe Walcott's age, whether Salinger's *The Catcher in the Rye* could be good *and* a Book-of-the-Month, how far Senator Joe McCarthy might go, was Calder Willingham overrated, how much it might set us back to motorcycle to Seville, was Alger Hiss lying, why wasn't Nathanael West more widely read, could Don Newcombe win thirty games, and was it disreputable of Max Brod to withhold Kafka's "Letter to My Father."

Piaf was big with us, as was Jacques Prévert's *Paroles,* the song *Les Feuilles mortes,* Trenet, and the films of Simone Signoret. Anything by Genet, or Samuel Beckett, was passed from hand to hand. I tried to read *La Nausée* in French, but stumbled and gave it up.

Early one Sunday morning in May, laying in a kitbag filled with wine, *pâté,* hardboiled eggs, quiches and salamis and cold veal from the charcuterie, cheeses, a bottle of armagnac and baguettes, five of us squeezed into a battered Renault quatre-chevaux and set off for Chartres and the beaches of Normandy. 1952 it was, but we soon discovered that the rocky beaches were still littered with the debris of war. Approaching the coast we bumped drunkenly past shelled-out, crumbling buildings, VERBOTEN printed on one wall and ACHTUNG! on another. This moved us to incredulous laughter, evoking old Warner Brothers films and dimly recalled hit parade tunes. But, once on the beaches, we were sobered and silent. Incredibly thick pill boxes, split and shattered, had yet to be cleared away. Others, barely damaged, clearly showed scorch-marks. Staring into the dark pill boxes, through gun slits that were still intact, was chilling, even though gulls now squawked reassuringly overhead. Barefoot, our trousers rolled to the knees, we roamed the beaches, finding deep pits and empty shell cases here and there. As the tide receded, concrete teeth were revealed still aimed at the incoming tanks and landing craft. I stooped to retrieve a soldier's boot from a garland of sea weed. Slimy, soggy, already sea-green, I could still make out the bullet hole in the toe.

Ikons.

We were not, it's worth noting, true adventurers, but followers of a romantic convention. A second *Aliyah*, so to speak. "History has not quite repeated itself," Brian Moore wrote in a review of *Exile's Return* for the *Spectator*. "When one reads of the passionate, naïve manifestos in Malcolm Cowley's 'literary odyssey of the 1920s,' the high ambitions and the search for artistic values which sent the 'lost generation' to Paris, one cannot help feeling a touch of envy. It would seem that the difference between the American artists' pilgrimage to Europe in the Twenties and in the Sixties is the difference between first love and the obligatory initial visit to a brothel.

"Moneyed by a grant from Fulbright, Guggenheim, or Ford, the American painter now goes to France for a holiday: he knows that the action is all in New York. Similarly, the young American writer abroad shows little interest in the prose experiments of Robbe-Grillet, Sarraute, and Simon; he tends to dismiss Britain's younger novelists and playwrights as boring social realists (*we finished with that stuff twenty years ago*), and as for Sartre, Beckett, Genet, or Ionesco, he has dug them already off-Broadway. It seems that American writers, in three short generations, have moved from the provincial (*we haven't yet produced any writing that could be called major*) to the parochial (*the only stuff worth reading nowadays is coming out of America*)."

Our group, in the Fifties, came sandwiched between, largely unmoneyed, except for those on the GI Bill, and certainly curious about French writing, especially Sartre, Camus, and, above all, Céline. We were also self-consciously aware of the Twenties. We knew the table at the Dôme that had been Hemingway's and made a point of eating at the restaurant on rue Monsieur le Prince where Joyce was reputed to have taken his dinner. Not me, but others regularly sipped tea with Alice Toklas. Raymond Duncan, swirling past in his toga, was a common, if absurd, sight. *Transition* still appeared fitfully.

Other connections with the Twenties were through the second generation. David Burnett, one of the editors of *New-Story*, was the son of Whit Burnett and Martha Foley, who had brought out the original *Story*. My own first publication was in *Points*, a little magazine that was edited by Sinbad Vail, the son of Lawrence Vail and Peggy Guggenheim. It wasn't much of a magazine, and though Vail printed 4,000 copies of the first issue, he was only able to peddle 400. In the same issue as my original mawkish short story there was a better one by Brendan Behan, who was described as "27, Irish. . . . Has been arrested several times for activities in the Irish Republican Army, which he joined in 1937, and in all has been sentenced to 17 years in gaol, has in fact served about 7 years in Borstal and Parkhurst Prison. Disapproves of English prison system. At present working as a housepainter on the State Railways."

Among other little magazines current at the time there were *Id* and *Janus* ("An aristocrat by his individualism, a revolutionary against all societies," wrote Daniel Mauroc, "the homosexual is both the Jew and the Negro, the precursor and the unassimilable, the terrorist and the *raffiné*. . . .") and *Merlin*, edited by Trocchi, Richard Seaver, Logue, and John Coleman, who is now the *New Statesman*'s film critic. *Merlin*'s address, incidentally, was the English Bookshop, 42 rue de Seine, which had once belonged to Sylvia Beach.

In retrospect, I cannot recall that anybody, except Alan Temko, perhaps, was as yet writing fantasy or satire. Mostly, the stories we published were realistic and about home, be it Texas, Harlem, Brooklyn, or Denver. Possibly, just possibly, everything can be stripped down to a prosaic explanation. The cult of hashish, for instance, had a simple economic basis. It was easy to come by and cheap, far cheaper than scotch. Similarly, if a decade after our sojourn in Paris a number of us began to write what has since come to be branded black humor, it may well be that we were not so much inspired as driven to it by mechanics. After all, the writer who opts out of the mainstream of American experience, self-indulgently luxuriating in bohemia, the pleasure of like-minded souls, is also cutting himself off from his natural material, sacrificing his sense of social continuity, and so when we swung round to writing about contemporary America, we could only attack obliquely, shrewdly settling on a style that did not betray knowledge gaps of day-to-day experience.

For the most part, I moved with the *New-Story* bunch: David Burnett, Terry Southern, Mason Hoffenberg, Alan

Temko, and others. One afternoon, Burnett told me, a new arrival from the States walked into the office and said, "For ten thousand dollars, I will stop in front of a car on the Place Vendôme and say I did it because *New-Story* rejected one of my stories. Naturally, I'm willing to guarantee coverage in all the American newspapers."

"But what if you're hurt?" he was asked.

"Don't worry about me, I'm a paraphrase artist."

"A what?"

"I can take any story in *Collier's*, rewrite it, and sell it to the *Post*."

New-Story, beset by financial difficulties from the very first issue, seldom able to fork out the promised two bucks a page to contributors or meet printer's bills, was eventually displaced by the more affluent *Paris Review*. But during its short and turbulent life *New-Story* was, I believe, the first magazine to publish Jean Genet in English. Once, browsing at George Whitman's hole-in-the-wall bookshop near Notre Dame, where Bernard Frechtman's translation of *Our Lady of the Flowers* was prominently displayed, I overheard an exasperated Whitman explain to a camera-laden American matron, "No, no, it's not the same Genet as writes for *The New Yorker*."

Possibly the most memorable of all the little magazines was the French publication *Ur, Cahiers pour un dictat culturel*. *Ur* was edited by Jean-Isador Isou, embattled author of *A Reply to Karl Marx*, a slender riposte hawked by gorgeous girls in blue jeans to tourists at Right Bank cafés—tourists under the tantalizing illusion that they were buying the hot stuff.

Ur was a platform for the Letterists, who believed that all the arts were dead and could only be resurrected by a synthesis of their collective absurdities. This, like everything else that was seemingly new or outrageous, appealed to us. And so Friday nights, our pockets stuffed with oranges and apples, pitching cores into the Seine, scuffling, singing *Adon Olam*, we passed under the shadows of Notre Dame and made our way to a café on the Ile St. Louis to listen to Isador Isou and others read poems composed of grunts and cries, incoherent arrangements of letters, set to an antimusical background of vacuum cleaners, drills, car horns, and train whistles. We listened, rubbing our jaws, nodding, looking pensive.

—Ça, alors.

—Je m'en fous.

—Azoi, Ginsberg. Azoi.

Ginsberg was the first to go home. I asked him to see my father and tell him how hard up I was.

"Sometimes," Ginsberg told him, "your son sits up all night in his cold room, writing."

"And what does he do all day?"

Crack peanuts on the terrace of the Café Royale. Ruminate over the baseball scores in the *Herald-Tribune*.

We were all, as Hemingway once said, at the right age. Everybody was talented. Special. Nobody had money. (Except, of course, Art Buchwald, the most openly envied ex-GI in Paris. Buchwald, who had not yet emerged as a humorist, had cunningly solved two problems at once, food and money, inaugurating a restaurant column in the *Herald-Tribune*.) We were all trying to write or paint and so there was always the hope, it's true, of a publisher's advance or a contract with a gallery. There was also the national lottery. There was, too, the glorious dream that today you would run into the fabled lady senator from the United States who was reputed to come over every summer and, as she put it, invest in the artistic future of five or six promising, creative youngsters. She would give you a thousand dollars, more sometimes, no strings attached. But I never met her. I was reminded of the days when as a kid in Montreal I was never without a Wrigley's chewing gum wrapper, because of that magic man who could pop up anywhere, stop you, and ask for a wrapper. If you had one with you, he gave you a dollar. Some days, they said, he handed out as much as fifty dollars. I never met him, either.

Immediately before Christmas, however, one of my uncles sent me money. I had written to him, quoting Auden, Kierkegaard, *The Book of Changes*, Maimonides, and Dylan Thomas, explaining we must love one another or die. "I can hear that sort of crap," he wrote back, "any Sunday morning on the Manischewitz Hour," but a check for a hundred dollars was enclosed, and I instantly decided to go to Cambridge for the holidays.

Stringent rationing—goose eggs, a toenail-size chunk of meat a week—was still the depressing rule in England and, as I had old friends in Cambridge, I arrived laden with foodstuffs, my raincoat sagging with contraband steaks and packages of butter. A friend of a friend took me along to sip sherry with E. M. Forster at his rooms in King's College.

Forster immediately unnerved me by asking what I thought of F. Scott Fitzgerald's work.

Feebly, I replied I thought very highly of it indeed.

Forster then remarked that he generally asked visiting young Americans what they felt about Fitzgerald, whose high reputation baffled him. Forster said that though Fitzgerald unfailingly chose the most lyrical titles for his novels, the works themselves seemed to him to be without especial merit.

Unaccustomed to sherry, intimidated by Forster, who in fact couldn't have been more kind or gentle, I stupidly knocked back my sherry in one gulp, like a synagogue schnapps, while the others sipped theirs decorously. Forster waved for my glass to be refilled and then inquired without the least condescension about the progress of my work. Embarrassed, I hastily changed the subject.

"And what," he asked, "do you make of Angus's first novel?"

Angus being Angus Wilson and the novel, *Hemlock and After.*

"I haven't read it yet," I lied, terrified lest I make a fool of myself.

I left Forster a copy of Nelson Algren's *The Man with the Golden Arm,* which I had just read and enormously admired. A few days later the novel was returned to me with a note I didn't keep, and so quote from memory. He had only read as far as page 120 in Algren's novel, Forster wrote. It had less vomit than the last American novel he had read, but . . .

At the time, I was told that the American novel Forster found most interesting was Willard Motley's *Knock on Any Door.*

Cambridge, E. M. Forster, was a mistake; it made me despair for me and my friends and our shared literary pretensions. In the rooms I visited at King's, St. Mary's, and Pembroke, gowned young men were wading through the entire *Faerie Queene,* they had absorbed *Beowulf,* Chaucer, and were clearly heirs to the tradition. All at once, it seemed outlandish, a grandiose *chutzpah,* that we, street-corner bohemians, kibbitzers, still swapping horror stories about our abominable Yiddish mommas, should even presume to write. Confirmation, if it had been needed, was provided by John Lehmann, who returned my first attempt at a sub-Céline novel with a printed rejection slip.

"Hi, keed," my brother wrote, "How are things in Gay

Paree?," and there followed a list of the latest YMHA basket-ball scores.

Things in Gay Paree were uncommonly lousy. I had contracted scurvy, of all things, from not eating sufficient fruit or vegetables. The money began to run out. Come mid-night, come thirst, I used to search for my affluent friend, Armstrong, who was then putting me up in his apartment in Étoile. I would seek out Armstrong in the homosexual pits of St. Germain and Montparnasse: the Montana, the Fiacre, L'Abbaye, the Reine Blanche. If Armstrong was sweetening up a butch, I would slip in and out again discreetly, but if Armstrong was alone, alone and sodden, he would comfort me with cognacs and ham rolls and take me home in a taxi.

Enormous, rosy-cheeked, raisin-eyed Armstrong was ad-dicted to acquired Yiddishisms. He'd say, "Oy, bless my little. I don't know why I go there, Mottel."

"Uh huh."

"Did you catch the old queen at the bar?"

"I'm still hungry. What about you?"

"*Zut.*"

"You know, I've never eaten at Les Halles. All this time in Paris . . ."

"I don't care a tit if you ever eat at Les Halles. We're going home, you scheming *yenta.*"

Armstrong and I had sat next to each other in Political Science 101 at Sir George Williams College. SYSTEMS OF GOVERNMENT, the professor wrote on the blackboard:

a. monarchy   c. democracy
b. totalitarianism   d. others

Canada is a ———

Armstrong passed me a note. "A Presbyterian twat."

At Sir George, Armstrong had taken out the most desirable girls, but I could never make out. The girls I longed for longed for the basketball players or charmers like Armstrong and the only ones who would tolerate me had been the sort who read Penguins on streetcars or were above using makeup. Or played the accordion at parties, singing about Joe Hill and *Los Quatro Generales*. Or demonstrated. Then, two years before, Armstrong had tossed up everything to come to Paris and study acting. Now he no longer put up with girls and had become an unstoppable young executive in a major advertising company. "I would only have made a mediocre actor," he was fond of saying to me as I sat amidst my rejection slips.

Once more I was able to wangle money from home, three hundred dollars, and this time I ventured south for the summer, to Haut-de-Cagnes. Here I first encountered American and British expatriates of the Twenties, shadowy remittance men, coupon-clippers, who painted a bit, sculpted some, and wrote from time to time. An instructive but shattering look, I feared, at my future prospects. Above all, the expatriates drank prodigiously. Twenties flotsam, whose languid, self-indulgent, bickering, party-crammed life in the Alpes-Maritimes had been disrupted only by World War II.

Bit players of a bygone age, they persisted in continuing as if it were still burgeoning, supplying the *Nice-Matin*, for instance, with guest lists of their lawn parties; and carrying on as if Cyril Connelly's first novel, *The Rockpool*, were a present scandal. "He was only here for three weeks altogether, don't you know," a colonel told me.

"I'm only *very* thinly disguised in it," a lady said haughtily.

Extremely early one morning I rolled out of bed in response to a knock on the door. It was Mr. Soon.

"I have just seen the sun coming up over the Mediterranean," he said.

In spite of the heat, Mr. Soon wore a crushed greasy

raincoat. Terry Southern, if I remember correctly, had given it to him. He had also thoughtfully provided him with my address. "Won't you come in?" I asked.

"Not yet. I am going to walk on the Promenade des Anglais."

"You might as well leave your coat here, then."

"But it would be inelegant to walk on the Promenade in Nice without a coat, don't you think?"

Mr. Soon returned late in the afternoon and I took him to Jimmy's Bar, on the brim of the steep grey hill of Haut-de-Cagnes.

"It reminds me most of California here," Mr. Soon said.

"But I had no idea you had ever been to California."

"No. Never. Have you?"

I watched, indeed, soon everyone on the terrace turned to stare, as Mr. Soon, his beard a filthy tangle, reached absently into his pocket for a magnifying glass, held it to the sun, and lit a Gauloise. Mr. Soon, who spoke several languages, including Chinese, imperfectly, was evasive whenever we asked him where he had been born in this, his twenty-third reincarnation. We put him down for Russian, but when I brought him along to Marushka's, she insisted that he spoke the language ineptly.

Marushka, now in her sixties, had lived in Cagnes for years. Modigliani had written a sonnet to her and she could recall the night Isadora had danced in the square. Marushka was not impressed by Mr. Soon. "He's a German," she said, as if it were quite the nastiest thing she could think of.

I took Mr. Soon home with me and made up a bed for him on the floor, only to be awakened at 2 a.m. because all the lights had been turned on. Mr. Soon sat at my table, writing, with one of my books, *The Guide for the Perplexed*, by his side. "I am copying out the table of contents," he said.

"But what on earth for?"

"It is a very interesting table of contents, don't you think?"

A week later Mr. Soon was still with me. One afternoon he caught me hunting mosquitoes with a rolled newspaper and subjected me to a long, melancholy lecture on the holy nature of all living things. Infuriated, I said, "Maybe *I* was a mosquito in a previous incarnation, eh?"

"No. You were a Persian Prince."

"What makes you say that?" I asked, immensely pleased.

"Let us go to Jimmy's. It is so interesting to sit there and contemplate, don't you think?"

I was driven to writing myself a letter and opening it while Mr. Soon and I sat at the breakfast table. "Some friends of mine are coming down from Paris the day after tomorrow. I'd quite forgotten I had invited them to stay with me."

"Very interesting. How long will they be staying?"

"There's no saying."

"I can stay at the Tarzan Camping and return when they are gone."

We began to sell things. Typewriters, books, wristwatches. When we all seemed to have reached bottom, when our credit was no longer good anywhere, something turned up. An ex-GI, Seymour, who ran a tourist office in Nice called SEE-MOR TOURS, became casting director for extra parts in films and we all got jobs for ten dollars a day.

Once more, Armstrong tolerated me in his Paris flat. One night, in the Montana, Armstrong introduced me to an elegant group of people at his table, including the Countess Louise. The next morning he informed me, "Louise, um, thinks you're cute, boychik. She's just dumped Jacques and she's looking for another banana."

Armstrong went on to explain that if I were satisfactory I would have a studio in Louise's flat and an allowance of one hundred thousand francs monthly.

"And what do I have to do to earn all that?"

"Oy vey. There's nothing like a Jewish childhood. Don't be so provincial."

Louise was a thin wizened lady in her forties. Glittering earrings dripped from her ears and icy rings swelled on the fingers of either hand. "It would only be once a week," Armstrong said. "She'd take you to first nights at the opera and all the best restaurants. Wouldn't you like that?"

"Go to hell."

"You're invited to her place for drinks on Thursday. I'd better buy you some clothes first."

On Thursday I sat in the sun at the Mabillion consuming beer after beer before I risked the trip to the Countess's flat. I hadn't felt as jumpy or been so thoroughly bright and scrubbed from the skin out since my bar-mitzvah. A butler took my coat. The hall walls were painted scarlet and embedded with precious stones. I was led into the drawing room, where a nude study of a younger Louise, who had used to be a patroness of surrealists, hung in a lighted alcove. Spiders and bugs fed on the Countess's ash-grey bosom. I heard laughter and voices from another room. Finally a light-footed American in a black antelope jacket drifted into the drawing room. "Louise is receiving in the bedroom," he said.

Possibly, I thought, I'm one of many candidates. I stalked anxiously round an aviary of stuffed tropical fowl. Leaning against the mantelpiece, I knocked over an antique gun.

"Oh, dear." The young American retrieved it gently.

"This," he said, "is the gun Verlaine used in his duel with Rimbaud."

At last Louise was washed into the room on a froth of beautiful boys and girls. She took my hand and pressed it. "Well, hullo," I said.

We sped off in two black Jaguars to a private party for Cocteau. All the bright young people, except me, had some accomplishment behind them. They chatted breezily about their publishers and producers and agents. Eventually one of them turned to me, offering a smile. "You're Louise's little Canadian, aren't you?"

"That's the ticket."

Louise asked me about Montreal.

"After Paris," I said, swaying drunkenly, "it's the world's largest French-speaking city."

The American in the black antelope jacket joined me at the bar, clapping me on the shoulder. "Louise will be very good to you," he said.

Azoi.

"We all adore her."

Suddenly Louise was with us. "But you must meet Cocteau," she said.

I was directed to a queue awaiting presentation. Cocteau wore a suede windbreaker. The three young men ahead of me, one of them a sailor, kissed him on both cheeks as they were introduced. Feeling foolish, I offered him my hand and then returned to the bar and had another whisky, and yet another, before I noticed that all my group, including my Countess, had gone, leaving me behind.

Armstrong was not pleased with me, but then he was a troubled man. His secretary, a randy little bit from Guildford, an ex-India Army man's daughter, was eager for him, and Armstrong, intimidated, had gone so far as to fondle her breasts at the office. "If I don't screw the bitch," he said to me, "she'll say I'm queer. Oy, my poor tuchus."

Armstrong's day-to-day existence was fraught with horrors. Obese, he remained a compulsive eater. Terrified of black-mailers and police *provocateurs*, he was still driven to cruising Piccadilly and Leicester Square on trips to London. Every day he met with accountants and salesmen, pinched men in shiny office suits who delighted in vicious jokes about queers, and Armstrong felt compelled to prove himself the most ferocious queer-baiter of them all.

"Maybe I should marry Betty. She wants to. Well, boy-chik?"

In the bathroom, I looked up to see black net bikini underwear dripping from a line over the tub. Armstrong pounded on the door. "We could have kids," he said.

The medicine cabinet was laden with deodorants and sweetening sprays and rolls of absorbent cotton and vaseline jars.

"I'm capable, you know."

A few nights later Armstrong brought a British boy home. A painter, a taschist. "Oy, Mottel," he said, easing me out of the flat. "Gevalt, old chap."

The next morning I stumbled into the bathroom, coming sharply awake when I saw a red rose floating in the toilet bowl.

After Armstrong had left for work, the painter, a tall fastidious boy with flaxen hair, joined me at the breakfast table. He misunderstood my frostiness. "I wouldn't be staying here," he assured me, "but Richard said your relationship is platonic."

I looked up indignantly from my newspaper, briefly startled, then smiled and said, "Well, you see I could never take him home and introduce him to my family. He's not Jewish."

Two weeks later my father sent me enough money for a ticket home and, regretfully, I went to the steamship office at L'Opéra. An advertisement in the window read:

> "liked Lisbon, loved Tahiti. But when it comes to
> getting the feel of the sea ..."
> give me the crashing waves and rugged rocks
> give me the gulls and nets and men and boats
> give me the harbours and homes and spires and quays
> GIVE ME NEW BRUNSWICK
>
> CANADA

I had been away two years.

Gordon Craig

*L*et me say at once that I hadn't the foggiest idea who
Edward Gordon Craig was when I met him in 1952. The first
time I saw Craig he was sitting in the sun at a café table on
the square in Vence playing patience. He wore, as was his
habit, a white linen suit, the jacket tumbling to his knees,
and a floppy-brimmed straw hat. My friend Jean-Luc introduced me. "Are you an artist?" Craig demanded immediately.

"Well," I said, fumbling, "I'm trying to write. I . . ."

"*Good*. I'm working on my memoirs."

A British publisher had commissioned the work, but
Craig was now on his third manuscript volume and had not
yet reached the literary age of nineteen. The publisher,
alarmed, had offered to buy all Craig's personal papers and
commission somebody else to write the biography. "But
would *you* let them have Isadora's love letters?" he asked me.

Isadora, I grasped, was Isadora Duncan. Before I could
reply, a man just returned from Vallauris came to the table.
He brought regards from Picasso.

"I *should* visit him," Craig said. "It would be very good
publicity for me to have my picture taken with him now.
Have you a car?"

"Sorry," I said.

Suddenly Craig slammed his cane across the table, a startling gesture, and indicated the initials "H.I." engraved on the gold band round the top. "This was the master's," he said. "Irving always had them imported. South American malacca."

We called for another round of beer.

"A young man was here yesterday to take pictures of me," Craig said. Then he paused, his eyes narrowed, and he studied the length of his cane. Just as he felt our attention had begun to wander, he leaned forward, a conspirator, and added, "He says he's my son."

I looked astonished. Obviously, this pleased Craig enormously. He smiled. "I don't think he's my son," he said. "Pity you haven't got a car."

Craig asked me, as I was a writer, if I could please explain why so many people came to take photographs of him and none was ever published. I couldn't tell him they were being held for his obituary notices. "I really don't know," I said.

Jean-Luc and I lived in Tourrettes-sur-loup, some four miles further up the winding mountain road, and we started back together, cutting through the hot, dusty olive groves. Jean-Luc, a playwright himself, told me that Craig was a theatrical genius. A neglected genius. He had begun his career as an actor in Henry Irving's Lyceum Theatre in 1889. When he was still young and unknown, W. B. Yeats used to come to see him in his room off the Euston Road. In 1904 he prepared designs for plays and masques for the Lessing Theatre in Berlin. Later he worked with Eleonora Duse and Isadora Duncan. At a public dinner given in his honor in London in 1911, by which time Craig was an acknowledged leader in the European theatre, celebrated for his theory (*The Art of the Theatre*, 1905; *On the Art of the Theatre*, 1911) as well as his revolutionary designs, W. B. Yeats said,

"A great age is an age which employs its men of genius; a poor age is an age which has no use for them. This age finds it difficult to employ men of genius like Mr. Craig." Craig first went to Russia in 1905, where he met Stanislavsky and Fokine. He returned to Russia in 1910, at the invitation of Stanislavsky, to design a production of *Hamlet*.

Craig had promised to visit us that night. He had a friend in Tourrettes, a Colonel Hiller.

The medieval village of Tourrettes-sur-loup, jutting natural as rock over a bony ravine, is in the foothills of the Alpes-Maritimes behind Nice. Our gritty little colony of foreigners there, in 1952, included Jean-Luc and his mistress; an ambitious Australian potter, his wife and child; a Viennese abstract painter; a would-be novelist from Texas who, to the unending delight of the boule players, was given to strolling across the village square in cowboy boots; and in the villas strewn over the surrounding hills some Twenties flotsam, a wash of retired British army and colonial service officers who spluttered into Tourrettes once a week in ancient cars to have their wine casks refilled.

Craig, to our surprise, arrived on the 6:15 bus. He looked around, briefly puzzled, a white rug slung over his shoulder. Then, recognizing us at a café table on the square, he waved his arms triumphantly, hooted, and scampered over to join us. He was eighty years old then. His mother, Ellen Terry, had died at the age of eighty-one, and Craig believed he was doomed to follow her. "She appeared at the foot of my bed in a dream last night," he said. "She often does, you know."

We asked him about his trip to Russia after the revolution.

"They're the most shocking prudes, you know. They were scandalized because my secretary was pregnant." He told us that the best *King Lear* he had ever seen had been performed by the Habima in Moscow. "The authorities wanted me to say theatre had improved since the revolution, but they couldn't trick me . . ."

It soon became obvious that Craig's world was filled with two sorts of people: artists and non-artists. The artists, ourselves included, were an adorable band of gypsies united against bad taste, though always willing to accept the protection of any politician or tycoon, be they fascist, communist, or what have you.

Craig talked endlessly, demonstratively impatient, even rude, when any of the others at the table even touched briefly on a subject that did not include him. He told us that when he had been living in Florence, where, from 1908 to 1929, he had edited, published, and, under various pseudonyms, written *The Mask*, Mussolini had summoned him to an interview. Craig had assumed the dictator was going to build him a theatre and elaborated on the sort he had wanted.

"But what did you think of Mussolini?" I interrupted.

"He had the most wonderful sense of theatre," Craig said.

He went on to describe, acting out both parts, how he had entered Mussolini's office and had seen him sitting behind an enormous desk at the end of a wide sweep of marble floor. Craig had approached, books under his arm, conscious of his footsteps resounding on the marble, the dictator's glare, and the humiliating distance he still had to cover. "Mussolini," he said, "picked up my book of sketches, flipped through them upside down, and muttered something to an adviser. He had thought I was an architect," Craig said, slamming his fist against the table. "No theatre."

Midnight came, it passed, and Craig was still with us. It had grown chilly, the last bus had gone. We began to whisper among ourselves. Shouldn't he be in bed? Two o'clock. The café closed and still Craig's large laughter filled the square.

Whenever our attention faltered—the truth was, *we* were getting tired—Craig banged the master's cane against the table to emphasize a point. At last a Hillman Minx pulled up across the square and Craig leaped to his feet. "Ah. My mistress!" He gathered his things together and hurried off. Before climbing into the car, however, he assured us, "Be back tomorrow morning."

He came on the first bus and sent a boy round to knock on our doors and wake us. Bleary-eyed, we gathered again.

Craig took us up, I think, because he was generally in the company of fading retired people. A condition he did not enjoy. He was, at the time, being shunted from one *pension* to another. Craig was a foul-tempered, demanding guest, a blight innkeepers shared, like the mistral.

Craig had brought an enormous collection of recent photographs of himself. "I want you to sift through them carefully, very carefully," he said, "and select the best." As he felt we ought to discuss the charms of each study, it proved a lengthy chore. Afterwards, however, he signed photographs—"Affectionately, E.G.C."—for each of us.

Craig never came to Tourrettes empty-handed; he always had something to show us. Once he appeared with a folio of precious cartoons and other items by Beerbohm. There was a drawing of the young handsome Craig leaping over a banquet table and—a jarringly childish prank, this—a double-page spread of photographs of company directors clipped from the *Illustrated London News* and altered by Beerbohm. The eyes of some had been crossed, a moustache or side-whiskers had been added to others, but all had been made to appear uniformly ridiculous. Beerbohm had also added one puncturing sentence to the capsule biography of each director that appeared under the photographs. Beerbohm was, at the time, still resident in Rapallo. The B.B.C. had invited several old friends to broadcast tributes to him on his eightieth birthday. The gist of Craig's reminiscence was, "Max is eighty, *I'm going on eighty-one,* and nobody has paid tribute to me . . ."

Another day Craig brought me copies of several of his books. There were penciled comments in all of them. To begin with, in the book about Henry Irving, there was a list of titles of Craig's previous books. Beside each title he had calculated in pencil how much each book had earned for him. All the sums were added up at the bottom and divided by the actual number of books to give him the average earnings of each one. Below, there was a notation in pencil saying, "What shoddy paper this book has been printed on. Will it have turned to dust in fifty years? E.G.C., Florence, 192–." All Craig's notes were initialed, dated, and precisely placed (on the road to Florence, Vence, et cetera). As soon as page 11 in a book ostensibly about Irving, Craig gives us a description of himself crossing the Atlantic with Ellen Terry. "If anybody is curious to see what I looked like at that time," he writes, "they will find me in a group photographed on board the 'Arizona,' in which we came back from America in 1885." A penciled footnote below further informs us, giving the date, that the photograph appeared in the New York *Herald-Tribune.* I should add that Craig was, at the time, all of thirteen years old. Elsewhere, various footnotes were penciled in *Henry Irving* over a span of thirty years. When he produced his first play in London, Craig recounts in the book, somebody with an outlandish feminine name wrote to say how inordinately bad the production was. "Could this letter," a penciled note reads, "have been from G.B.S. in disguise?" Another note, written years later, reads, "It must have been." In another passage, Craig suggests in a printed footnote that if anyone wanted to know what he and his friends were up to in the theatre they might read books by Allardyce Nicoll and Glenn Hughes. A footnote reflects on how much in royalties this recommendation must have earned the two men and yet they never wrote to thank Craig. A further note, written some years later, observes that you'd think they would have written by this time. The final note, written in Vence, says, "They still haven't written."

When I turned to another page of the book, a typewritten letter fell out. It was written in English, to Craig, from Sergei Eisenstein. Eisenstein wrote to say how much he had enjoyed their last meeting in Paris and how he was looking forward to seeing Craig again in Moscow.

Craig told me, "Oh yes, Eisenstein. He studied my book on Irving like a Bible. He had made elaborate notes and he questioned me all night about Irving's technique."

Craig never threw anything out. He still retained all the sketches he had ever made when he had used to go to the music halls in London as a youth. His friend, Colonel Hiller, told me that several years earlier the Victoria and Albert Museum in London had made Craig a considerable offer for all his letters, manuscripts, woodcuts, and memorabilia, but he had turned them down. Later he was to sell everything to the Bibliothèque Nationale in Paris.

He was, I remember, often disturbed by newspaper accounts that referred to him as the late Edward Gordon Craig. One day he came to Tourrettes, infuriated. A press agent's story in the Paris edition of the *Herald-Tribune* had described an encounter between Orson Welles and Craig in the American Express. Welles, according to the story, bowed deeply and said, "Master. My Master."

"Very flattering, I suppose," Craig said, "but I never met Welles."

I left Tourrettes a week later and my last glimpse of

Craig, from the bus, was on the square in Vence. He was playing patience. He looked bored and eager for an interruption.

When I returned to Tourrettes four years later, in 1956, the first person I saw there was Craig. He sat at the café on the square, seemingly unchanged, talking to Colonel Hiller. I did not expect him to recognize me and he didn't. I had to introduce myself again. "I've brought you regards," I said.

"Who?" he said, cupping an ear.

"I've been asked to bring you regards from a friend of yours."

"A gift! You've brought me a gift!"

"Regards," I said, flushing.

"REGARDS," Colonel Hiller shouted. "NOT A GIFT."

"Oh," Craig said, his head dropping, dejected.

Since I had last seen him, Craig had enjoyed a revival of sorts. Many of his early books had been reissued and he was much better off, financially, than he had been in 1952. He had also moved from Vence to an inn on the edge of the Tourrettes ravine. The inn was run by a retired French army officer, an opium-eater, and his teenage Arab boyfriend. Craig adored sitting on the terrace, talking about art and artists, his white hair flowing in the wind and his chin resting on H.I.'s cane.

One of Edward Gordon Craig's dearest ambitions had still not been realized—he hadn't been knighted.

In the final chapter of *Henry Irving*, after Craig has, so to speak, finished the book, the master's spirit appears in his study.

"You must not think I exaggerate," Craig wrote. "I was alone; the wind, 'tis true, was howling down the valley outside my house—how it howwwled—yet all was cosy and well-lit in my room—nothing dusky, nothing weird: yet there—there stood Irving."

After man and ghost discoursed for a while, Irving observed, "Er—yes: by the bye, I see you have been knighted, my boy—very good—very good."

Craig protested vehemently that he had not been knighted.

"Not knighted—but it's in the papers!"

"No, Henry . . . that was somebody else . . . an Ernest Gordon Craig."

"Ah! Ernest—Ernest," repeated Irving—"Wilde pointed to the er-r—importance of that. . . ."

Craig was included in the Queen's Honours List in 1956 and his Companion of Honour (C.H.) was presented to him by the British consul in Nice. At the small party for Craig, I'm told, the consul began to recite a verse by Browning.

"Byron?" Craig interrupted. "Is that Byron?"

"BROWNING!"

"I don't care for Browning."

One day during that last summer in Tourrettes an eager young off-Broadway producer in Bermuda shorts turned up on the square. "You mean to say Craig is still alive?" he said.

"There he is now."

The producer took Craig to dinner, and he suggested, his manner breathless, that the old man might do a few sketches for his next production. Craig refused. But the last time I saw Craig the flabby young man was at his elbow. "Why don't we drive down to see Picasso?"

"Not today," Craig said, wearily.

Writing
for the Movies

*O*nce, *it was ruled that any serious novelist or play-*
wright who tried his hand at film-writing was a sellout. Indeed, many a novelist-turned-screenwriter next proffered a
self-justifying, lid-lifting novel about Hollywood, wherein the
most masculine stars were surreptitiously (not to say gratifyingly) queer, the most glamorous girls were empty inside,
deep inside, but lo and behold, the writer, on the last page,
had left the dream palace, fresh winds rippling through his
untamed hair, to write the book-of-the-month you had just
finished reading. Later, the novelist returned to Hollywood,
but *on his own terms*, to do the screenplay of his novel. It
was filmed frankly, outspokenly, and everybody felt better
inside, deep inside.

Hollywood is one thing, London another. No better than
the archetypal boss's son, I started out at the bottom in films.
I got work as a reader for a studio script department. For
two quid, in 1955, a reader was expected to write a ten-page
synopsis of a book followed by a shrewd evaluation of its
film potential. Like, Harold Robbins is visual, but Proust isn't.
Experts, I discovered, managed to zip through and report on
as many as four books a day. I never got to be an expert.

One day a script editor handed me a book for which, she said, I would be paid a double fee. It was Brecht's *Mother Courage*. "The play's only sixty pages," I said. "Why can't the producer read it himself?"

I did not yet know that it was no more expected of most producers to actually read books than it was, say, of Walter O'Malley to chop down trees to make baseball bats. So I took the play home, wrote a synopsis, and mailed it off. The next morning the script editor phoned me, outraged. "But you haven't said whether or not you think it would make a good film," she said.

That ended my career as a reader, but shortly afterwards I was hired to write a script for the TV serial mill. The hero of the series was a free-lance sea captain (tough, fearless, jaunty), and my script took him to Spain for some smuggling. The producer didn't like it one bit. "You call this a script? What's this here? Two guys talking. *Talking?* Yak-yak-yak for two whole pages. Where's the action?"

I bought a book with three screenplays in it by Graham Greene and set to work again. I made absolutely no plot or dialogue changes, but, whereas a page of my first draft script read,

> CARLOS: Things are very quiet here tonight. I do not like it, Nick.
> NICK: I was just wondering . . .

my revised, professional version read,

> CARLOS: Things are very quiet here tonight. I do not like it, Nick.
> SOUND: *It is very quiet.*
>   CUT TO CU NICK. *He lights a cigarette. He inhales.*
> NICK: «with a far-off, wondering look» I was just wondering . . .

I had arrived. Another writer, hired to do two half-hour comedies, pilots for a possible series for Peter Sellers (Sellers, at the time, had made only one feature-length film, *The Lady*

Killers), made me his collaborator. He wanted company. He executed all the routines meant for Sellers. I learned to say, "Why, that's swell. A great gag." I did the typing and brewed the tea. Eventually, we were summoned to a script conference. Present were Sellers, the director, the producer, two assistants, my collaborator, and I. We sat solemnly round an enormous table in a boardroom overlooking Hyde Park. Before each of us there were a pad, a pencil, and a glass of water. The producer, a tiny wizened man with pebble-glasses, told us, "Gentlemen, we are here to exchange ideas. To my right is our director. Need I say, a *great* talent. A talent I have engaged, I might say, for a pretty penny."

The director, who hadn't worked in years, said, "I consider this series a challenge."

The rest of us were fulsomely introduced. "Now about the script . . ." Squinting, the producer held the script no more than two inches from his face. "Page twenty-nine, boys. We've slowed down here. We need a gimmick. Well, if you saw *Love Happy* with the Marx Brothers you will recall there was a great scene in that picture. Harpo is leaning against a wall. Groucho comes by and says, what are you doing, holding up the building? Harpo nods. He moves away and the building collapses."

Sellers was silent.

"Now, boys, ours is a small-budget film. What I think we could do on page twenty-nine is this: Instead of a building, Mr. Sellers could be leaning against a lamppost. When he moves away," the producer said, already beginning to break up with laughter, "the lamppost falls down."

Sellers lit one cigarette off another.

"Page thirty-two, boys. Have you ever had the good fortune to see Mr. Danny Kaye, a great comedian, in *Up in Arms*?"

To my astonishment, the two films were made and distributed. I never saw them, but within months I was working on my first feature film, a mediocre thriller that required rewrites. The director wasn't jumpy, he was panic-stricken, and he insisted that I work with him at his flat every day. Together we raked each scene over and over again.

"Mn," he'd say, reading a page just ripped out of the typewriter, "jolly good . . . Well, not bad. But would he say *that?* Is it really in character for him to say 'thank you' at that moment?"

I'd look pensive. Wearily I'd say, "I think you're on to something, you know. It *is* out of character. I think he'd say 'thanks,' not 'thank you.' "

"But isn't that too American-y?"

"Exactly. But that's the point. *He's American-oriented.*"

The director sometimes kept me all day without doing any writing. Nervously, he would dig out his copy of *Spotlight*, a catalogue with photographs of almost every actor and actress in the country, and solicit my opinion on casting. My opinion was worthless and, if you figured it at a day's pay, worthless *and* expensive.

"What would you think of John Mills?"

"He's all right."

"What do you mean all right? Are you holding something back? Do you know something?"

I swore I didn't.

"What about Jack Hawkins?"

"Sure."

"If you don't like Jack Hawkins, tell me. This is very important."

Like most novelists, I am conditioned to working for months on material I discuss with nobody, because to talk about it is to risk losing it. To adjust from that to scriptwriting, where you are bound to meet once a week with a director or pro-ducer or both to discuss work in shaky first-draft form and work yet to be done, is more than unnerving, it's indecent.

Here it is necessary to make a sharp distinction between the entertainment and the so-called art film, each presenting the novelist-turned-scriptwriter with special problems. I'd like to deal with the entertainment first because it's simpler, a straightforward street corner deal. Money is time, and writing an entertainment can buy a novelist a very sweet chunk of it.

As a general rule, the writer who adapts a thriller or a best-seller for the screen is the most lowly and expendable of technicians; in fact most take-charge, can-do producers don't feel secure until they've hired and fired one writer after another, licking the script into shape, as they say. Once I was summoned by a producer who had already hired a writer for an adventure film he was going to make. Although the writer had not yet begun work, the producer wanted to know if I could take over within twelve weeks. "What," I asked, "if the man you've got turns in a script that doesn't require more work?"

"Don't worry," the producer replied immediately, "he can only go seven innings."

Traditionally, producers are the butt of most film jokes, but in my limited dealings I've found many of them engaging and surprisingly forthright about their needs. In the Sixties, too, they were running touchingly scared. Commercial pro-ducers were baffled by the new films, they didn't understand their success. Arty directors, writers, and actors, whom the big production units had been shunning for years, were not only making pix but some of their pix were making money. Wowsy in Denver, boffo in Cincy. Suddenly art was good biz. So the call is out for no-saying playwrights, black humor-ists, and dirty-minded novelists. Only the producers still want the same old stuff, the good old stuff, but tarted up, modishly done, with frozen frames, action speeded up here, slowed down there, clichés shot through a brandy glass or as seen reflected in a cat's eye, and performers talking directly to the audience. It's much as if, instead of printing the best take, they had now begun to print the take before the last, the one wherein the actors sent up the film, including jokes that were hitherto private, limited to the studio unit. Which, incidentally, often brought the bewildered producers full circle, right back to where many of them started out years and years ago, making Robert Benchley and Edgar Kennedy shorts.

The problems involved in writing a screenplay for a seriously meant film are at once more intricate and perplexing, assuming that you are adapting somebody else's novel or play. To begin with, there's your relationship with the director. A talented director does not eat a batch of interchangeable writers; he seeks out, and is prepared to wait for, the writer he wants and who, he feels, will see a screenplay through from beginning to end. He will treat a writer well, protecting him from prying, nervy producers, stars who want a peek at the script-in-progress, and other occupational hazards; but in return he demands that you do your best for him. Let me put it another way. He has actually read your novels, not your screenplays, and that's why he wants you.

Flattering. But how far do you go with such a director? How many of your own original ideas do you contribute to an adaptation of somebody else's work? I have, for instance, twice worked for Jack Clayton, on the final script for *Room at the Top* and doing the screenplay for John Le Carré's *The Looking Glass War*. I've also worked with Ted Kotcheff, writing the screenplay for *Life at the Top*. In each case, as a novelist myself, with split loyalties, I couldn't help feeling that no matter what I added to Braine or Le Carré the written work remained essentially theirs, justifiably so. Why, then, do more than adapt? Why turn in a scene or an idea or a character you've been hoarding and can very nicely use in one of your own novels?

Ideally, I used to believe, the thing would be to get yourself commissioned to write an original screenplay, but I no longer think so, if only because even under the most ideal circumstances film is not a writer's medium. Filmmaking belongs more than anything to the writer-director, say Fellini, and, failing that, to the truly gifted director, always remembering that the director, no matter how inspired, who cannot write his own scripts is an incomplete artist.

One comes away from filmmaking with an increasing respect for the serious director, one who needs somebody else for the script. I speak here of the director who will not make any film, even any worthwhile film, unless it touches him. To watch him between films, devouring novels and plays, reading scripts, is to witness the anguish of a sadly dependent man. Why wait for novels or plays, then, why not get something of his own going? Sometimes he does, but the sort of writer such a director would like to commission to write an original screenplay is also the kind who presents the most difficulties. In the nature of things, he won't or can't submit an idiotic four-page synopsis to be sent on to a producer for financing. More seriously, he is loath to write an original screenplay because his ego, like the director's, tends to be discomfortingly large, and the same concept committed to a novel remains in his control.

Even given an admirable screenplay, my sympathies remain with the director. The writer leads a comparatively sheltered life, everything happens in his room. The director, equally proud and sensitive, if you like, is almost always on. Performing. Not only must he be able to con producers and flatter actors, but, ultimately, he has to be up to making his mistakes in public. The writer, having done a scene badly, rips it out of his typewriter and tries again or goes out to shoot pool for the rest of the day. Nobody knows. The director, botching a scene, does it before a crowd. His off-days are shared and possibly savored by an entire studio unit, and there may not be time or money left to redo the scene.

As recently as 1962, Daniel Fuchs was driven to defending his abandonment of fiction for the movies. "Generations to come," he wrote in *Commentary*, "looking back over the years, are bound to find that the best, the most solid creative effort of our decades was spent in the movies, and it's time someone came clean and said so."

Today, no apologies are asked for or given. The movies have become increasingly, almost insufferably modish, especially among writers, intellectuals, and students. In fact, the sort of student who once used to help put out a little magazine is nowadays more likely to be making a movie with a hand-held camera. His mentors are Antonioni, Resnais, Godard, Losey, Bergman, Fellini, Polanski, etc. He also studies corny old movies, resuscitated as camp.

This is not to say that in *our* student days, in the Forties, we did not cut morning lectures to watch the Marx Brothers or guffaw at inspirational war films—say, *The Pride of the Marines* with John Garfield. In an early scene, as I recall it, Garfield has a Jap grenade explode smack in his face, but he continues to fire his machine gun heroically with Dane Clark's help. Shipped back to a military hospital in San Francisco, blinded but unscarred(!), Garfield dictates a letter to his sweetheart saying he never wants to see her again, he's found somebody else. The truth is, Garfield is too proud to become a burden to such a nice girl as Eleanor Parker. He tells Dane

Clark bitterly, "Nobody will give a blind man a job," and Clark replies, if I remember correctly, "*I've* always had that problem. My name is Shapiro."

This era of treacly, brother-loving films, in which so many of the good guys were Jews or Negroes and nearly all the shits were Wasps, broke up with the coming of McCarthyism. Ultimately Senator McCarthy—so despicable in his time, seen to be such a buffoon in retrospect—may come to be appreciated as the most effective of cultural brooms. He did more than *Cahiers du Cinema* or *Sight & Sound* to clean the liberal hacks as well as some talented men out of Hollywood.

But the point I was really trying to make here was that we, too, laughed at jingoism, bad taste, and enjoyed slapstick; however, as we took this to be altogether unexceptionable, we did not go on and on about it. We did not enshrine it, calling it camp. I should add, incidentally, that we also went in for screwing in the afternoon. Or, as a thought-provoking *Time* essayist might put it, we had sex without love. But we did not think for a minute that this made us revolutionaries. Or alienated. Or that it was happening for the first time. We put it down to being horny, that's all.

I throw this in because so much that is praised in the new, serious films is dependent on an appallingly ignorant, mistaken belief that things are happening for the first time. The truth is, they are only happening for the first time on film. But we are so grateful for even a modicum of originality on the screen, we are so flattered to be addressed directly, that we seldom realize the so-called serious film is, for the most part, shamelessly derivative, taking up a position abandoned by novelists years ago.

Notes on an Endangered Species

S*trolling down to the Carlton Hotel beach, suffi*-ciently early to claim a place in the sun on the first morning of the Cannes Film Festival in 1972, I immediately espied a hirsute belly boiling out of the sands, knobby arms glistening with suntan oil, thumbs hooked into plaid Bermuda shorts that caught the belly necessarily low, yet punishingly tight all the same. The man's face was at once pouchy but rutted with wrinkles, cupped by a spreading silver foil reflector aimed at the sun. Unmistakably Bronstein.

No sooner did I settle onto my own mattress than the gnats began to buzz around him. Three overeager Englishmen, Wardour Street hustlers, deep into skin flicks.

"What have you got for us this year?" Bronstein sang out.

Attaché cases flick open, brochures fly out.

"Well, we've got some werewolves, a monster, but no tits. That market's played out, you know."

"I'm thinking of buying *Homo Vampire*," Bronstein allowed, amazed at himself. "You heard?"

Yes; they'd heard.

"Who do you think made it? The Germans, naturally.

It's all about a fag witch," Bronstein continued, disgusted, "who faints at the sight of blood."

Though Bronstein now buys exploitation films for American distribution, he was once a producer. An independent. When I'd last seen him, some six months earlier, he was ensconced in his Belgravia Mews flat, the furnishings out of the most modish King's Road antique shops, provisions laid on by Harrod's Food Emporium, a Bentley idling in the garage, a taxproof portfolio fattening in a Swiss account, the number swallowed and committed to memory, and the latest Mrs. Bronstein not only a pleasure to look at, but his youngest wife yet. He seemed the most enviable of middle-aged men. But now Bronstein's a wreck. The world he took so long to knit is unraveling again.

Bronstein's one of a brood of show business Americans now rooted in London. Years ago, serving his Hollywood apprenticeship, he churned out two-reelers. The Three Stooges were not unknown to him; neither were the Ritz Brothers. In the early Fifties, he began to produce, albeit only for Monogram, but Metro was making sweet noises. Things were looking up. Forearming himself, intent on self-improvement, Bronstein devoured The Great Books, he acquired a taste for claret, and learned to eschew Gershwin for Bach. Then, for the first time, things flew apart. Senator Joe McCarthy led his vigilantes into town and Bronstein—hitherto a professional yes-man, a fully accredited forelock-toucher—stiffened. With nothing to gain, everything to lose, something in his Brownsville background wouldn't yield. Memories of the Spanish Civil War, maybe, or his father demonstrating. To his own astonishment, Bronstein refused to talk to the Committee on Un-American Activities. He would not name names. Driven out of the industry, blacklisted, he packed his wife and children and set out for London, which is where I, a published but decidedly impecunious novelist, first met him in 1954. I shall always cherish Bronstein as he was then, adrift, stunned, even as he propelled me toward the Hampstead Public Library. "You've got an education," he said. "Go in there, to the stacks, and find me something. Have you ever been in a library? It's a goddamn goldmine. All those books in the public domain. But you've got to know what to reach for."

Bronstein, in those days, was prepared to start on the bottom rung again. Riding the TV serial mill maybe. But in London, lo and behold, he was no longer scorned as a schlock artist; instead, he was celebrated as a producer for all seasons. Other blacklisted men, Academy Award–winning directors and writers, began to shove things his way. And, over the years, Bronstein's name came to be associated with quality pictures, festival candidates, Academy nominees. Sir Laurence Olivier's agent was pleased to have lunch with him. If he waved to David Niven in the Mirabelle, Niven waved back. Once, at the White Elephant, Richard Burton actually stopped at his table: he had a project . . .

Then, suddenly, brutally, the quality films Bronstein took such immense pride in, each one elegantly made, flopped one after another. The audience had gone elsewhere. Bronstein, taking to Valium, threw his own money into a motorcycle movie a year too late and then surfaced with a love story a year too soon. Meanwhile, the art house cinema that had flattered him for a season was devoting itself to a "golden age of comedy" anthology—the Ritz Brothers, The Three Stooges, *the crap he had overcome*—and packing them in, yes, packing them in. And now Bronstein was afraid to make a move, any move, because one more mistake and he was out.

Noon. Even those who didn't stagger out of the Casino until 4 a.m. have now risen to their restorative glasses of hot water, honey, and lemon, taken with pills (one color for energy, another for tranquility), and driven their sagging bodies to the waterside. The action. The Carlton Hotel beach is now littered with baking filmmakers. Rex Reed has been seen. Groucho's arrival is rumored. Harry Saltzman, it is promised, will soon appear. Bronstein, suddenly mindful of his burning belly, rises, shifts to the shelter of his umbrella, and flops down on another mattress. He is now part of a group, among them Bernie Lindman, who ventures, "Hey, what about a remake of *Gone with the Wind*, retold from the *schwartze* point of view? You know, the slave market, whippings, interracial screwing, the whole *shmear*. Scarlett is kinky."

"Are you making fun of me?" Bronstein demands.

"To tell you the truth, I don't know. I'm not sure. But it's one hell of a market now."

They are joined by Schwartz, who has just been to see *Mona*, a hard-core porn film, ending in an orgy. The large screen swollen with close-ups of genitalia.

"They're actually showing that stuff in drive-ins now," Schwartz says. "You're looking at it and getting it at the same time. How are you going to top that, baby?"

Like the kangaroo or, more appropriately, perhaps, the blue whale, film producers are now an endangered species. In their beleaguered world, nothing is sure-fire any more. Neither a big-budget blockbuster adorned by the most dazzling constellation of stars, nor a cheap but explicit skin flick. The trouble is that nothing is box-office-sacred any more, not even the frontal nude. Gone, gone forever, are the fat years, when to shoot a film, any film, was, for openers, to cream $200,000 off the top of the budget.

A diminishing form of wildlife, increasingly starved for sustenance, the independent producers have been driven from pastures traditionally green, by television, by the unaccountable tastes of the ungrateful young, and, to an even larger extent, by their own stupidity and consuming greed. Through the long cold winter in Rome, Hollywood, Paris, and London, delaying payment on the long-distance phone bill, they have been sustained by miracles proven (last year *The Godfather*, this year *Last Tango in Paris*) and the dizzying dream of connecting in Cannes in May. For if absolutely nothing but chicanery is assured any more, then the Cannes Film Festival is still where the producers come to spawn in the springtime. Those who can afford it sink into luxury suites in the Carlton, the Majestic, or Antibes' Hotel de Cap, and the others, the hustlers who have flown the Atlantic economy class, toting reels of unsold film under their arms, hunker down in nondescript back street *pensions*. Ostensibly they have all come to watch the films being officially shown at the festival, but actually to reassure each other, spitball and, above all, buy and sell. And why not? As Gilbert de Goldschmidt, director of Unifrance, the association of French producers, put it, "All through history peasants who have wanted to sell have had to bring their pigs to market."

More than four hundred films are screened during the festival, most of them porn, hard and soft, shown out of prize competition in back street cinemas, distribution rights readily available. The real marketplace, by common consent, is a Victorian wedding cake of a hotel, the Carlton, baking on the sea-front. The market spills out of the churning lobby, onto the overflowing terrace, running down to the beach and the yachts moored beyond. The independent producer approaches it armed with hope, appetite, optioned screenplays, and rented starlets; he comes to meet and haggle with distributors, exhibitors, and potential investors from every continent, assuring them, hand held over his heart, that he, and he alone, has the biggie going into production, and will surface as next year's *Godfather*'s godfather. Climb on board today, baby, or cry tomorrow.

To the uninformed onlooker, the terrace might seem unusually crowded with roistering middle-aged men during the festival, but otherwise unremarkable. To the initiated, its hierarchy is as intricate as that of any medieval court, festooned with power brokers, the rare cardinal, and a plethora of fringe film people hustling here, there, and everywhere.

Morning again; and scuttering from table to table are the flacks, dispensing the most coveted luncheon, party, and film invitations to the anointed, shaking disdainfully free of pleading, coat-pulling outsiders. Modishly braless hookers, nipples by Eversharp, are rooted here and there, the empty coffee cups before them unfailingly lipstick-stained. Occasionally, a cardinal deigns to appear—say, seemingly benign, cubby Harry Saltzman, begetter of the James Bond films; and Saltzman's eyes do not dart as he sails between tables, raining smiles on acolytes, blessing less fortunate men. Saltzman is immediately embraced by a director with an official entry in the festival. "Harry Saltzman is a great producer, the greatest," he proclaims again and again, "and I don't say that just because he's here."

Saltzman, not inclined to disagree, settles into an empty table, waiting for the world, his inheritance, to come to him, and, within minutes, he is indeed besieged.

"Would you believe," he says, "that it took me twenty minutes to get from the front desk to this table? Everybody stops me, they've got a deal. And within the next half-hour, just sitting here, I will be offered stars, scripts, directors, armies in Yugoslavia, studios in Tel Aviv, and five-million-dollar co-production deals, and at the end of it what will I have? A stack of bills this high, nobody even picks up his own coffee tab."

Saltzman recognizes that these are economy-minded days,

even for him. "I make no more seven-limousine pictures. You know," he adds, shaking his head, astonished at himself, "on the last Bond picture, *I used my own car.*"

Which was when Norm Flecker, a fringe producer, bore down on us. Flecker endeared himself to me years ago in London when he took an option on Evelyn Waugh's *Scoop* and was sufficiently intrepid to commission the novelist to do a screen treatment of the book for him. Waugh accepted his several thousand pounds gleefully and, in return, sent Flecker a treatment at once as comprehensive as it was unique: the Penguin edition of his novel pasted up on postcards. For Flecker, his briefcase bulging with projects unfulfilled, the Carlton terrace is that heart-hammering one-chance-of-the-year. All through the punishing winter he has been humiliated and scorned, unable to get past Warner's front office or even get the assistant head of overseas production at MGM on the phone; and now, suddenly—look, look —everybody's here, on the terrace, tantalizingly vulnerable, unable to hide behind secretaries. Uninvited and uninsultable, his skin thicker than bear hide, he moves in on them one by one.

The terrace is charged with risks and interruptions for those who have come to do serious business, among them Buck Dane *né* Dankowitz. Greying, pear-shaped Dane, fifty-two years old and a natty dresser, is a veteran of radio and TV and has, he is fond of saying, written two hundred screenplays and fourteen novels. Written out, perhaps, he is now in charge of London production for an American exploitation film company, an adroit two-way dealer, peddling his company's product for European, Asian, and African distribution, and buying foreign schlock for release in America. Habitually, Dane is ensconced at the table that lies right against the glass doors to the bar and sits with his back to the terrace. "This way," he says, "I can watch the bodies float by, reflected in the glass, and if a loser is bearing down on my table, I signal the waiter, two fingers up, and he summons me to a long-distance call." Dane keeps his tape recorder prominently displayed on his table. "I warn them, I tell them it's here, but, listen, I've got every offer made down on tape. It helps prevent misunderstandings later on. Even so, the terrace is a bummer. Too many schnorrers."

So Dane is filled with admiration for John Heyman, of World Film Sales, who, in 1971, beat the terrace crush with considerable panache. Heyman rented Elizabeth Taylor's yacht for £3,000 a week, and moored offshore. "You know," Dane said, "it wasn't that everybody wanted to make deals with him, but they all went out to the yacht. They're only human, you know, they wanted to see Elizabeth Taylor's bidet. And then the next thing you know, they're out to sea, floating on champagne, and contracts are out, it's sunny, and maybe you close a deal . . ."

A young Canadian filmmaker descends on Dane and invites him to a screening of his film, *Cannibal Girls*. Dane, agreeing to go, makes a note. "I'll tell you," he says, "it's a subject that could really go. I've been pushing for cannibalism for two years now."

The first Cannes Film Festival, in 1939, was conceived as a democratic response to the older festival in Venice, then thought to be controlled by Mussolini. It was to be a glittering affair, charged with glamour. MGM dispatched a shipload of stars. In the pre-opening ceremonies, Norma Shearer and George Raft danced in the streets. But the festival, actually scheduled to open on September 1, 1939, was upstaged by a bigger, more dramatic production to the north, the Nazi invasion of Poland, and didn't get under way again until 1946.

Some serious reputations have been made at Cannes,

including that of Michelangelo Antonioni, who showed *L'Avventura* there in 1960, and Godard, who was there the same season with *Breathless*. Once, stars used to adorn the sea-front cafés, pursued everywhere by fans, and fabled champagne-and-caviar parties were the rule. In 1956, an unknown starlet flung herself at Robert Mitchum, shedding her bikini top, and her photograph, a shocker at the time, traveled round the world. But on last season's beaches topless girls abound, hardly rating a second glance.

"There are no more stars, not in the old and accepted sense," said the festival's most seasoned publicist. "Robert Redford is here, you know. I watched him sitting on the terrace for maybe an hour, and not one person came over to ask for his autograph."

No more stars and, Harry Saltzman laments, no more showmanship. But, as recently as 1969, Commonwealth United, a film company backed by I.O.S.—and buried with it —ran guests in and out of Cannes by chartered jet, and threw a lavish party for hundreds at the casino, presenting all the men with gold Dunhill lighters and all the ladies with expensive evening bags, each with one hundred dollars' worth of chips thoughtfully tucked inside. Most of the ladies, rather sensibly, didn't play, but cashed in their chips instead. A harbinger of things to come, perhaps. For last May most of the parties were distinctly on the chintzy side. Nothing more than *vin ordinaire* and cold fish salad at the luncheon for Jeanne Moreau. From United Artists, at their cocktail party, not Beluga caviar but sliced eggs or tomatoes on crackers. MGM didn't entertain, Columbia passed, and Paramount, the Chosen Studio, saw fit to send forth to Cannes only its tabernacles, white-on-black ceiling-high placards mounted on pillars in the Carlton lobby, saying *"The Godfather* is now a phenomenon." So it was left to Samuel Z. Arkoff, the ebullient head of A.I.P., with *Frogs* jumpin' in nine house multiples and *Spider Woman* yet to come, to offer a first-class lunch, lobster followed by filet, and strawberries with cream. "Last year we had more than fifty Arabs here," Arkoff said, "but I didn't invite any this time. I've got nothing against them. But if you sell distribution rights to your film in Lebanon, it ends up playing in Jordan, Libya, and Egypt as well. They're some crowd."

After twenty-five years, the festival differs from a shoe salesmen's convention only in that it is more subdued, without funny hats or door prizes, the money tighter. Something even the hookers, who wouldn't accept credit cards, grasped as early as the fifth day, when they abandoned the impecunious producers for the cash-paying sailors of the Sixth Fleet. Of course, there's still the competition for the Grand Prix International, but that's no more than window dressing now, like the small cigar store that fronts for the larger bookie's office behind. Yesteryear's glamour was grotesquely parodied last May by the frequent appearance on the beach and the terrace of a six-foot transvestite, silvery-wigged, wearing a frilly bolero, Pucci-type floral slacks, and platform shoes. Encouraged by the *paparazzi*, he pirouetted along the Carlton pier, using it as a model's catwalk, pausing here and there to mock the poses usually affected by bikini-clad starlets.

Prominent on the terrace at all hours are the so-called distress merchants, those men grim as they are bronzed, who offer new methods, just this side of usury, of financing films. One of the most thrusting, Alberti, maintains offices in the capitals of three continents. Producers, rejected by all the major studios, come to him with projects. He listens, he nods, he makes notes on his scratch pad. The producer says he's got a director, a star, and a honey of a script, but no money. He must have a million two. Alberti, if he savors the project, phones Athens and Tokyo, Paris, Toronto, and Madrid. From his agents in each country, he extracts a promissory note, a guarantee against the rights to distribute the finished film in their territory, say $50,000 from Greece, $100,000 from Japan, and so on. He delivers the notes to the producer, less eighteen percent, his cut for raising the money. The producer, grasping the notes in his hot hand, then breaks for the bank, where the notes are usually discounted for another ten percent. But he's in business, shooting a film. Likely as not, flying over Geneva, he shakes the budget bag, just to see how much will stick to his numbered account, and in the end produces his film for only $900,000. He will charge a year's office overhead, his mistress's new car, his father-in-law's heart specialist, and his son's orthodontia bill to the production. He cajoles his director into taking only $25,000 up front, against a whacking share of profits that he knows will never materialize, and his star, if he's French, may work for nothing, acquiring all rights to the film in France in lieu of payment.

Alas, most of the films financed through this method, beginning with *Shalako*, a Western starring Sean Connery and Brigitte Bardot, and running through *Trotsky* with Richard Burton, have done poorly at the box office. Even so, the initial investors, the men who forked out for the territories in advance, were probably in need of a tax write-off. Most likely, they have also visited the sets, and now boast photographs of themselves actually shaking hands with Richard Burton or sitting at the very same table as Brigitte Bardot. Alberti has creamed his eighteen percent off the top, the producer is hardly out of pocket, the director and actors have earned something. Everybody's worked.

Another distress merchant, a febrile American in London called Seigal, has succeeded in making a large number of films, selling the territories in advance, but all of them have been critical failures as well as box office losers. He is grudgingly admired, if only because, as Bronstein puts it, he climbs up the ladder of success from failure to failure. But, if that's the case, he's not the least bit fazed. "I'm a great promoter of money," he told me. "Each time out, I put together a very impressive package."

Yes, yes, I protested, but none of your films have earned money.

"Oh yeah, well look here, even before I had my own company, when I was still producing for one of the majors, I made two losers in one year, big ones, and I still came out 450,000 dollars ahead. There's more than one way to skin a cat, you know."

The distributors, it must be said, do not sit on the Carlton terrace primarily to invest in films hopefully to be made, but rather to buy a finished product. The most astute, whether they be from South America or Greece, are in persistent quest of a "locomotive," a proven box office winner, for which they will overpay, if only because it enables them to hitch many wagons to it, cheaply bought duds, which they will force-feed to cinema chains who want the big one.

Something else: The producer, who cheats gleefully, is gleefully swindled in turn by most distributors. In a typical deal, a distributor will buy a film for, say, Brazil, signing a check for $10,000 against a guaranteed further $40,000 to come out of receipts. No sooner has he issued the check than he phones his bank and stops payment on it. Then, still on the line to Brazil, he hustles various cinema chains, trying to unload the film he has just purchased. If he succeeds, making a profit, he will ultimately let his check go through; if not, not. But the seller knows, without a doubt, that he will never see his further $40,000. "Then why does he insist on it?" I ask Harry Saltzman.

"Because when he returns to his backers, and they shout, why did you sell so cheap, what's ten thousand for Brazil, he says, yes, but look, there's another forty to come. He takes his contract to the bank and uses the forty for collateral. They'll advance him more money against it to finance his next film. And the secret of this business is to have a new film going on the floor before your last disaster has been released. That way you can go on for years."

Such convoluted dealings are especially demanding of the fledgling filmmaker, but some make it, among them the young Canadian director of *Cannibal Girls* ("They eat men!"), which he sold before the festival was done. Buck Dane, it's true, walked out, disgusted, after twenty minutes' viewing, but he returned another day with Samuel Z. Arkoff, who bought American distribution rights.

"Let me tell you," Dane said, "that kid is something. He sat with Arkoff, an old pro, the boy's only twenty-six years old, he talked grosses, percentages, cooperative advertising, never giving an inch. Those things you don't learn at school in Toronto. His film is awful, but he'll go far. You wait and see."

Finally, there were some stars in Cannes last May, the real McCoy, but they were all grand old men, none of whom had films showing in competition. John Huston, Groucho, and Alfred Hitchcock. No sooner did Huston loom on the terrace, a compelling, craggy-faced man in a white safari suit, pursued by celebrity-starved photographers, than lesser men thrust themselves at him, smiling not at the director, but into the photographers' flashing bulbs, only to have their faces clipped out of the next morning's *Nice-Matin*.

Late one night I ran into Seigal at the Carlton bar. "Listen here," he said, "even if they do go to cassettes, somebody will still have to produce, direct, and write them, don't you think?"

On the last day of the festival, after most people had scattered, a giggly girl, young, but far from pretty, suddenly shed her bikini top—seemingly crazed—and raced to and fro, to and fro, on the Carlton pier for the benefit of the remaining photographers, no more than two or three.

Even as the billboards and sales booths began to come down, carpenters hammering everywhere, Bronstein, his nose peeling, finally connected. He made a deal. He slipped a waiter ten francs and in return collected a wad of bar bills with which to pad his expense account. I had run into him earlier at the official French gala, where wristwatches had been presented to all the ladies. He had passed in and out of the reception twice, collecting as many watches. All in all, he wasn't flying off empty-handed.

The Great Comic
Book Heroes

"Q uiet! A revolution is brewing," begins a recent
advertisement for the New Book of Knowledge. "This is
Gary. Age 11. He's a new breed of student. A result of the
'quiet revolution' in our schools. He's spent happy hours on
his project. Away from TV. Away from horror comics. Completely absorbed. Learning! Reading about cocoons, larvae,
butterflies. . . ."

No, no, Gary is no new breed. I recognize him. In my
day he always did his homework immediately he came home
from school. He never ate with his elbows on the table. Or
peeked at his sister in the bath. Or shoplifted. Or sent un-
wanted pianos, ambulances, firemen, and bust developers to
the class teacher, the unspeakable Miss Ornstein, who made
us suffer creative games, like Information Please or Increasing
Your Word Power with the Reader's Digest. Gary ate his
spinach. He was made president of the Junior Red Cross
Club and pinned The Ten Rules of Hygiene over his sink.
He didn't sweat, he perspired. And he certainly never swiped
a hard-earned dime from his father's trousers, the price of a
brand-new comic book. Oh, the smell of those new comic

books! The sheer, the glossy feel! *Tip-Top*, *Action*, *Detective*, and *Famous Funnies*.

Each generation its own nostalgia, its own endearing fantasy figures. For my generation, born into the Depression, beginning to encourage and count pubic hairs during World War II, there was nothing quite like the comic books. While bigger, more mature men were cunningly turning road signs to point in the wrong direction in Sussex, standing firm at Tobruk, Sending for More Japs, holding out at Stalingrad, making atomic bombs, burning Jews and gassing Gypsies; while General ("Old Blood and Guts") Patton was opening the Anglo-American service club in London, saying, "The idea of these clubs could not be better because undoubtedly it is the destiny of the English and American people to rule the world" and Admiral William F. ("Bull") Halsey was saying off the record, "I hate Japs. I'm telling you men that if I met a pregnant Japanese woman, I'd kick her in the belly"; we, the young, the hope of the world, were being corrupted by the violence in comic books. Ask Dr. Frederic Wertham, who wrote in *Seduction of the Innocent*:

> . . . a ten-year-old girl . . . asked me why I thought it was harmful to read Wonder Woman. . . . She saw in her home many good books and I took that as a starting point, explaining to her what good stories and novels were. "Supposing," I told her, "you get used to eating sandwiches made with very strong seasonings, with onions and peppers and highly spiced mustard. You will lose your taste for simple bread and butter and for finer food. The same is true for reading strong comic books. If later you want to read a good novel it may describe how a young boy and girl sit together and watch the rain falling. They talk about themselves and the pages of the book describe what their innermost little thoughts are. This is what is called literature. But you will never be able to appreciate that if in

comic book fashion you expect that any minute someone will appear and pitch both of them out of the window."

Or Kingsley Martin, who wrote that Superman was blond and saw in him the nefarious prototype of the Aryan Nazi. Never mind that Superman, the inspired creation of two Jewish boys, Jerome Siegal and Joe Shuster, was neither blond nor Aryan; it was a good theory. We were also being warped by Captain Marvel, The Human Torch, The Flash, Sheena, Queen of the Jungle, Hawkman, Plastic Man, Sub Mariner, and Batman and Robin. Our champions; our revenge figures against what seemed a gratuitously cruel adult world.

This is not to say our street was without intellectual dissent. After all, social realism was the thing, then.

"There's Tarzan in the jungle, week in and week out," Solly said, "and he never once has to shit. It's not true to life."

"What about Wonder Woman?"

"Wonder Woman's a dame, you shmock."

Wonder Woman was also a waste of time. Uncouth. Like ketchup in chicken soup. Or lighting up cigarette butts retrieved from the gutter. Reading was for improving the mind, my Aunt Ida said, and to that end she recommended *King's Row* or anything by John Gunther. Wonder Woman, according to Dr. Wertham, was a dyke as well. For boys, a frightening image. For girls, a morbid ideal. Yes, yes, but as Jules Feiffer observes in his nostalgic *The Great Comic Book Heroes*, "Whether Wonder Woman was a lesbian's dream I do not know, but I know for a fact she was every Jewish boy's unfantasied picture of the world as it really was. You mean men weren't wicked and weak? . . . You mean women didn't have to be *stronger* than men to survive in the world? Not in *my* house!"

Batman and Robin, the unsparing Dr. Wertham wrote, were also kinky: "Sometimes Batman ends up in bed injured and young Robin is shown sitting next to him. At home they lead an idyllic life. They are Bruce Wayne and 'Dick' Grayson. Bruce Wayne is described as a 'socialite' and the official relationship is that Dick is Bruce's ward. They live in sumptuous quarters with beautiful flowers in large vases. . . . Batman is sometimes shown in a dressing gown. . . . It is like a wish dream of two homosexuals living together."

Unfortunately I cannot personally vouch for the sexual proclivities of socialites, but I don't see anything necessarily homosexual in "beautiful flowers in large vases." This strikes me as witch-hunting. Sexual McCarthyism. Unless the aforesaid flowers were pansies, which would, I admit, just about clinch the good doctor's case. As, however, he does not specify pansies, we may reasonably assume they were another variety of flora. If so, what? Satyric rambling roses? Jewy yellow daffodils? Droopy impotent peonies? Communist-front orchids? More evidence, please.

Of more significance, perhaps, what Dr. Wertham fails to grasp is that we were already happily clued in on the sex life of our comic book heroes. As far back as 1939, publishers (less fastidious than the redoubtable Captain Maxwell) were offering, at fifty cents each, crude black-and-white comics which improvised pornographically on the nocturnal, even orgiastic, adventures of our champions. I speak here of GASOLINE ALLEY GANG BANG, DICK TRACY'S NIGHT OUT, BLIND DATE WITH THE DRAGON LADY, and the shocking but liberating CAPTAIN AMERICA MEETS WONDER WOMAN, all of which have long since become collector's items. It is worth pointing out, however, that I never came across anything juicy about Superman and Lois Lane, not even gossip, until dirty-minded intellectuals and Nazis had their say.

Item: Richard Kluger writes (*Partisan Review,* Winter

1966): "He could, of course, ravish any woman on earth (not excluding Wonder Woman, I daresay). . . . Beyond this, there is a tantalizing if somewhat clinical and highly speculative theory about why Superman never bedded down with Lois, never really let himself get hotted up over her; Superman, remember, was the Man of Steel. Consider the consequences of supercoitus and the pursuit of The Perfect Orgasm at the highest level. So Supe, a nice guy, had to sublimate. . . ."

Item: When Whiteman, one of the many Superman derivatives, this one published by the American Nazi Party, is asked whatever became of the original Superman, he replies: "Old Supey succumbed to the influence of Jew pornography. . . . It seems Superman was putting his X-ray vision to immoral use and was picked up by the vice squad as a Peeping Tom."

Superman, of course, was the original superhero. "Just before the doomed planet Krypton exploded to fragments, a scientist placed his infant son within an experimental rocket-ship, launching it toward earth!" Here Superman was discovered and finally adopted by the Kents, who gave him the name Clark. When they died, "it strengthened a determination that had been growing in his mind. Clark decided he must turn his titanic strength into channels that would benefit mankind. And so was created . . . SUPERMAN, champion of the oppressed, the physical marvel, who had sworn to devote his existence to helping those in need." Because Superman was invincible, he soon became something of a bore . . . until Mort Weisinger, a National Periodical Publications vice-president who has edited the strip since 1941, thought up an Achilles' heel for him: when exposed to fragments from the planet Krypton, Superman is shorn of his powers and reduced to mere earthly capabilities. A smooth touch, but the fact is, the real Superman controversy has always centered on his assumed identity of Clark Kent, a decidedly fainthearted reporter. Kent adores Lois Lane, who has no time for him. Lois is nutty for Superman, who in true "aw shucks" tradition has no time for any woman. "The truth may be," Jules Feiffer writes, "that Kent existed not for purposes of the story but the reader. He is Superman's opinion of the rest of us, a pointed caricature of what we, the non-criminal element, were really like. His fake identity is our real one." Well, yes, but I'm bound to reveal there's more to it than that. Feiffer, like so many before him, has overlooked a most significant factor: the Canadian psyche.

Yes. Superman was conceived by Toronto-born Joe Shuster, originally worked not for the *Daily Planet* but for a newspaper called *The Star*, modeled on the Toronto *Star*. This makes his assumed identity of bland Clark Kent not merely understandable, but artistically inevitable. Kent is the archetypal middle-class Canadian Wasp, superficially nice, self-effacing, but within whom there burns a hate-ball, a would-be avenger with superhuman powers, a smasher of bridges, a breaker of skyscrapers, a potential ravisher of wonder women. And (those who have scoffed at Canadian culture in the past, please take note) a universal hero. Superman, first drawn by Shuster in 1938, now appears in twenty languages. This spring, God willing, Lois Lane, who has pined for him all these years, will be married off to a reformed mad scientist, Dr. Lex Luther. I am indebted to another *aficionado*, Alexander Ross, a *Macleans* editor, for all this information. Last March, Ross went to visit Joe Shuster, fifty and still single ("I have never met a girl who matched up to Lois Lane," he has said), at Forest Hills, Long Island, where he lives with his aged mother. Shuster, sadly, never did own the rights on his creation. It is the property of NPP, who say that by 1948 the legendary Shuster was no longer able to draw the strip because of failing eyesight. He was discharged and now earns a living of sorts as a free-lance cartoonist. "He is trying," Ross writes, "to paint pop art—serious comic strips —and hopes eventually to promote a one-man show in some chic Manhattan gallery." Such, Ross might have added, is the inevitable fate of the artistic innovator under capitalism.

If Superman, written and drawn by a hard-faced committee with 20/20 vision these days, continues to flourish, so do the imitations; and here it is worth noting how uncomfortably the parodies of the anarchistic left and broad Jewish humor have come to resemble the earnestly meant propaganda of the lunatic right.

On the left, *The Realist* has for some time now been running a comic strip about LeRoi Jones called Supercoon. Little LeRoi becomes mighty Supercoon, threat to the virtue of white women everywhere, by uttering the magic curse, "Mother-fucker." Jones, I'm told, was so taken with this parody that he wrote the script for an animated cartoon called *Supercoon* which he wished to have made and released with the film version of his play *Dutchman*. It has, however, yet to be produced. On a more inane level, *Kosher Comics*, a one-shot parody, published in New York, which runs strips called The Lone Arranger (with the masked marriage broker and Tante), Tishman of the Apes, and Dick Shamus, also includes Supermax, who is called upon to defeat invaders from the planet Blech. The invaders are crazy for matzoh balls.

Meanwhile, back at American Nazi headquarters in Arlington, Virginia, the *Stormtrooper* magazine has recently given us Whiteman. "Jew Commies Tremble . . . Nigger Criminals Quake In Fear . . . Liberals Head For The Hills . . . Here Comes Whiteman." In his first adventure Whiteman, whose costume is a duplicate of Supey's, except that the emblem on his chest is a swastika rather than an S, "fights an interplanetary duel with a diabolical fiend . . . THE JEW FROM OUTER SPACE." He also does battle with SUPERCOON. In

real life, Whiteman is a milkman named Lew Cor ("Rockwell" spelled backwards, for Nazi Commander George Lincoln Rockwell) and is transformed into Whiteman by speaking the secret words, "Lieh Geis!" "With my super-vision,"
Whiteman says, "I can see three niggers have been caught
in the act of trying to burn down a Negro church. If they had
not been caught in the act, some poor southern white man
would have been blamed for it." He soon beats up the Negro
arsonists ("Sweet dreams, Jigaboo"), but meanwhile, inside
a mysterious spacecraft, MIGHTY MOTZA is creating SUPERCOON
with an atomic reverse-ray gun. The emblem on Supercoon's
chest, incidentally, is a half-peeled banana, and naturally he
is no match for Whiteman, who quickly eliminates him. "So
long, Supercoon! You just couldn't make the grade with your
second-class brain. With my white man intelligence, I have
reduced you to a super-revolting protoplasmic slime. Ugh!
Looks like a vile jellyfish."

In the past, comic strips, or derivatives thereof, have been
put to less extreme political purpose. All of us, I'm sure, remember the late Vicky's Supermac. Parralax, publishers of
Kosher Comics, have also brought out *Great Society Comics*,
with Super LBJ and Wonderbird; and *Bobman and Teddy
Comics*, featuring the Kennedy brothers. Then day by day,
in the Paris edition of the New York *Herald-Tribune*, Wash-
ington *Post*, and hundreds of other newspapers, Steve Canyon
and Buzz Sawyer risk their lives for us in Vietnam. Canyon,
a more politically conscious type than Sawyer, has recently
had some sour things to say about dovelike congressmen and
student peaceniks: neither fighter has yet had anything to say
about Whiteman. If and when the crunch comes on the
Mekong Delta, it remains an open question whether or not
Buzz and Steve would accept Whiteman's support.

Canyon's political past, incidentally, is not unblemished.
When he came to serve at a U.S. Air Force base in northern

Canada in 1960, the Peterborough (Ontario) *Examiner* took umbrage. "We have become disturbed by the political implications of the strip. The hero and his friends were on what was obviously Canadian soil, but it seemed to be entirely under the domination of American troops who were there as a first-line defense against the Russians." There was only one manly answer possible: Canadian-made strips such as Larry Brannon, a non-starter, who was to glamourize the face of Canada. In his first adventure, Brannon visited "Toronto, focus of the future, channel for the untold wealth of the north, communications centre of a vast, rich hinterland, metropolis of rare and precious metals." The last time we were asked to make do with Canadian comics was during the war years when in order to protect *our* balance of payments the government stopped the import of American comic books. The Canadian comic books hastily published to fill the gap were simply awful; we wouldn't have them. Banning American comic books was a typically unimaginative measure, for whatever pittance the government made up in U.S. currency, it lost in home front morale. Comics, as Feiffer has written, were our junk. Our fix. And before long a street corner black market in *Detective* and *Action* comics began to flourish. Just as we had come to the support of Americans during the Prohibition years, thereby founding more than one Canadian family fortune, so the Americans now saw that we didn't go without. Customs barriers erected against a free exchange of ideas never work.

I have no quarrel with Feiffer's selection from the comics for his *The Great Comic Book Heroes*, but his text, the grammar and punctuation quirky, seems to me somewhat thin. Feiffer is most knowledgeable, a veritable Rashi, on the origins and history of the comic books. He is at his most absorbing when he writes about his own experience as a comic book artist. He learned to draw in the schlock houses, the art

schools of the business. "We were a generation," he writes.
"We thought of ourselves the way the men who began the
movies must have." And indeed they went to see *Citizen
Kane* again and again, to study Welles's use of angle shots.
Rumors spread that Welles in his turn had read and learned
from the comic books. Fellini was certainly a devotee.

In the schlock houses, Feiffer writes, "Artists sat lumped
in crowded rooms, knocking it out for a page rate. Penciling,
inking, lettering in the balloons for ten dollars a page, sometimes less. . . ."; decadence setting in during the war. The
best men, Feiffer writes, went off to fight, hacks sprouting up
everywhere. "The business stopped being thought of as a
life's work and became a stepping stone. Five years in it at
best, then on to better things: a daily strip, or illustrating for
the *Saturday Evening Post*, or getting a job with an advertising agency. . . . By the end of the war, the men who had been
coloring our childhood fantasies had become archetypes of
the grown-ups who made us need to have fantasies in the
first place."

But it was Dr. Wertham, with his *Seduction of the Innocent*, who really brought an end to an era. His book led to
the formation of a busybody review board and an insufferable
code that amounted to the emasculation of comic books as we
had known them:

1. Respect for parents, the moral code, and for honourable behaviour, shall be fostered.
2. Policemen, judges, government officials and respected institutions shall never be presented in such a way as to create dis-
   respect for established authority.
3. In every instance, good shall triumph over evil and the criminal
   punished for his misdeeds.

To be fair, there were uplifting, mind-improving side-
effects. Culture came to the newsstands in the shape of *True*

Comics, *Bible Comics*, and the unforgettable series of *Classic Comics* from which Feiffer quotes the death scene from *Hamlet:*

> Fear not, queen mother!
> It was Laertes
> And he shall die at my hands!
> . . . Alas! I have been poisoned
> And now I, too, go
> To join my deceased father!
> I, too—I—AGGGRRRAA!

Today, men in their thirties and forties trade old comic books with other addicts and buy first issues of *Superman* and *Batman* for fifty dollars or more. Although the original boyhood appeal of the comic books was all but irresistible to my generation, I have not gone into the reasons until now, for they seemed to me obvious. Superman, The Flash, The Human Torch, even Captain Marvel, were our *golems.* They were invulnerable, all-conquering, whereas we were puny, miserable, and defeated. They were also infinitely more reliable than real-life champions. Max Schmeling could take Joe Louis. Mickey Owen might drop that third strike. The Nazi Rats could bypass the Maginot Line, and the Yellow-Belly Japs could take Singapore; but neither dared mix it up with Captain America, the original John Bircher, endlessly decorated by FBI head J. Arthur Grover, and sponsor of the Sentinels of Liberty, to which we could all belong (regardless of race, color, or creed) by sending a dime to Timely Publications, 330 West 42nd St., N.Y., and signing a pledge (the original loyalty oath?) that read: "I solemnly pledge to uphold the principals [sic] of the Sentinels of Liberty and assist Captain America in his war against spies in the U.S.A."

Finally, many of our heroes were made of paltry stuff when they started out. The World's Mightiest Man, Power-

ful Champion of Justice, Captain Marvel, was mere Billy
Batson, newsboy, until he uttered the magic word, "Shazam!"
The Flash is another case in point.

> Faster than the streak of lightning in the sky . . . Swifter than
> the speed of light itself . . . Fleeter than the rapidity of thought
> . . . is *The Flash*, reincarnation of the winged Mercury . . .
> His speed is the dismay of scientists, the joy of the oppressed—
> And the open mouthed wonder of the multitudes!

Originally, however, he was as weak as you or I. A decidedly forlorn figure. He was Jay Garrick, "an unknown student at a midwestern university . . ." and, for my money, a
Jew. The creators of *The Flash*, Gardner Fox and Harry
Lampert, even like Arthur Miller, wrote at a time, remember,
when Jews were still thinly disguised as Gentiles on the stage,
in novels, and in comic books. There is no doubt, for instance,
that *The Green Lantern* has its origin in Hassidic mythology.
Will Eisner's *The Spirit*, so much admired by Feiffer, is given
to cabalistic superstitions and speaking in parables. With
The Flash, however, we are on the brink of a new era, a
liberated era. Jay Garrick is Jewish, but Reform. Semi-
assimilated. In the opening frame, lovely Joan (significantly
blonde) won't date him, because he is only a scrub on the
university football team while Bull Tyron is already a captain.
"A man of your build and brains," she says, "could be a
star. . . . A scrub is just an old washwoman! You won't put
your mind to football. . . . !" Jay, naturally, is intellectually
inclined. Probably he is taking freshman English with Leslie
Fiedler. An eye-opener! Huck Finn and Nigger Jim, like Batman and Robin, are fags. Jay, however, spends most of the
time in the lab with his professor. Then one day an experiment with hard water goes "Wrong." Jay, overcome by
fumes, lurches forward. ("It's . . . it's . . . too much for
me. . . .") He lies between life and death for weeks, coming

out of it endowed with superhuman powers. "Science," the doctor explains, "knows that hard water makes a person act much quicker than ordinarily. . . . By an intake of its gases, Jay can walk, talk, run and think swifter than thought. . . . He will probably be able to outrace a bullet!! He is a freak of science!" Briefly, he is now The Flash.

How puerile, how unimaginative, today's comic strips seem by comparison. Take Rex Morgan, M.D., for instance. In my day, to be a doctor was to be surrounded by hissing test tubes and vile green gases. It was to be either a cackling villain with a secret formula that would reduce Gotham City to the size of a postage stamp, or a noble genius, creator of behemoths who would bring hope to the oppressed multitudes. The best that can be expected of the loquacious Dr. Morgan is that he will lecture us on the hidden dangers of Medicare. Or save a student from LSD addiction. There's no magic in him. He's commonplace. A bore.

The Catskills

*A*ny account of the Catskill Mountains must begin
with Grossinger's. The G. On either side of the highway out
of New York and into Sullivan County, a two-hour drive
north, one is assailed by billboards. DO A JERRY LEWIS—COME
TO BROWN'S. CHANGE TO THE FLAGLER. I FOUND A HUSBAND
AT THE WALDEMERE. THE RALEIGH IS ICIER, NICIER, AND
SPICIER. All the Borscht Belt billboards are criss-crossed with
lists of attractions, each hotel claiming the ultimate in golf
courses, the latest indoor and outdoor pools, and the most
tantalizing parade of stars. The countryside between the signs
is ordinary, without charm. Bush land and small hills. And
then finally one comes to the Grossinger billboard. All it says,
sotto voce, is GROSSINGER'S HAS EVERYTHING.

"On a day in August, 1914, that was to take its place
among the red-letter days of all history," begins a booklet
published to commemorate Grossinger's fiftieth anniversary,
"a war broke out in Europe. Its fires seared the world. . . .
On a summer day of that same year, a small boarding house
was opened in the Town of Liberty." The farmhouse was
opened by Selig and Malke Grossinger to take in nine people
at nine dollars a week. Fresh air for factory workers, respite

for tenement dwellers. Now Grossinger's, spread over a thousand acres, can accommodate fifteen hundred guests. It represents an investment of fifteen million dollars. But to crib once more from the anniversary booklet, "The greatness of any institution cannot be measured by material size alone. The Taj Mahal cost a king's ransom but money in its intrinsic form is not a part of that structure's unequalled beauty."

Grossinger's, on first sight, looks like the consummate kibbutz. Even in the absence of Arabs, there is a security guard at the gate. It has its own water supply, a main building—in this case Sullivan County Tudor with picture windows —and a spill of outlying lodges named after immortals of the first Catskill *Aliyah*, like Eddie Cantor and Milton Berle.

I checked in on a Friday afternoon in summer, and crossing the terrace to my quarters stumbled on a Grossinger's Forum of the Air in progress. Previous distinguished speakers —a reflection, as one magazine put it, of Jennie Grossinger, in whom the traditional reverence for learning remains undimmed—have included Max Lerner and Norman Cousins. This time out the lecturer was resident hypnotist Nat Fleischer, who was taking a stab at CAN LOVE SURVIVE MARRIAGE? "I have a degree in psychology," Fleischer told me, "and am now working on my doctorate."

"Where?"

"I'd rather not say."

There were about a hundred and fifty potential hecklers on the terrace. All waiting to pounce. Cigar-chompers in Bermuda shorts and ladies ready with an alternative of the New York *Post* on their laps. "Men are past their peak at twenty-five," Fleischer shouted into the microphone, "but ladies reach theirs much later and stay on a plateau, *while the men are tobogganing downhill.*" One man hooted, another guffawed, but many ladies clapped approval. "You think," Fleischer said, "the love of the baby for his momma is natural—*no!*" A man, holding a silver foil sun reflector to his face, dozed off. The lady beside him fanned herself with *From Russia, With Love.* "In order to remain sane," Fleischer continued, "what do we need? ALL OF US. Even at sixty and seventy. LOVE. A little bit of love. If you've been married for twenty-five years you shouldn't take your wife for granted. Be considerate."

A lady under a tangle of curlers bounced up and said, "I've been married twenty-*nine* years, and my husband doesn't take me for granted."

This alarmed a sunken-bellied man in the back row. He didn't join in the warm applause. Instead he stood up to peer at the lady. "I'd like to meet her husband." Sitting down again, he added, "The schmock."

There was to be a get-together for singles in the evening, but the prospects did not look dazzling. A truculent man sitting beside me in the bar said, "I dunno. I swim this morning. I swim this afternoon—indoors, outdoors—my God, what a collection! When are all the beauties checking in?"

I decided to take a stroll before dinner. The five lobbies at Grossinger's are nicely paneled in pine, but the effect is somewhat undermined by the presence of plastic plants everywhere. There is plastic sweet corn for sale in the shop beside the Olympic-size outdoor pool, and plastic grapes are available in the Mon Ami Gift and Sundry Shop in the main building. Among those whose pictures hang on the Wall of Fame are Cardinal Spellman and Yogi Berra, Irving Berlin, Governors Harriman and Rockefeller, Ralph Bunche, Zero Mostel, and Herman Wouk. The indoor pool, stunningly simple in design, still smelled so strongly of disinfectants that I was reminded of the more modest "Y" pool of my boyhood. I fled. Grossinger's has its own post office and is able to stamp all mail "Grossinger, N.Y." There is also Grossinger Lake, "for your tranquil togetherness"; an eighteen-hole golf course; stables; an outdoor artificial ice rink; a ski and to-boggan run; a His 'n Hers health club; and of course a land-ing strip adjoining the hotel, the Jennie Grossinger Field.

The ladies had transformed themselves for dinner. Gone were the curlers, out came the minks. "Jewish security blankets," a guest, watching the parade with me, called the wraps, but fondly, with that sense of self-ridicule that re-deems Grossinger's and, incidentally, makes it the most slippery of places to write about.

I suppose it would be easiest, and not unjustified, to present the Catskills as a cartoon. A Disneyland with knishes. After all, everywhere you turn, the detail is bizarre. At the Concord, for instance, a long hall of picture windows over-looks a parking lot. There are rooms that come with two adjoining bathrooms. ("It's a gimmick. People like it. They talk about it.") All the leading hotels now have indoor ice skating rinks because, as the lady who runs The Laurels told me, our guests find it too cold to skate outside. True, they have not yet poured concrete into the natural lakes to build artificial filtered pools above, but, short of that, every new convenience conspires to protect guests from the countryside. Most large hotels, for instance, link outlying lodges to the main building through a system of glassed-in and sometimes even subterranean passages, all in the costly cause of pro-tecting people from the not notoriously fierce Catskills out-doors.

What I'm getting at is that by a none too cunning process of selected detail one can make Grossinger's, the Catskills, and the people who go there appear totally grotesque. One doesn't because there's more to it than that. Nothing, on the other hand, can prevent Sullivan County from seeming outlandish, for outlandish it certainly is, and it would be condescending, the most suspect sort of liberalism, to overlook this and instead celebrate, say, Jennie Grossinger's maudlin "warmth" or "traditional reverence" for bogus learning.

Something else. The archetypal Grossinger's guest belongs to the most frequently fired-at class of American Jews. Even as *Commentary* sends out another patrol of short story writers the *Partisan Review* irregulars are waiting in the bushes, bayonets drawn. Saul Bellow is watching, Alfred Kazin is ruminating, Norman Mailer is ready with his flick-knife, and who knows what manner of tripwires the next generation of Jewish writers is laying out at this very moment. Was there ever a group so pursued by such an unsentimental platoon of chroniclers? So plagued by moralists? So blamed for making money? Before them came the *luftmenschen*, the impecunious dreamers—tailors, cutters, corner grocers—so adored by Bernard Malamud. After them came Philip Roth's confident college boys on the trot, Americans who just happen to have had a Jewish upbringing. But this generation between, this unlovely spiky bunch that climbed with the rest of middle-class America out of the Depression into a pot of prosperity, is the least liked by literary Jews. In a Clifford Odets play they were the rotters. The rent collectors. Next Jerome Weidman carved them up and then along came Budd Schulberg and Irwin Shaw. In fact, in all this time only Herman Wouk, armed with but a slingshot of clichés, has come to their defense. More of an embarrassment, I'd say, than a shield.

Well now, here they are at Grossinger's, sitting ducks for satire. Manna for sociologists. Here they are, breathless, but at play, so to speak, suffering sour stomach and cancer scares, one Israeli bond drive after another, unmarriageable daughters and sons gone off to help the Negroes overcome in Mississippi. Grossinger's is their dream of plenty realized, but if you find it funny, larger than life, then so do the regulars. In fact, there is no deflating remark I could make about minks or matchmaking that has not already been made by visiting comedians or guests. Furthermore for an innocent goy to even think some of the things said at Grossinger's would be to invite the wrath of the B'nai Brith Anti-Defamation League.

At Grossinger's, guests are offered the traditional foods, but in superabundance, which may not have been the case for many of them in the early years. Here, too, are the big TV comics, only this is their real audience and they appreciate it. They reveal the authentic joke behind the bland story they had to tell on TV because Yiddish punchlines do not make for happy Nielsen ratings.

The "ole swimmin' hole," as one Catskill ad says, was never like this. Or, to quote from an ad for Kutsher's Country Club: "You wouldn't have liked The Garden of Eden anyway—it didn't have a golf course. Kutsher's, on the other hand . . ." There are all the knishes a man can eat and, at Brown's Hotel, they are made more palatable by being called "Roulade of Fresh Chicken Livers." In the same spirit, the familiar chicken soup with *lockschen* has been reborn as "essence of chicken broth with fine noodles" on yet another menu.

The food at Grossinger's, the best I ate in the Catskills, is delicious if you like traditional kosher cooking. But entering the vast dining room, which seats some 1,600 guests, creates an agonizing moment for singles. "The older men want young girls," David Geivel, the headwaiter, told me, "and the girls want presentable men. They want to line up a date for New York, where they sit alone all week. They've only got two days, you know, so they've got to make it fast.

After each meal they're always wanting to switch tables. The standard complaint from the men runs . . . 'Even when the girls are talking to me, they're looking over my shoulder to the dentist at the next table. Why should I ask her for a date, such an eye-roamer.'"

I picked up a copy of the daily *Tattler* at my table and saw how, given one bewitching trip through the hotel Gestetner, the painfully shy old maid and the flat-chested girl and the good-natured lump were transformed into "sparkling, captivating" Barbara; Ida, "the fun-loving frolicker"; and Miriam, "a charm-laden lass who makes a visit to table 20F a must." I also noted that among other "typewriter boys" who had stayed at "the G." there were Paddy Chayefsky and Paul Gallico. Dore Schary was a former editor of the *Tattler* and Shelley Winters, Betty Garrett, and Robert Alda had all once worked on the special staff. Students from all over the United States still compete for jobs at the hotel. They can clear as much as $150 a week and, as they say at the G., be nice to your busboy, next year when he graduates he may treat your ulcer. My companions at the table included two forlorn bachelors, a teenager with a flirtatious aunt, and a bejeweled and wizened widow in her sixties. "I hate to waste all this food," the widow said, "it's such a crime. My dog should be here, he'd have a wonderful time."

"Where is he?"

"Dead," she said, false eyelashes fluttering, just as the loudspeaker crackled and the get-together for singles was announced. "Single people *only*, please."

The teenager turned on her aunt. "Are you going to dance with Ray again?"

"Why not? He's excellent."

"Sure, sure. Only he's a *faigele*." (A homosexual.)

"Did you see the girl in the Mexican squaw blanket? She told her mother, 'I'm going to the singles. If I don't come back to the room tonight, you'll know I'm engaged.' What an optimist!"

The singles get-together was thinly attended. A disaster. Bachelors looked in, muttered, pulled faces, and departed in pairs. The ladies in their finery were abandoned in the vast ballroom to the flatteries of staff members, twisting in turn with the hairdresser and the dance teacher, each of whom had an eye for tomorrow's trade. My truculent friend of the afternoon had resumed his station at the bar. "Hey," he said, turning on a "G-man" (a staff member), "where'd you get all those dogs? You got a contract with New York City maybe, they send you all the losers?"

The G-man, his manner reverent, told me that this bar was the very place where Eddie Cantor had discovered Eddie Fisher, who was then just another unknown singing with the band. "If you had told me in those days that Fisher would get within even ten feet of Elizabeth Taylor—" He stopped short, overcome. "The rest," he said, "is history."

Ladies began to file into the Terrace Room, the husbands trailing after them, with the mink stoles now slung nonchalantly over their arms. Another All-Star Friday Nite Revue had finished in the Playhouse.

"What was it like?" somebody asked.

"Aw. It goes with the gefilte fish."

Now the spotlight was turned on the Prentice Minner Four. Minner, a talented and militant Negro, began with a rousing civil rights song. He sang, "From San Francisco to New York Island, this is your land and mine."

"Do you know 'Shadrack'?" somebody called out.

" 'Old Man River'?"

"What about 'Tzena Tzena'?"

Minner compromised. He sang "Tzena Tzena," a hora, but with new lyrics. CORE lyrics.

A G-man went over to talk to my truculent friend at the

bar. "You can't sit down at a table," he said, "and say to a lady you've just met that she's, um, well stacked. It's not refined." He was told he would have to change his table again.

"All right. O.K. I like women. So that makes me a louse."

I retired early, with my G. fact sheets. More than 700,000 gallons of water, I read, are required to fill the outdoor pool. G. dancingmasters, Tony and Lucille, introduced the mambo to this country. Henry Cabot Lodge has, as they say, graced the G. roster. So has Robert Kennedy. Others I might have rubbed shoulders with are Baron Edmond de Rothschild and Rocky Marciano. It was Damon Runyon who first called Grossinger's "Lindy's with trees." Nine world boxing champions have trained for title bouts at the hotel. Barney Ross, who was surely the first Orthodox Jew to become lightweight champion, "scrupulously abjured the general frolicsome air that pervaded his camp" in 1934. Not so goy-boy Ingemar Johansson, the last champ to train at Grossinger's.

In the morning I decided to forgo the recommended early riser's appetizer, a baked Idaho potato; I also passed up herring baked and fried, waffles and watermelon, blueberries, strawberries, bagels and lox, and French toast. I settled for orange juice and coffee and slipped outside for a fast cigarette. (Smoking is forbidden on the Sabbath, from sunset Friday to sundown Saturday, in the dining room and the main lobbies.) Lou Goldstein, Director of Daytime Social Activities, was running his famous game of Simon Says on the terrace. There were at least a hundred eager players and twice as many hecklers. "Simon says, put up your hands. Simon says, bend forward from the waist. The *waist*, lady. You got one? Oi. *That's* bending? What's your name?"

"Mn Mn," through buttoned lips.

"All right. Simon says, what's your name?"

"Sylvia."

"Now that's a good Jewish name. The names they have these days: Désirée. Drexel. Where are you from?"

"Philadelphia."

"*Out.*"

A man cupped his hands to his mouth and called out, "Tell us the one about the two *goyim.*"

"We don't use that word here. There are people of every faith at Grossinger's. In fact, we get all kinds here. (All right, lady, sit down. We saw the outfit.) Last year a lady stands here and I say to her, What do you think of sex? Sex, she says, it's a fine department store." Goldstein announced a horseshoe toss for the men, but there were no takers. "Listen here," he said, "at Grossinger's you don't work. You toss the horseshoe but a member of our staff picks it up. Also you throw downhill. All right, athletes, follow me."

I stayed behind for a demonstration on how to apply makeup. A volunteer was called for, a plump matron stepped forward, and was helped onto a makeshift platform by the beautician. "Now," he began, "I know that some of you are worried about the expression lines round your mouth. Well, this putty if applied correctly will fill all the crevices . . . There, notice the difference on the right side of the lady's face?"

"No."

"*I'm sure* the ladies in the first four rows can notice."

Grossinger's has everything—and a myth. The myth of Jennie, LIVING SYMBOL "HOTEL WITH A HEART," as a typical *Grossinger News* headline runs. There are photographs everywhere of Jennie with celebrities. "A local landmark," says a Grossinger's brochure, "is the famous smile of the beloved Jennie." A romantic though mediocre oil painting of Jennie hangs in the main lobby. There has been a song called "Jennie" and she has appeared on *This Is Your Life,* an occasion so thrilling that as a special treat on rainy days guests are sometimes allowed to watch a rerun of the tape. But Jennie, now in her seventies, can no longer personally bless all the honeymoon couples who come to the hotel. Neither can she "drift serenely" through the vast dining room as often as she used to, and so a younger lady, Mrs. Sylvia Jacobs, now fills many of Jennie's offices. Mrs. Jacobs, in charge of Guest Relations, is seldom caught without a smile. "Jennie," she told me, "loves all human beings, regardless of race, color, or creed. Nobody else has her vision and charm. She personifies the grace and dignity of a great lady."

Jennie herself picked Mrs. Jacobs to succeed her as hostess at the G.

"God, I think, gives people certain gifts—God-given things like a voice," Mrs. Jacobs said. "Well, I was born into this business. In fifty years I am the one who comes closest to personifying the vision of Jennie Grossinger. The proof of the pudding is my identification here." Just in case further proof was required, Mrs. Jacobs showed me letters from guests, tributes to her matchmaking and joy-spreading powers. You are, one letter testified, T-E-R-R-I-F-I-C. You have an atomic personality. "There's tradition," she said, "and natural beauty and panoramic views in abundance here. We don't need Milton Berle. At Grossinger's, a seventy-five dollar a week stenographer can rub shoulders with a millionaire. This is an important facet of our activities, you know."

"Do you deal with many complaints?" I asked.

Mrs. Jacobs melted me with a smile. "A complaint isn't a problem—it's a challenge. I thank people for their complaints."

Mrs. Jacobs took me on a tour of Jennie's house, Joy Cottage, which is next door to Millionaire's Cottage and across the road from Pop's Cottage. A signed photograph of Chaim Weizmann, first president of Israel, rested on the piano, and a photograph of Jack Benny, also autographed, stood on the table alongside. One wall was covered from ceiling to floor with plaques. Interfaith awards and woman-of-the-year citations, including The Noble Woman of the Year Award from the Baltimore Noble Ladies' Aid Society. There was also a Certificate of Honor from *Wisdom* magazine. "Jennie," Mrs. Jacobs said, "is such a modest woman. She is always studying, an hour a day, and if she meets a woman with a degree she is simply overcome . . ." Jennie has only one degree of her own: an honorary Doctor of Humanities awarded to her by Wilberforce University, Ohio, in 1959. "I've never seen Jennie so moved," Mrs. Jacobs said, "as when she was awarded that degree."

Mrs. Jacobs offered me a box of cookies to sustain me for my fifteen-minute drive to "over there"—*dorten*, as they say in Yiddish—the Concord.

If Jennie Grossinger is the Dr. Schweitzer of the Catskills, then Arthur Winarick must be counted its Dr. Strangelove. Winarick, once a barber, made his fortune with Jerris Hair Tonic, acquired the Concord for $10,000 in 1935, and is still, as they say, its guiding genius. He is in his seventies. On first meeting I was foolish enough to ask him if he had ever been to any of Europe's luxury resorts. "Garages with drapes," he said. "Warehouses."

A guest intruded; he wore a baseball cap with sunglasses fastened to the peak. "What's the matter, Winarick, you only put up one new building this year?"

"*Three.*"

One of them is that "exciting new sno-time rendezvous," King Arthur's Court, "where every boy is a Galahad or a Lancelot and every damsel a Guinevere or a fair Elaine." Winarick, an obsessive builder, once asked comedian Zero Mostel, "What else can I do? What more can I add?"

"An indoor jungle, Arthur. Hunting for tigers under glass. On *shabus* the hunters could wear *yarmulkas*." (Skullcaps.)

It is unlikely, however, that anyone at the Concord would ever wear a skullcap, for to drive from the G. to *dorten* is to leap a Jewish generation; it is to quit a *haimishe* (homey) place, however schmaltzy, for chrome and concrete. The sweet though professional people-lovers of one hotel yield to the computer-like efficiency of another. The Concord, for instance, also has a problem with singles, but I would guess that there is less table-changing: Singles and marrieds, youngs and olds, are identified by different-colored pins plugged into a war plan of the dining room.

The Concord is the largest and most opulent of the Catskill resorts. "Today," Walter Winchell recently wrote, "it does 30 million Bux a year." It's a fantastic place. A luxury liner permanently in dry dock. Nine stories high with an enormous lobby, a sweep of red-carpeted stairway, and endless corridors leading here, there, and everywhere, the Concord can cope with 2,500 guests who can, I'm assured, consume 9,000 *latkes* and ten tons of meat a day. Ornate chandeliers drip from the ceiling of the main lobby. The largest of the hotel's three nightclubs, the Imperial Room, seats 2,500 people. But it is dangerous to attempt a physical description of the hotel. For even as I checked in, the main dining room was making way for a still larger one, and it is just possible that since I left, the five interconnecting convention halls have been opened up and converted into an indoor spring training camp for the Mets. Nothing's impossible. "Years ago," a staff member told me, "a guest told Winarick, 'You call this a room, at home I have a toilet nicer than such a room.' And Winarick saw that he was right and began to build. 'We're going to give them city living in the country,' he said. Look at it this way. Everybody has the sun. Where do we go from there?"

Where they went was to build three golf courses, the last with eighteen holes; hire five orchestras and initiate a big-name nightclub policy (Milton Berle, Sammy Davis Jr., Judy Garland, Jimmy Durante, etc.); install a resident graphologist in one lobby ("Larry Hilton needs no introduction for his humorous Chalk-talks. . . .") and a security officer, with revolver and bullet belt, to sit tall on his air-cushion before the barred vault in another; hire the most in lifeguards, Director of Water Activities Buster Crabbe ("This magnificent outdoor pool," Crabbe recently wrote, "makes all other pools look like the swimming hole I used to take Jane and the chimps to. . . ."); buy a machine, *the first in the Catskills*, to spew artificial and multi-colored snow on the ski runs ("We had to cut out the colored stuff, some people were allergic to it."); and construct a shopping arcade, known as Little Fifth Avenue, in the lower lobby.

Mac Kinsbrunner, the genial resident manager, took me on a tour beginning with the shopping arcade. A sign read:

SHOW YOUR TALENT
Everyone's Doing It
PAINT A PICTURE YOURSELF
The Spin Art Shop
50 cents
5 × 7 oil painting
Only Non Allergic Paints Used

Next door, Tony and Marcia promised you could walk in and dance out doing the twist or the bossa nova or pachanga or cha cha.

"We've got five million bucks worth of stuff under construction here right now. People don't come to the mountains for a rest any more," Kinsbrunner said, "they want *tummel*."

Tummel in Yiddish means "noise," and the old-time nonstop Catskill comics were known as *tummlers,* or "noisemakers."

"In the old days, you know, we used to go in for calis-

thenics, but no more. People are older. Golf, O.K., but—
well, I'll tell you something—in these hotels we cater to what
I call food-coholics. Anyway, I used to run it—the calisthenics
—one day I'm illustrating the pump, the bicycle pump exer-
cise for fat people—you know, in-out, in-out—zoom—her guts
come spilling out. A fat lady. Right out. There went one
year's profits, no more calisthenics."

We went to take a look at the health club. THRU THESE
PORTALS, a sign read, Pass The Cleanest People In The
World. "I had that put up," Kinsbrunner said. "I used to be
a schoolteacher."

Another sign read:

FENCE FOR FUN
Mons. Octave Ponchez
Develop Poise—Grace—Physical Fitness

In the club for singles, Kinsbrunner said, "Sure they're
trouble. If a single doesn't hook up here, she goes back to
New York and says the food was bad. She doesn't say she's
a dog. Me, I always tell them you should have been here
last weekend. Boy."

The Concord, indeed most of the Catskill resorts, now do
a considerable out-of-season convention business. While I
was staying at the hotel a group of insurance agents and their
wives, coming from just about every state in the union, were
whooping it up. *Their* theme-sign read:

ALL THAT GLITTERS
IS NOT GOLD
EXCEPT ANNUITIES

Groups representing different sales areas got into gay
costumes to march into the dining room for dinner. The
men wore cardboard moustaches and Panama hats at rakish
angles, and their wives wiggled shyly in hula skirts. Once

inside the dining room they all rose to sing a punchy sales song to the tune of "Mac the Knife," from *The Threepenny Opera* by Bertolt Brecht and Kurt Weill. It began, "We're behind you/ Old Jack Regan/ To make Mutual number one. . . ." Then they bowed their heads in prayer for the company and held up lit sparklers for the singing of the national anthem.

The Concord is surrounded by a wire fence. It employs some thirty security men. But Mac Kinsbrunner, for one, is in favor of allowing outsiders to stroll through the hotel on Sundays. "Lots of them," he told me, "can't afford the Concord yet. People come up in the world, they want to show it, you know. They want other people to know they can afford it here. So let them come and look. It gives them something to work toward, something to look up to."

The Concord must loom tallest from any one of a thousand *kochaleins* (literally, "cook-alone's") and bungalow colonies that still operate in Sullivan County. Like Itzik's Rooms or the Bon-Repos or Altman's Cottages. Altman's is run by Ephraim Weisse, a most engaging man, a refugee, who has survived four concentration camps. "The air is the only thing that's good in the Catskills," Ephraim said. "Business? It's murder. I need this bungalow colony like I need a hole in the head." He shrugged, grinning. "I survived Hitler, I'll outlast the Catskills."

Other large hotels, not as celebrated as Grossinger's or the Concord, tend to specialize. The Raleigh, for instance, has five bands and goes in for young couples. "LIVE 'LA DOLCE VITA' " (the sweet life), the ads run, "AT THE RALEIGH." "We got the young swingers here," the proprietor told me.

Brown's, another opulent place, is more of a family hotel. Jerry Lewis was once on their social staff, and he still figures in most of their advertisements. Brown's is very publicity-conscious. Instead of playing Simon Says or the

Concord variation, Simon Sez, they play Brown's Says. In fact, as I entered the hotel lobby a member of the social staff was entertaining a group of ladies. "The name of the game," he called out, "is not bingo. It's BROWN'S. You win, you yell out BROWN'S."

Mrs. Brown told me that many distinguished people had stayed at her hotel. "Among them, Jayne Mansfield and Mr. Haggerty." Bernie Miller, *tummler*-in-residence, took me to see the hotel's pride, the Jerry Lewis Theatre-Club. "Lots of big stars were embryos here," he said.

Of all the hotels I visited in the Catskills, only The Laurels does not serve kosher food and is actually built on a lake. Sackett Lake. But, oddly enough, neither the dining room nor the most expensive bedrooms overlook the lake, and, as at the other leading resorts, there are pools inside and out, a skating rink, a health club, and a nightclub or two. "People won't make their own fun any more," said Arlene Damen, the young lady who runs the hotel with her husband. "Years ago, the young people here used to go in for midnight swims, now they're afraid it might ruin their hairdos. Today nobody lives like it's the mountains."

Finally, two lingering memories of the Sullivan County Catskills.

As I left The Laurels, I actually saw a young couple lying under a sun lamp by the heated indoor pool on a day that was nice enough for swimming in the lake outside the picture window.

At Brown's, where THERE'S MORE OF EVERYTHING, a considerable number of guests ignored the endless run of facilities to sit on the balcony that overlooked the highway and watch the cars go by, the people come and go. Obviously, there's still nothing like the front-door stoop as long as passersby know that you don't have to sit there, that you can afford everything inside.

Jews in Sport

Good news. *The bar mitzvah gift book has come of age.* In my time, we had to make do with Paul de Kruif's inspirational medical books or a year's subscription to *National Geographic.* Since then, but too late for me, a spill of treasuries has become available: of Jewish Thought, of Jewish Wisdom, of Jewish Humor. Now, after many years of research, filling "a glaring void in the long record of Jewish achievement," comes the *Encyclopedia of Jews in Sports* by Bernard Postal, Jesse Silver, and Roy Silver (Bloch, 526 pp., $12.95), "the first all-inclusive volume to tell the complete story of Jews in professional and amateur sports all over the world, from Biblical times to Sandy Koufax's no-hitter in September."

The compendium comes lavishly recommended. "It is," Mel Allen writes on the jacket flap, "a noteworthy contribution to mankind's ever-growing quest for knowledge"; while Senator Abraham Ribicoff, former Secretary of Health, Education and Welfare, writes in a foreword, "Interest in sports among Jews—as among all Americans—has intensified as

opportunities for leisure activities have increased." Continuing in the same thoughtful, controversial vein, he adds,
"For sports are a healthy part of American life, and Jews are
involving themselves fully in all aspects of American life."

The encyclopedia should first of all be judged by its own
exacting standards. If I am not guilty of misunderstanding
editors Postal, Silver, and Silver, they compiled it not to
turn a buck in the non-book trade, but for two altogether
admirable reasons: that Jews might be made more aware
of their sports heritage and to dispel "one of the oldest
myths about the Jew . . . the curious belief that he was a
physical coward and a stranger to athletics," or, as Senator
Ribicoff puts it, that he is "nimble in the head, perhaps, but
not too nimble with the feet." On this test alone, the encyclopedia fails. It will, I fear, make trouble for *us* with
them. It's dynamite! Rotten with proof of Jewish duplicity
and athletic ineptitude.

Until I read the encyclopedia, for instance, I had no idea
that Mushy Callaghan (World Junior Welterweight Champion, 1926–30) was really born Vincente Morris Schneer, and
I wonder if this will also be a revelation to his Irish Catholic
fans. Neither did I suspect that anybody called Al McCoy
(World Middleweight Champion, 1914–17) answered more
properly to the name Al Rudolph, and was actually the son
of a kosher butcher who changed his name because his
parents objected to his boxing activities.

Then, consider these far from untypical baseball entries:

COHEN, HYMAN 'HY.' Pitcher, b. Jan. 29, 1931 in Brooklyn, N.Y.
Played for Chicago Cubs in 1955. Total Games: 7. Pitching
record: 0–0. Right-hander.

HERTZ, STEVE ALLAN. Infielder, b. Feb. 26, 1945 in Dayton, Ohio.
Played for Houston in 1964. Total Games: 5. Batting Average:
.000.

Is this the stuff the Jewish Hall of Fame is made of? Doesn't it suggest that in order to fill only 526 pages with Jewish athletic "Achievement," Messrs. Postal, Silver, and Silver were driven to scraping the bottom of the barrel, so to speak? Still worse. Put this volume in the hands of an anti-Semitic sportsman and can't you just hear him say, "Nimble with the feet? Ho ho! Among them o–o pitchers and nothing hitters count as *athletes.*"

Orthodox Jews will also be distressed by certain entries in the encyclopedia. Was it necessary, for example, to include Cardinal, Conrad Ceth, a pitcher with an o–1 record when he is only half-Jewish? Or the playboy pitcher Belinsky, Robert "Bo," just because he is the son of a Jewish mother? This is more than a purist's racial quibble. Such entries could lead, if this volume is the first of a series, to the inclusion of, say, Elizabeth Taylor in a compilation of Jewish Playmates from Biblical Times to Today.

Of course there is another possibility: half-Jewish players of dubious achievement were included in the book because the editors are not only racialists, but cunning ones at that, and what they intended by listing Belinsky and Cardinal was an oblique but penetrating comment on the capabilities of the issue of mixed marriages.

Something else: You and I might be pleased in our hearts to know that the first man to take money for playing baseball, the first real pro, was a Jew, Lipman E. "Lip" Pike, whose name appeared in a box score for the first time only one week after his bar mitzvah in 1864, but anti-Semites could easily make something unfortunate out of this information. Neither was I proud to discover that, according to a Talmudic scholar at the Jewish Theological Seminary of America, Jews—as early as the second century c.e.—had a special prayer for horse players; and that the bettor was advised to "take this [prayer] tablet and bury it in the ground of the hippodrome where you want to win."

There are some regrettable omissions. While Joe Reichler earns an entry because he is a baseball writer and Allen Roth, resident statistician with the Montreal Canadiens, is also included there is no mention anywhere of Mailer, Norman, who has reported memorably on boxing for *Esquire*. Neither could I find the names of Malamud, Bernard, author of a baseball novel, or Schulberg, Budd, who has written a novel about boxing. Does this suggest an anti-intellectual bias on the part of Messrs. Postal, Silver, and Silver?

This is not to say that the *Encyclopedia of Jews in Sports* is entirely without merit. The three-page ice hockey section pleased me enormously, if only because it included my favorite Jewish defenseman, one-time National League player, the astute Larry Zeidal. An issue of *Jewish Press*, a New York publication, once carried the following Canadian report: "ONLY JEW IN PRO HOCKEY PLAYS A ROUGH GAME." "Larry Zeidal," the story began, "owns a scar for every one of the 20 years he marauded through organized hockey. 'When you're the only Jew in this bloody game,' he said, 'you have to prove you can take the rough stuff more than the average player.'" The story went on to say that Zeidal, in contrast to his teammates, read *Barron's Business Weekly* between periods, perhaps taking "Lip" Pike as his inspiration. Pike, the encyclopedia notes, played baseball at a time when other players were usually gamblers and drunkards. "However, Pike was an exception. Throughout his career contemporary journals commented on his sobriety, intelligence, wit, and industry."

Finally, if the encyclopedia fails, on balance, to rectify the oldest myth about the Jew—that he is "a stranger to athletics"—it must be allowed that this is a pioneering work and a step in the right direction. Let us hope that Messrs.

Postal, Silver, and Silver, thus encouraged, will now take on other foul anti-Semitic myths, for instance, that Jews don't drink or practice homosexuality widely enough. I, for one, look forward to an encyclopedia (for delinquent bar mitzvah boys, perhaps) on Jewish Drunks, High School Dropouts, and Thugs from Noah to Today. I would also like to see a compilation of Famous Jewish Homosexuals, Professional and Amateur, Throughout History.

II. KOUFAX THE INCOMPARABLE

Within many a once-promising, now suddenly command-generation Jewish writer, there is a major league ball player waiting to leap out; and come Sunday mornings in summer, from the playing fields of East Hampton to the Bois de Boulogne to Hyde Park, you can see them, heedless of tender discs and protruding bellies, out in the fresh air together, playing ball. We were all raised on baseball. While today there do not seem to be that many Jewish major league stars about, when I was a kid there were plenty we could identify with: Sid Gordon and Al Rosen and of course Hank Greenberg. Even in Montreal we had, for a time, one of our own in the outfield, Kermit Kitman. Kitman, alas, was all field and no hit and never graduated from the Royals to the parent Dodgers, but it was once our schoolboy delight to lie in wait for him over the clubhouse at Saturday afternoon games and shout, "Hey, Kermit, you *pipick*-head, you think it's right for you to strike out on *Shabbes?*"

Baseball was never a bowl of cherries for the Jewish player. *The Encyclopedia of Jews in Sports* observes that while the initial ballplayer to accept money for playing was a Jew, Lipman E. Pike, there were few known Jewish players. The *Sporting News*, in 1902, wrote of one player, "His name

was Cohen and he assumed the name of Kane when he became a semi-professional, because he fancied that there was a
popular and professional prejudice against Hebrews as ball
players." Other major-leaguers were more militantly Jewish.
Barney Pelty, for instance, who pitched for the St. Louis
Browns from 1903 to 1912, seemingly did not object to
being known as "The Yiddish Curver." Still, the number of
our players in any era has been small, possibly because, as
Norm Sherry, once a catcher with the Dodgers, has said,
"Many boys find opposition at home when they want to go
out for a ballplaying career." Despite opposition at home
or in the game, the Jew, as the *Encyclopedia* happily notes,
has won virtually every honor in baseball. If there remains a
Jewish Problem in the game today, it hinges on the Rosh
Hashanah–Yom Kippur syndrome, for the truth we all have
to live with is that much as the Reform temple has done to
lighten our traditional Jewish burdens, the rush for the
pennant and Rosh Hashanah, the World Series and Yom
Kippur, still sometimes conflict.

Should a nice Jewish boy play ball on the High Holidays?
Historical evidence is inconclusive. Harry Eisenstadt, once a
pitcher for the Dodgers, was in uniform but not scheduled to
pitch on Rosh Hashanah, 1935, but when the Giants began
to hurt his team he was called into the game and his first
pitch was hit for a grand slam home run. And yet—and yet—
one year earlier, Hank Greenberg, with the Tigers close to
their first pennant since 1909, played on Rosh Hashanah
and hit two home runs. Greenberg went to *shul* on Yom
Kippur, alas, and the Tigers lost. The whole country, rabbis
and fans at odds, was involved in the controversy, and Edgar
Guest was sufficiently inspired to write a poem the last verse
of which reads:

> Come Yom Kippur—holy fast day
> world-wide over to the Jew—

And Hank Greenberg to his teaching
and the old tradition true
Spent the day among his people
and
he didn't come to play.
Said Murphy to Mulrooney "We
shall lose the game today!
We shall miss him in the infield
and
shall miss him at the bat,
But he's true to his religion—
and
I honor him for that!"

Honor him, yes, but it is possible that Greenberg, the only Jew in the Hall of Fame, was also tragically inhibited by his Jewish heritage. I'm thinking of 1938, when he had hit 58 home runs, two short of Babe Ruth's record, but with five games to play, failed to hit another one out of the park. Failed . . . or just possibly held back, because Greenberg just possibly understood that if he shattered the Babe's record, seemingly inviolate, it would be considered pushy of him and given the climate of the times, not be such a good thing for the Jews.

Greenberg, in any event, paved the way for today's outstanding Jewish player, the incomparable Sandy Koufax. So sensitive is the Dodger front office to Koufax's religious feelings that Walter Alston, the Dodgers' manager, who was once severely criticized for scheduling him to play on Yom Kippur, is now reported to keep a Jewish calendar on his desk.

Koufax, who has just published his autobiography, is not only the best Jewish hurler in history, he may well be the greatest pitcher of all time, regardless of race, color, or creed. His fast ball, Bob Feller has said, "is just as good as mine," and Casey Stengel was once moved to comment, "If that young fella was running for office in Israel, they'd have a whole new government over there . . ." Koufax has won the National League's Most Valuable Player Award, the Cy Young Award as the outstanding major league pitcher of the year, and the Hickok Pro Athlete of the Year Award. He has pitched four no-hit games, more than any other major league pitcher. He holds the major league record for both the most shutouts and the most strikeouts in one season and also the major league record for the number of seasons in which he has struck out more than three hundred batters. He has tied the major league record for most strikeouts in a nine-inning game, and also tied World Series records. I could go on and on, but a nagging question persists. This, you'd think, was enough. Koufax, at least, has proved himself. He is accepted. But is he?

Anti-Semitism takes many subtle shapes, and the deprecating story one reads again and again, most memorably recorded in *Time*, is that Sandy Koufax is actually something of an intellectual. He doesn't mix. Though he is the highest-paid player in the history of the game, improving enormously on Lipman E. Pike's $20 a week, he considers himself above it. Fresco Thompson, a Dodger vice-president, is quoted as saying, "What kind of a line is he drawing anyway—between himself and the world, between himself and the team?" Another report quotes Koufax himself as saying, "The last thing that entered my mind was becoming a professional athlete. Some kids dream of being a ball player, I wanted to be an architect. In fact, I didn't like baseball. I didn't think I'd ever like it." And the infamous *Time* story relates that when Koufax was asked how he felt after winning the last game in the 1965 World Series, he said, "I'm glad it's over and I don't have to do this again for four whole months."

In *Koufax*, which the pitcher wrote with the dubious relief help of one Ed Linn, he denies the accuracy of most of these stories. In fact, looked at one way, Koufax's autobiography can be seen as a sad effort at self-vindication, a forced attempt to prove once and for all that he is the same as anybody else. Possibly, Koufax protests too much. "I have nothing against myths," he begins, "but there is one myth that has been building through the years that I would just as soon bury without any particular honors: the myth of Sandy Koufax, the anti-athlete." He goes on to state flatly that he is no "dreamy intellectual" lured out of college by a big bonus, which he has since regretted, and as if to underline this point, he immediately lapses into regular-guy English: "Look, if I could act that good I'd have signed with 20th Century Fox instead of Brooklyn. . . ." Koufax protests that though he is supposed to read Aldous Huxley and Thomas Wolfe, and listen to Beethoven, Bach, and Mendelssohn, if anybody dropped in at his place they would more likely find him listening to a show tune or a Sinatra album. All the same, he does own up to a hi-fi. "I wish," he writes, "my reading tastes were classier, but they happen to run to the bestseller list and the book-club selections," which strikes this reader as something of an evasion. Which book clubs, Sandy? Literary Guild or Readers' Subscription?

Koufax insists the only thing he was good at in school was athletics (he captained the basketball team which won the National Jewish Welfare Board hoop tournament in 1951–52) and denies, to quote *Time* again, that he is an anti-athlete "who suffers so little from pride that he does not even possess a photograph of himself." If you walk into his room, Koufax writes, "you are overwhelmed by a huge, immodest action painting," by which he means a picture which shows him in four successive positions of delivery. Furthermore, he denies that "I'm mightily concerned about projecting a sparkling all-American image," and yet it seems to me this book has no other purpose. Examined on any other level, it is a very bush-league performance, thin, cliché-ridden, and slapped together with obnoxiously clever chapter headings such as, "Where the Games Were," "*La Dolce Vita* of Vero Beach," "Suddenly That Summer," and "California, Here We—Oops—Come." A chapter called "The Year of the Finger," I should hasten to add in this time of Girodias and Grove Press books, actually deals with Koufax's near-tragic circulatory troubles, his suspected case of Raynaud's phenomenon.

Projecting an All-American image or not, Koufax hasn't one unkind or, come to think of it, perceptive word to say about the game or any of his teammates. Anecdotes with a built-in twinkle about this player or that unfailingly end with "That's John" (Roseboro), or "That's Lou" (Johnson), and one of his weightiest observations runs "Life is odd," which, *pace* Fresco Thompson, is not enough to imply alienation.

Still true to the All-American image, Koufax writes, nicely understating the case, that though there are few automobiles he couldn't afford today, nothing has given him more joy than the maroon Rollfast bicycle his grandparents gave him for his tenth birthday when he was just another Rockville Centre kid. "An automobile is only a means of transportation. A bike to a ten-year-old boy is a magic carpet and a status symbol and a gift of love." Self-conscious, perhaps, about his towering salary, which he clearly deserves, considering what a draw he is at the gate, he claims that most of the players were for him and Drysdale during their 1966 holdout. "The players felt—I hope—that the more we got paid, the more they would get paid in the future," which may be stretching a point some.

Koufax was not an instant success in baseball. He was, to begin with, an inordinately wild pitcher, and the record for his 1955 rookie year was 2–2. The following year he won two more games, but lost four, and even in 1960 his record was only 8–13. Koufax didn't arrive until 1961, with an 18–13 record, and though some accounts tell of his dissatisfaction with the earlier years and even report a bitter run-in with the Dodgers' general manager, Buzzy Bavasi—because Koufax felt he was not getting sufficient work—he understandably soft-pedals the story in his autobiography. Koufax is also soft on Alston, who, according to other sources, doubted that the pitcher would ever make it.

If Koufax came into his own in 1961—becoming a pitcher, he writes, as distinct from a thrower—then his transmogrification goes some way to belie the All-American image; in fact, there is something in the story that will undoubtedly appeal to anti-Semites who favor the Jewish-conspiracy theory of history: Koufax, according to his own account, was helped most by two other Jews on the team, Allen Roth, the resident statistician, and Norm Sherry, a catcher. The turning-point, Koufax writes, came during spring training, at an exhibition game, when Sherry told him, "Don't try to throw hard, because when you force your fast ball you're always high with it. Just this once, try it my way . . ."

"I had heard it all before," Koufax writes. "Only, for once, it wasn't blahblahblah. For once I was rather convinced . . ." Koufax pitched Sherry's way and ended up with a seven-inning no-hitter and went on from there to superstardom. The unasked question is, would Norm Sherry have done as much for Don Drysdale?

III. POSTSCRIPT

"Koufax the Incomparable" appeared in *Commentary*, November 1966, and led to a heated correspondence:

MARSHALL ADESMAN, BROOKLYN, N.Y., WROTE:

As a professional athlete in the highest sense of the word, Hank Greenberg would never have purposely failed to tie or break Ruth's record. The material gain he could have realized by attaining this goal would have been matched only by the great prestige and glory that naturally come along with the magical figure of sixty home runs. Greenberg failed only because the pressure, magnified tenfold by the press, weighed too heavily on his shoulders. Very rarely is one able to hit the ball into the seats when he is seeking to do so. Home runs come from natural strokes of the bat, and Greenberg's stroke in those last five games was anything but natural. The pitchers, also, were not giving the Detroit slugger anything too good to hit, not wishing to have the dubious honor of surrendering number sixty. In short, it was the pressure that made Greenberg's bat too heavy, not the political atmosphere. Perhaps Mr. Richler should check his facts before his next article on the National Pastime.

SAMUEL HEFT, LONG BEACH, N.Y., WROTE:

I am stunned by . . . some startling statements made by Mordecai Richler. . . .

Even to hint at the possibility that the Hall of Fame baseball player, Hank Greenberg, "held back" in his efforts to break Babe Ruth's home run record, for any reason, is shocking. To state that Greenberg considered it would be "pushy" of him to do so, is almost too silly for comment. I shudder to think of a player in the Hall of Fame being accused of not giving his all. . . .

Richler states that "many boys found opposition at home" when they went out for sports. This is understandable. Our parents were not sports-minded, because of their European sufferings. . . . I'm sure our people didn't get many opportuni-

ties to play ball in the *shtetl*, while running away from pogroms.

I disagree that there is a Jewish problem in baseball today.
If Walter Alston keeps a Jewish calendar on his desk . . . it is
because he is a good administrator, and needs this reminder in
his scheduling of pitchers' rotations, and not because of
"sensitivity."

So far as playing baseball on the Jewish holidays goes, and
yelling *pipickhead* at Kermit, this is not a baseball problem.
I see with my own eyes too many Jews of all denominations
mowing lawns, shopping, and doing numerous other chores
on the *Shabbes*. . . .

Mr. Richler's article may do serious harm in the struggle
against discrimination. . . . Maybe, according to Richler, even
Kermit Kitman might have been a good hitter, but he was
afraid the Montreal non-Jewish population would think he
was "pushy."

E. KINTISCH, ALEXANDRIA, VIRGINIA, WROTE:

. . . Richler very obviously doesn't think much of Koufax.
Then why did he bother reading the Koufax book, or writing
about it? . . .

JEROME HOLTZMAN, CHICAGO SUN-TIMES, CHICAGO, ILL., WROTE:

I am but one of approximately two-to-three dozen Jewish
baseball writers—writers from big city newspapers—who cover
major league baseball teams from the beginning of spring
training through the World Series—and as such should in-
form your readers that Mordecai Richler was off base quite
a few times in his "Koufax the Incomparable." (November
1966)

Richler indicates that Hank Greenberg was "tragically
inhibited by his Jewish heritage" and thus held back and hit

58 home runs instead of breaking Babe Ruth's record of 60 because the breaking of such a record ". . . would be considered pushy of him . . . and not a good thing for the Jews." Balderdash! Greenberg didn't hit 60 because pitchers stopped giving him anything good to hit at—probably because he was Jewish, and probably also because no pitcher wants to be remembered for throwing historic home run balls. We must assume also that the pressure was a factor, as it always is; what also hurt was that a season-ending doubleheader (in Cleveland) had to be moved to a bigger ball park with a longer left field, and that the second game wasn't played to a nine-inning finish. . . .

I agree that the *Time* magazine cover story on Koufax was distorted, but to accuse *Time* of anti-Semitism is presumptuous. *Time* has erred on plenty of other sports cover stories as have many of the other slicks. The image of Koufax as an intellectual (which he is not) was featured, I suspect, because it made "a good angle" and probably because a *Time* stringer spotted a bookshelf. Moreover, that Koufax likes his privacy isn't unusual. Many star players, Feller, Musial, Williams *et al.*, roomed alone in their later years and did their best to avoid the mob.

Author Richler is looking too hard, also, when he emphasizes that Koufax, in his autobiography, points out that he was helped most by two other Jews. . . . Sherry, a catcher, advised Koufax not to throw hard, advice I'm sure Sherry has given to dozens and dozens of Gentile pitchers, and advice which previously had been given to Koufax by Gentile coaches. Sherry simply happened to mention this at precisely the right moment, before a meaningless exhibition game, and when Koufax was . . . eager to listen. . . .

As for Allen Roth, he was a statistician with the Dodgers, the only full-time statistician employed by a big league club. Roth borders on genius in this field. It was his job to keep and translate his findings to the Dodger players and the Dodger management. Whatever information Roth gave Koufax (and I don't know what this was), I'm sure was part of the routine. Richler's attitude is disgusting if he thinks that Roth would favor Koufax because both are Jews. In effect, Richler is saying that Roth would withhold significant statistics from Gentiles such as Drysdale, Newcombe, or Podres.

I agree that from a so-called Jewish standpoint, the Koufax book is disappointing, and I agree with Richler that Koufax protesteth too much in emphasizing that he is not anti-athlete. It is unfortunate that Koufax didn't control his anger, not only at the *Time* story but at several minor pieces that preceded it. In his book, Koufax tells us almost nothing about his Jewishness; that he is Jewish is mentioned almost in passing. But he doesn't owe us any detailed explanations. As a baseball book, and as a text in pitching, I found it excellent.

I should think that *Commentary*, in this rare instance when it did touch on sports, could have done better than offer the long-distance musings of a novelist. . . .

AMRAM M. DUCOVNY, NEW YORK CITY, WRITES:

I am shocked that Mr. Richler in his treatise on Curve Balls: Are They Good or Bad for the Jews? overlooked Willie Davis's three errors in one inning behind Koufax in the 1966 World Series—which was one of the most flagrant acts of Negro anti-Semitism since the Panic of 1908.

He does get somewhere in pointing out the Jewish-con-spiracy angle in the Norm Sherry-Koufax cabal; however, he does not really go deep enough. What of Norm's brother Larry—also a Dodger pitcher at the time—stopped from the advice that made a super star because of piddling sibling rivalry? There's one for Bill Stern!

And yea, verily, let us weep for the likes of Don Drysdale

—disenfranchised Wasp—alone in a sea of Gentile coaches whose knowledge of baseball never had the benefit of the secret indoctrination into the *Protocols of the Elders of Swat.* By the way, what is that resident genius, Norm Sherry, doing today? Have I somehow missed his name among the current great pitching coaches of baseball?

And finally, finally, the true story of the whispered Greenberg caper, wherein he was visited by representatives of the Anti-Defamation League, the American Jewish Committee and Congress, and the many, many Friends of the Hebrew University, who said unto him: "Hershel, thou shalt not Swat; whither Ruth goest, thou goest not."

I am looking forward with great anticipation to Mr. Richler's exposure of Mike Epstein (the self-labeled "super-Jew" rookie of the Baltimore Orioles) who all "insiders" know is a robot created at a secret plant in the Negev and shipped to Baltimore for obvious chauvinistic reasons.

FINALLY, DAN WAKEFIELD
WROTE A MOST AMUSING LETTER THAT BEGAN:

I greatly enjoyed Mordecai Richler's significant comments on Sandy Koufax, and the profound questions he raised about the role of Jews in American sports. Certainly much research still needs to be done in this area, and I hope that some of the provocative points raised by Richler will be picked up and followed through by our social scientists, many of whom are capable of turning, say, a called strike into a three-volume study of discrimination in the subculture of American athletics.

I REPLIED:

The crucial question is: did Hank Greenberg hold back (possibly for our sake), or was the pressure too much for him? Mr. Adesman, obviously a worldly man, suggests that Greenberg couldn't have held back, because of "the material gain he could have realized" by hitting sixty home runs. This, it seems to me, is gratuitously attributing coarse motives to an outstanding Jewish sportsman.

Mr. Heft is stunned by my flattering notion that Greenberg might have placed the greater Jewish good above mere athletic records and goes on to nibble at a theory of Jewish anti-gamesmanship based on our parents' "running away from pogroms." This theory, clearly unattractive if developed to its logical big league conclusion, would surely have resulted in a more noteworthy Jewish record on the base paths. Mr. Heft is also of the opinion that if Walter Alston keeps a Jewish calendar on his desk, it is because he is a good administrator. Yom Kippur, Mr. Heft, comes but once a year, and surely Alston doesn't require a calendar to remind him of one date. If Koufax had also been unwilling to take his turn on the mound on Tisha be'Av or required, say, a *chometz*-free resin bag for the Passover week, then Alston would have had a case. As things stand, the calendar must be reckoned ostentatious.

About Kermit Kitman: I'm afraid his poor hitting had no racial origins, but was a failure all his own, regardless of race, color, or creed. His superb fielding, however, was another matter: a clear case of the overcompensating Jew. Briefly put, Kitman was a notorious *chapper*, a grabber, that is to say any fly ball hit into the outfield had to be *his* fly ball, if you know what I mean.

Mr. Kintisch errs. I admire Koufax enormously and shall miss him sorely this season. He was undoubtedly the greatest pitcher of our time, and yet—and yet—now that he has retired so young is it possible that carping anti-Semites have already begun the whispering campaign: great, yes, but *sickly*.

Without the staying power of Warren Spahn. An unnatural athlete.

Jerome Holtzman, a dazzling intellectual asset to the sports department of the Chicago *Sun-Times*, raises darker questions. Greenberg, he says, would never have held back. He "didn't hit 60 because pitchers stopped giving him anything good to hit at—*probably because he was Jewish. . . .*" Now there's something nasty even I didn't think of: the possibility that Bob Feller, Red Ruffing, and others threw bigoted anti-Semitic curve balls at Hank Greenberg while a later generation of American League pitchers fed Roger Maris pro-Gentile pitches. . . . Next season I would implore Holtzman and other Jewish baseball writers to keep a sharp eye on the racial nature of pitches thrown to (or God forbid, even at) Mike Epstein.

As for *Time*, if it is not anti-Semitic then it is certainly Machiavellian; otherwise, why second-best Juan Marichal on a cover last summer when Koufax was also available? Either as a back-of-the-hand to Jewish achievement or as a shameful, possibly Jewish-motivated, attempt to apply the famous *Time* cover jinx to the one Gentile who might have won more games than Koufax.

Messrs. Ducovny and Wakefield are another matter. They think I would joke about Jews in sport, which strikes me as presumptuous.

Mr. Ducovny cunningly introduces Willie Davis's three errors behind Koufax in one inning and immediately claims this was a case of Negro anti-Semitism. Not necessarily. It depends on whether Davis dropped the three fly balls in his character as a Negro or in his office as an outfielder. Me, I'm keeping an open mind on the incident.

On the other hand, Mr. Wakefield is right when he says there is much more research to be done about Jews in sport. Not only Jews, but other minority and out-groups. Allen

Roth, *pace* Jerome Holtzman, may border on genius in his field, but though it may seem to some fans that baseball is already stifled with statistics, these are only statistics of a certain kind, safe statistics. It has been left to me to establish, haphazardly I admit, the absorbing statistic that homosexuals in both major leagues prefer playing third base over all other positions. As a group, they hit better in night games and are more adroit at trapping line drives than catching flies. They do not, as the prejudiced would have it, tend to be show-boats. They are a group with a gripe. A valid gripe. Treated as equals on the field, cheered on by teammates when they hit a homer, they tend to be shunned in the showers. On road trips, they have trouble finding roomies.

Finally, since I wrote my article, so unexpectedly controversial, world events have overtaken journalism.

1. Sandy Koufax has retired.
2. Ronald Reagan has been elected governor of California.
3. Tommy Davis has been traded to the Mets.
4. Maury Wills has been given, it would seem, to Pittsburgh.

I'm not saying that Ronald Reagan, who in the unhappy past has been obliged to play second-best man again and again for Jewish producers, has been harboring resentments . . . or is behind the incomparable Koufax's departure from California. I'm not saying that image-conscious Governor Reagan, mindful of right-wing support, was against being photographed shaking hands with Captain Maury Wills on opening day. I'm also not saying that after Willie Davis dropped the three flies, Mr. O'Malley turned to one of his minions and said, "Davis belongs with the Mets." Furthermore, I'm not saying that the aforementioned front-office minion could not tell one Davis from another. . . . Just remember, as they said in the sports pages of my boyhood, that you read it here first.

Intimate Behaviour

In a public dispute with Stephen Spender last year, W. H. Auden insisted that no novel or poem, however remarkable, had ever changed anything. Yes, probably, but I daresay Auden would agree that other books, say those of Freud or Marx, have effected profound changes in our consciousness or society. And now, sailing irresistibly down the anthropological turnpike, along comes zoologist Desmond Morris with *Intimate Behaviour*, after which the female navel, at any rate, will never be the same again:

> Since their reappearance, the naked navels of the Western world have undergone a curious modification. They have started to change shape. In pictorial representations, the old-fashioned circular aperture is tending to give way to a more elongated, vertical slit. Investigating this odd phenomenon, I discovered that contemporary models and actresses are six times more likely to display a vertical navel than a circular one, when compared with the artists' models of yesterday. A brief survey of two hundred paintings and sculptures showing female nudes, and selected at random from the whole range of art history, revealed a proportion of 92 per cent of round navels to 8 per cent vertical ones. A similar analysis of pictures

of modern photographic models and film actresses shows a striking change: now the proportion of the vertical ones has risen to 46 per cent. . . . How this change has come about, and whether it has been unconsciously arrived at or knowingly encouraged by modern photographers, is not entirely clear. . . . The ultimate significance of the new navel is, however, reasonably certain. The classical round navel, in its symbolic orifice role, is rather too reminiscent of the anus. By becoming a more oval, vertical slit, it automatically assumes a much more genital shape, and its quality as a sexual symbol is immensely increased.

But then the female form, as Morris sees it, can be fairly said to bristle with genital substitutes, the mouth being by far the most important of these, as it "transmits a great deal of pseudo-genital signaling during amorous encounters." Morris then alludes to the unique development of everted lips in our species, and goes on to say that their fleshy pink surfaces have developed as a labial mimic at the biological, rather than purely cultural level. "Like the true labia they become redder and more swollen with sexual arousal, and like them they surround a centrally placed orifice."

Yes, quite, but the implications are unnerving. For, if we allow that evolution is a continuing process (as witness the astonishing percentile leap of genital-shaped female navels), encouraged not only by modern photographers but novelists as well, and then take into account the contemporary novelist's propensity for describing fellatio, it seems possible that the labia, compensating, will eventually emerge as a mouth mimic. One day women, like egg-timers, will be the same rightside up as upside down. What I'm suggesting is that not in our time, certainly, but when our great-grandchildren pass from self-intimacy (head scratching, leg-crossing, masturbation) to the joys of full-scale pair-bonding, they may encounter true serendipity, that is to say, a laughing labia, or possibly one that can even tell stories. In a word, a pseudo-mouth substitute.

If this seems fanciful or farfetched, let me hastily add that Morris has already established, as it were, that women, unique among primates, possess a pair of swollen hemispherical mammary glands that can "better be thought of as another mimic of a primary sexual zone; in other words, as biologically developed copies of the hemispherical buttocks." These pseudo-buttocks, his researches have satisfied him, are enhanced when pushed together to "make the cleavage between them more like that between real buttocks." Furthermore, with his trained zoologist's eye, he has ascertained that they transmit sexual signals.

The eye, often used for eye-to-eye contacts in face-to-face encounters, that is to say, looking, is also rather more than it appears to be, for tears, in the opinion of Morris, have evolved into substitute urine, a plea for Mother to dry you.

In fairness, I shouldn't have said "in the opinion of," for in his introduction Morris states, "I shall endeavor to keep my opinions to myself, and to describe human behaviour as seen through the objective eyes of a zoologist. The facts, I trust, will speak for themselves." All the facts, or "quantitative statements," he adds elsewhere, "are based on personal observations backed up by a detailed analysis of 10,000 photographs taken at random from a wide variety of recent news magazines and newspapers."

This method, as productive as it is novel, has yielded the following revelations. Between adults in public, a partial embrace is six times as likely to occur as a full embrace. It is possible to identify 650 different types of hand-to-head contacts. By the time he dies, the average clean-shaven man will have spent well over two thousand hours scraping and rubbing his face. Two-thirds of all hand-shaking is done between males, but when it comes to clasping one's own thigh with the hand, a survey of a large number of such hand-to-thigh contacts has revealed that 91 percent were female and only 9 percent male. Another random count, this one of leg-crossing, shows that 53 percent were female and 47 percent male. The latter statistic, I fear, cries out for more data. It does not take into account homosexuals or bisexuals; neither does it tell us how many of the female leg-crossers were wearing mini-skirts and, therefore, not practicing self-intimacy, but once again transmitting sexual signals.

Even so, it is these statistics, I take it, that led Arthur Koestler, among others, to be so scornful of *Intimate Behaviour*. Koestler wrote in the London *Observer*, "The Germans have a word for it: *Die Wissenschaft des nicht Wissenwerten*—the science of what is not worth knowing."

Rather unfair, I think, for, based on his scale of 10,000, Morris has established that the face is the most expressive region of the entire human body. He has also concluded that the female body and limb skin are less hairy than those of the male and, in courtship, kissing on the mouth combined with full frontal embrace is a major step forward. With consummate good sense, he recommends that breast manipulation (a pair-bonding hand-to-pseudo-buttock-hemispherical-mammary-gland contact) and body fondling should not be conducted in public places. Without actually taking sides, he also ventures that for a man to nibble another man's ear in a public place might lead outsiders to make snap sexual judgments about the pair, which is also sensible advice, I think.

To a writer so fixated on substitutes—breasts for buttocks, tears for urine, cigarettes for nipples—I am tempted to reply that his zany conjectures are substitutes for thought and that *Intimate Behaviour* is, on balance, a pseudo-book. I am tempted, but, finally, unwilling. For as William Saroyan once observed, even the most abominable book is not without its uses.

Intimate Behaviour is charged with facts new to me. Reading it, I learned that a man's head-hairs number roughly 100,000 and grow at a rate of nearly five inches a year, which is nice going, I think. I also found out that each time I spit, my ordinary saliva contains between ten million and one billion bacteria in every cubic centimeter.

It should also be said that Morris, clearly nobody's fool, isn't kidded for a minute by all the funny stuff going on in discothèques. "The special role that social dancing plays in our society is that it permits, in its special context, a sudden and dramatic increase in body intimacy in a way that would be impossible elsewhere."

Finally, to those who are bound to be skeptical of some of Morris's more daring conclusions, I should say that the author, having formulated these conclusions, promises, at a later date, to publish a detailed study proving them. Which is to say, having devised an unintentionally risible key to human intimacy, he will now go on to construct a suitably incredible machine to fit it. A challenging task, I daresay.

Following the
Babylonian Talmud,
After Maimonides...

*Rabbi Stuart Rosenberg on the History of the Jewish
Community in Canada*

*I*f Rabbi Stuart Rosenberg, sole begetter of *The Jewish
Community in Canada*,[1] Volume 1, a History, had instead
undertaken to write an account of the assassination of John
Kennedy, it would have run as follows:

"President John F. Kennedy (who was boosted in his
campaign for office by such Jewish luminaries as Norman
Mailer, of writing-fame, Senator Abe Ribicoff, and Danny
Kaye, of film-fame) drove into Dallas on November 22, 1963.
Dallas, it is worth noting, was the birthplace of Izzy Lubin,
the first Jew to be arrested for jaywalking in Macon County.
The city is also the setting for Neiman-Marcus, of department store-fame, and home of the Chevra Kadisha congrega-
tion, president Benjy Taub. Indispensable community leaders
are Hy Green, Sam Farber, Mort Weiner, the Fiedler family,
and Norm Levi.

"Tooling into downtown Dallas, which welcomes Jewish

1 Toronto, McClelland & Stewart, Limited, 1971.

shopkeepers, among them Sid's Deli, President Kennedy rode in an open Lincoln Continental, a Ford product. The Ford Company is not ashamed to advertise in *Commentary* and numbers many of our brethren among its distributors, not to say, shareholders, most of whom support the annual Israeli Bond drive, the Red Cross, Mother's Day, and oil depletion allowances. As the car passed the Texas Public School Book Depository, with lots of titles by Jewish authors in stock, somebody called Oswald shot and killed Kennedy.

"A day to remember!

"And, I am now free to reveal, that among the crowd who will remember, there was a goodly sprinkling of Jews, prominent among them the Shapiros of San Antonio; Barney Kugler, a descendant of the first Jewish postmaster of Waco; and Seymour Freed, the distinguished past treasurer of the United Jewish Appeal in Shreveport and a wholesale gunsmith whose cultural contribution to that proud city is second to none!

"Oswald, not a Jew himself, numbered among his acquaintances one Jack Ruby, who was to shoot him dead in turn, though not on the Sabbath. A report was issued following the assassination and shoot-up, the so-called Warren Commission Report, though the real digging was done by counselors David Bellin, Melvin Eisenberg, Arlen Spector, and Alfred Goldberg, with somebody called O'Brien to empty the ashtrays."

In other words, what Rabbi Rosenberg has wrought is not so much a history as a catalogue, ostensibly boring, but inadvertently hilarious. Writing in the language of Shakespeare, as well as that of the Geritol commercial, the author owes something to Polonius, even more to the school of failed advertising copywriters. But his compendium, to be fair, radiates generosity. For if, as Rabbi Rosenberg claims, there are some 280,000 Jews in Canada, then it seems that at least half of them are enshrined in the history, and even to be mentioned by the rabbi is to be fulsomely praised. The author, whatever else can be held against him, has a heart of gold. If, for instance, he had cast his perceptive eye on Jack Ruby, what would have been revealed was a dedicated social worker, especially concerned with the lot of itinerant strippers and underpaid, thirsty cops.

True, an ungracious nit-picker might question the Rabbi's system of values and the relevance, beyond their undisputed office as potential book-buyers, of the plethora of names mentioned, as well as some serious omissions. That is to say, if Karl Marx had been a Canadian-born rather than a German Jew, his name would not have been inscribed in the history unless, like Sydney Maislin, Ben Beutel, or Maxwell Cummings, he was one of "a handful of leaders who could be regarded as wielders of wide and crucial powers in the life and direction of Montreal Jewry." Similarly, Franz Kafka, arguably a born outpatient, would not have rated an entry, unless he had been appointed to the board of governors of the Jewish General Hospital.

Given the abundantly dramatic, even ennobling, story of that heroic generation of Jews who came to Canada in steerage, largely penniless, without English or French, to gather scrap in alleys, peddle shoelaces, and teach socialist doctrine on the Canadian steppes (some of them succumbing to penury in basement tailor shops, others, with an eye on the main chance, emerging as robber barons, poets, fabled bootleggers, gamblers, wizards financial or medical), it has been Rabbi Rosenberg's uncommon achievement to render their history bland as frozen processed peas, no color tolerated unless it be artificial.

Here, for instance, is how he disposes of the rise of the Bronfmans: "One of the major incidents in Montreal history in the 1880's took place, interestingly enough, over two thousand miles west of the city. Yehiel Bronfman and his wife moved from Bessarabia, Russia, to Wampella, Saskatchewan, one of the first members of the Jewish farm colony established there. Later moving to Brandon and finally to Winnipeg, Bronfman was to father eight children, of which his four sons—Abe, Harry, Sam, Allan—were to become millionaire financiers, philanthropists and major leaders of Jewish causes in Montreal in the following century." Thereby reducing a tale, the natural material of Isaac Babel, to absolutely nothing.

Though there is hardly a nondescript alderman or community pillar from coast to coast who is not hailed in the history, there is no mention made of Fred Rose, the communist M.P., or his trial, actually the first of the postwar atom-bomb trials. Montrealers, especially, will be astonished to discover that, amidst so many nonentities blessed, there was also no space for Michael Buhay, a more engaging communist politician, or that fabulous gambler of the late Forties, Harry Ship. Neither is there a word spoken on behalf of our boyhood sports hero, boxer Maxie Berger. Good enough to enter the ring with Ike Williams, but obviously not the stuff to fire the Rabbi's imagination, any more than that good local featherweight Louis Alter, who once fought Willie Pep.

This is not to suggest that *The Jewish Community in Canada* is officiously polite, a snow job, or that it only celebrates the bland—in the age of the common man, a commonplace book. No, no. The shattering truth is that the author, ostensibly our people's PR supreme, has disturbed a hive laden with honey for anti-Semites.

The first Jewish settler in Canada, Rabbi Rosenberg reveals, was not, as Bruce McKelvie, an authority on British Columbia history, has ventured, a wandering Chinese hassid-cum-prospector, a member of one of the ten tribes lost in Babylonian captivity, staking a claim to Victoria as early as

2000 B.C. No. The first Jewish settler, Esther Brandeau, was a transvestite. Anticipating Myra Breckenridge, she arrived in 1738, disguised as a man and going by the name of Jacques La Farge. Even more compromising news: many years before Steinberg's had even been dreamed of, the miracle marts to both Generals Montcalm and Wolfe were Jewish-owned. Montcalm's foodstuffs were supplied by one M. Abe Grandis and Wolfe, a comparison shopper, learned to depend on Sir Alexander Schomberg. More gratifyingly, Rabbi Rosenberg reveals that the very first Jewish writer in Canada was a man called Mordecai. He was, in fact, the incomparable Adolphus Mordecai Hart, author of *Practical Suggestions on Mining Rights and Privileges in Lower Canada,* a seminal chunk of Canadiana too long out of print.

The author, no pussyfoot, is most rewarding on our city, Montreal, Montreal, which he comes right out and claims as . . . The Capital of Jewish Canada, and that, sir, is what I call standing up to René Lévesque and other French-Canadian squatters. "The social life of the Jews of Montreal over the past century," Rabbi Rosenberg writes with his accustomed assurance, "has centred around its 'clubs.' The two most worthy of note are the Montefiore and the de Sola."

The social life of the very rich, perhaps, but not of the majority of the Jewish populace. Indeed, I could argue, citing names and accomplishments, a much better case for the informal gatherings that were once held at Wilensky's Cigar & Soda, corner of Fairmount and St. Urbain, and that the most distinguished Jews ever to emerge from Montreal were shaped on the playing fields of Baron Byng High School—our Eton. But I would feel miserable, considering how good-hearted the Rabbi is, to end on a sour note. He is, above all, to be prized as a man who has taken 280,000 Jews to his bosom and found only beautiful things to say about all of them. I, for one, would be unable to do as much for an equal number of Protestants or Catholics. On the other hand, washing our Jews whiter than the purest snow, sanitizing them, as it were, it is also possible Rabbi Rosenberg has dehumanized a truly compelling bunch, whose colorful history has yet to be written.

Wait, wait. This is only the first volume of Rabbi Rosenberg's testimonial, and it ends with a rhetorical question: "In Canada, Jews have come a long way, and more specifically, in a very, very short time: since World War II. But will material achievements diminish their cultural and spiritual possibilities? Will success spoil them?

"We turn our attention to this theme, in the volume that follows. Can Jews and Judaism flourish and grow in the midst of freedom?"

Watch this space.

With the Trail Smoke Eaters in Stockholm

*I*n *1963 the world ice hockey championships were not* only held in Stockholm but, for the third time, the Swedes were the incumbent champions and the team to beat. Other threatening contenders were the Czechs and the Russians, and the team everyone had come to see humiliated was our own peppery but far from incomparable Trail Smoke Eaters.

"No nations can form ties of friendship without there being personal contact between the peoples. In these respects sports builds on principles of long standing," Helge Berglund, president of the Swedish Ice Hockey Association, wrote warmly in the world hockey tournament's 1963 program. Berglund's bubbly letter of greeting continued, "I do hope the ice hockey players will feel at home here and that you will take advantage of your leisure to study Swedish culture and Swedish life. Welcome to our country."

Yes indeed; but on the day I arrived in Stockholm a poster advertising a sports magazine on kiosks everywhere announced THE CANADIANS WANT TO SEE BLOOD. Only a few days later a headline in the Toronto *Star* read UGLY ROW IN SWEDEN OVER OUR HOCKEY TEAM.

I checked into the Hotel Continental, a well-lit teak-ridden place where well on a hundred other reporters, radio and television men, referees, a hockey priest, and a contingent of twenty-seven Russians, were staying; and immediately sought out Jim Proudfoot of the Toronto *Star*. Proudfoot had just returned from a cocktail party at the Canadian embassy. "What did the players have to say?" I asked.

"The players weren't invited."

The next morning things began to sizzle. On Saturday night, according to the most colorful Swedish newspapers, a substitute player with the Canadian team, Russ Kowalchuk, tried to smuggle a girl into his room and was knocked senseless by an outraged hall porter. Kowalchuk, enthusiastically described as a "star" in one Swedish newspaper and "a philandering hoodlum" in another, was not flattered: he denied that there had been a girl involved in the incident and claimed he had been flattened by a sneak punch.

Two things worried me about this essentially commonplace story. While it seemed credible that a hotel porter might be shocked if a hockey player tried to sneak a stuffed rabbit into the elevator, it did seem absurd that he would be shaken to his roots if a man, invited by Helge Berglund to study Swedish life, tried to take a girl to his room. And if the Canadians were such a rough-and-ready lot, if they were determined to crush Swedish bones in Friday night's game, wasn't it deflating that one of their defensemen could be knocked out by a mere porter? More important, mightn't it even hurt the gate?

The Trail Smoke Eaters, as well as the Czech, Russian, and American players, were staying at the Malmen—not, to put it mildly, the most elegant of hotels, a feeling, I might add, obviously shared by the amateur hockey officials associated with the Smoke Eaters, which group sagaciously put up at the much more commodious Grand Hotel.

When I finally got to the Malmen at noon on Sunday, I

found the sidewalk outside all but impassable: kids clutching autograph books, older boys in black leather jackets, and fetching girls who didn't look like they'd need much encouragement to come in out of the cold, jostled each other by the entrance. An American player emerged from the hotel and was quickly engulfed by a group of autograph-hungry kids. "Shove off," he said, leading with his elbows; and if the kids (who, incidentally, learn to speak three languages at school) didn't grasp the colloquialism immediately then the player's message, I must say, was implicit in his tone. The kids scattered. The American player, however, stopped a little further down the street for three girls and signed his name for them. I knew he *could* sign too, for, unlike the amateurs of other nations, he was neither a reinstated pro, army officer, or sports equipment manufacturer, but a bona fide student. Possibly, he could sign *very well*.

In the lobby of the Malmen, Bobby Kromm, the truculent coach of the Smoke Eaters, was shouting at a Swedish journalist. Other players, reporters, camp followers, cops, *agents provocateurs*, and strong-armed hotel staff milled about, seemingly bored. Outside, kids with their noses flattened against the windows tried to attract the attention of the players who slouched in leather chairs. Suddenly the Russian team, off to a game, emerged from the elevators, already in playing uniforms and carrying sticks. A Canadian journalist whispered to me, "Don't they look sinister?" As a matter of fact, if you overlooked the absence of facial stitches, they closely resembled the many Canadians of Ukrainian origin who play in the National Hockey League.

Bobby Kromm and his assistant manager, Don Freer, were also off to the game, but they agreed to meet me at eight o'clock.

When I returned to the Malmen that evening I saw a car parked by the entrance, three girls waiting in the back seat. Kids, also hoping to attract the players' attention, were banging pennies against the lobby windows. The players ignored them, sucking on matchsticks. Kromm, Freer, and I went into the dining room, and while I ordered a cognac I was gratified to see that the reputedly terrifying Smoke Eaters, those behemoths who struck fear into the hearts of both Swedish mothers and Russian defensemen, stuck to coffee and pie.

Kromm, assuming our elderly waiter could understand English, barked his order at him and was somewhat put out —in fact he complained in a voice trained to carry out to center ice—when the waiter got his order wrong. The waiter began to mutter. "You see," Kromm said, "they just don't like Canadians here."

I nodded sympathetically.

"Why do they serve us pork chops, *cold* pork chops, *for breakfast?*"

"If you don't like it here, why don't you check out and move right into another hotel?"

This wasn't possible, Kromm explained. Their stay at the Malmen was prepaid. It had been arranged by John Ahearne, European president of the International Ice Hockey Federation, who, as it turned out, also ran a travel agency. "If they treat us good here," Kromm said, "we'd treat them good."

Freer explained that the Smoke Eaters had nothing against the Swedes, but they felt the press had used them badly.

"They called me a slum," Kromm said. "Am I a slum?"

"No. But what," I asked, "is your big complaint here?"

Bobby Kromm pondered briefly. "We've got nothing to do at night. Why couldn't they give us a Ping-pong table?"

Were these men the terror of Stockholm? On the contrary. It seemed to me they would have delighted the heart of any YMCA athletic director. Freer told me proudly that nine of the twenty-one players on the team had been born and raised in Trail and that ten of them worked for the C.M. and S.

"What does that stand for?" I asked.

"I dunno," he said.

It stands for Consolidated Mining & Smelting, and Bobby Kromm is employed as a glass blower by the company. All of them would be compensated for lost pay.

Kromm said, "We can't step out of the hotel without feeling like monkeys in a cage. People point you out on the streets and laugh."

"It might help if you didn't wear those blazing red coats everywhere."

"We haven't any other coats."

I asked Kromm why European players didn't go in for body-checking.

"They condone it," he said, "that's why."

I must have looked baffled.

"They condone it. Don't you understand?"

I did, once I remembered that when Kromm had been asked by another reporter for his version of the girl-in-the-lobby incident, he had said, "O.K., I'll give you my impersonation of it."

Kromm and Freer were clear about one thing. "We'd never come back here again."

Jackie McLeod, the only player on the team with National Hockey League experience, didn't want to come back again either. I asked him if he had, as reported, been awakened by hostile telephone calls. He had been wakened, he said, but the calls weren't hostile. "Just guys in nightclubs wanting us to come out and have a drink with them."

While Canadian and Swedish journalists were outraged by Kowalchuk's misadventures, the men representing international news agencies found the tournament dull and Stock-

holm a subzero and most expensive bore. Late every night
the weary reporters, many of whom had sat through three
hockey games a day in a cold arena, gathered in the makeshift press club at the Hotel Continental. Genuine melancholy usually set in at 2 a.m.

"If only we could get one of the Russian players to defect."

"You crazy? To work for a lousy smelting factory in
Trail? Those guys have it really good, you know."

The lowest-paid of all the amateurs were the Americans,
who were given twenty dollars spending money for the entire
European tour; and the best off, individually, was undoubtedly
the Swedish star, Tumba Johansson. Tumba, a ten-dollar-a-
game amateur, had turned down a Boston Bruin contract
offer but not, I feel, because he was intent on keeping his
status pure. A national hero, Tumba earns a reputed $40,000
a year through a hockey equipment manufacturer. First night
on the ice not many Swedish players wore helmets. "Don't
worry," a local reporter said, "they'll be wearing their helmets
for Tumba on Wednesday. Wednesday they're on TV."

It was most exhilarating to be a Canadian in Stockholm.
Everywhere else I've been in Europe I've generally had to
explain where and what Canada was, that I was neither quite
an American nor really a colonial. But in Sweden there was
no need to fumble or apologize. Canadians are known, widely
known, and widely disliked. It gave me a charge, this—a real
charge—as if I actually came from a country important enough
to be feared.

The affable Helge Berglund, president of the Swedish Ice
Hockey Association, claims there are more than a hundred
thousand active players and about seven thousand hockey
teams in Sweden. How fitting, he reflects, that the Johan-
neshov *isstadion* should be the scene of the world champion-

ship competition. "The stadium's fame as the Mecca of ice hockey," he continues in his own bouncy style, "is once more sustained."

My trouble was I couldn't get into Mecca.

"You say that you have just come from London for the *Macleans*," the official said warily, "but how do I know you are not a . . . chancer?"

With the help of the Canadian embassy I was able to establish that I was an honest reporter.

"I could tell you were not a chancer," the official said, smiling now, "a man doesn't flow all the way from London just for a free ticket."

"You're very perceptive," I said.

"They think here I am a fool, that I do everybody favors —even the Russians. But if I now go to Moscow they do me a favor and if I come to London," he said menacingly, "you are happy to do me a favor too."

Inside the *isstadion*, the Finns were playing the West Germans. A sloppy, lackluster affair. Very little bodily contact. If a Finn and a West German collided, they didn't exactly say excuse me; neither did any of them come on in rough National League style.

I returned the same night, Monday, to watch the Smoke Eaters play the exhausted, dispirited Americans. Down four goals to begin with, the Canadians easily rallied to win ten to four. The game, a dull one, was not altogether uninstructive. I had been placed in the press section, and in the seats below me agitated agency men, reporters from Associated Press, United Press International, Canadian Press, and other news organizations sat with pads on their knees and telephones clapped to their ears. There was a scramble round the American nets and a goal was scored.

"Em, it looked like number ten to me," one of the agency men ventured.

"No—no—it was number six."

"Are you sure?"

"Absolutely."

"I'm with Harry," the man from another agency said. "I think it was number ten."

A troubled pause.

"Maybe we ought to wait for the official scorer?"

"Tell you what, as long as we all agree it was number ten—"

"Done."

All at once, the agency men began to talk urgently into their telephones.

". . . and the Smoke Eaters add yet another tally. The second counter of the series for . . ."

The next game I saw—Canada vs. Czechoslovakia—was what the sporting writers of my Montreal boyhood used to call the big one, a four-pointer. Whoever lost this one was unlikely to emerge world champion. Sensing the excitement, maybe even hoping for a show of violence, some fifteen thousand people turned up for the match. Most of them were obliged to stand for the entire game, maybe two hours.

This was an exciting contest, the lead seesawing back and forth throughout. The Czech amateurs are not only better paid than ours, but play with infinitely more elegance. Superb stick-handlers and accurate passers, they skated circles round the Smoke Eaters, overlooking only one thing: in order to score frequently it is necessary to shoot on the nets. While the Czechs seemed loath to part with the puck, the more primitive Canadians couldn't get rid of it quickly enough. Their approach was to wind up and belt the puck in the general direction of the Czech zone, all five players digging in after it.

The spectators—except for one hoarse and lonely voice that seemed to come from the farthest reaches of Helge

Berglund's Mecca—delighted in every Canadian pratfall. From time to time the isolated Canadian supporter called out in a mournful voice, "Come on, Canada."

The Czechs had a built-in cheering section behind their bench. Each time one of their players put stick and puck together a banner was unfurled and at least a hundred chunky broad-shouldered men began to leap up and down and shout something that sounded like, "Umpa-Umpa-Czechoslovakia!"

Whenever a Czech player scored, their bench would empty, everybody spilling out on the ice to embrace, leap in the air, and shout joyously. The Canadian team, made of cooler stuff, would confine their scoring celebration to players already out on the ice. With admirable unself-consciousness, I thought, the boys would skate up and down poking each other on the behind with their hockey sticks.

The game, incidentally, ended in a 4–4 tie.

The Canadians wanted to see blood, the posters said. Hoodlums, one newspaper said. The red jackets go hunting at night, another claimed. George Gross, the Toronto *Telegram*'s outraged reporter, wrote, "Anti-Canadian feeling is so strong here it has become impossible to wear a maple leaf on your lapel without being branded ruffian, hooligan and— since yesterday—sex maniac."

A man, that is to say, a Canadian man, couldn't help but walk taller in such a heady atmosphere, absorbing some of the fabled Smoke Eaters' virility by osmosis. But I must confess that no window shutters were drawn as I walked down the streets. Mothers did not lock up their daughters. I was not called ruffian, hooligan, or anything even mildly deprecating. Possibly, the trouble was I wore no maple leaf in my lapel.

Anyway, in the end everything worked out fine. On Tuesday morning Russ Kowalchuk's virtue shone with its radiance restored. Earlier, Art Potter, the politically astute president of the Canadian Amateur Hockey Association, had confided to a Canadian reporter, "These are cold war tactics to demoralize the Canadian team. They always stab us in the back here." But now even he was satisfied. Witnesses swore there was no girl in the lobby. The Malmen Hotel apologized. Russ Kowalchuk, after all, was a nice clean-living Canadian boy. In the late watches of the night he did not lust after Swedish girls, but possibly, like Bobby Kromm and Don Freer, yearned for nothing more depraved than a Ping-pong table. A McIntosh apple maybe.

Finally, the Smoke Eaters did not behave badly in Stockholm. They were misunderstood. They also finished fourth.

Going Home

"*Why do you want to go to university?" the student* counselor asked me.

Without thinking, I replied, "I'm going to be a doctor, I suppose."

A doctor.

One St. Urbain Street day cribs and diapers were cruelly withdrawn and the next we were scrubbed and carted off to kindergarten. Though we didn't know it, we were already in pre-med school. School-starting age was six, but fiercely competitive mothers would drag protesting four-year-olds to the registration desk and say, "He's short for his age."

"Birth certificate, please?"

"Lost in a fire."

On St. Urbain Street, a head start was all. Our mothers read us stories from *Life* about pimply astigmatic fourteen-year-olds who had already graduated from Harvard or who were confounding the professors at M.I.T. Reading *Tip-Top Comics* or listening to *The Green Hornet* on the radio was as good as asking for a whack on the head, sometimes administered with a rolled-up copy of the *Canadian Jewish Eagle*, as if that in itself would be nourishing. We were not supposed to memorize baseball batting averages or dirty limericks. We were expected to improve our Word Power with the *Reader's Digest* and find inspiration in Paul de Kruif's medical biographies. If we didn't make doctors, we were supposed to at least squeeze into dentistry. School marks didn't count as much as rank. One wintry day I came home, nostrils clinging together and ears burning cold, proud of my report. "I came rank two, Maw."

"And who came rank one, may I ask?"

Mrs. Klinger's boy, alas. Already the phone was ringing. "Yes, yes," my mother said to Mrs. Klinger, "congratulations, and what does the eye doctor say about Riva, poor kid, to have a complex at her age, will they be able to straighten them . . ."

Parochial school was a mixed pleasure. The old, under-paid men who taught us Hebrew tended to be surly, impatient. Ear-twisters and knuckle-rappers. They didn't like children. But the girls who handled the English-language part of our studies were charming, bracingly modern, and concerned about our future. They told us about *El Campesino*, how John Steinbeck wrote the truth, and read Sacco's speech to the court aloud to us. If one of the younger, unmarried teachers started out the morning looking weary, we assured each other that she had done it the night before. Maybe with a soldier. Bareback.

From parochial school, I went on to a place I call Fletcher's Field High in the stories and memoirs that follow. Fletcher's Field High was under the jurisdiction of the Montreal Protestant School Board, but had a student body that was nevertheless almost a hundred percent Jewish. The school became something of a legend in our area. Everybody, it seemed, had passed through FFHS: Canada's most famous gambler. An atom bomb spy. Boys who went off to fight in the Spanish Civil War. Miracle-making doctors

and silver-tongued lawyers. Boxers. Fighters for Israel. All
of whom were instructed, as I was, to be staunch and bold,
to play the man, and, above all, to

> Strive hard and work
> With your heart in the doing.
> Up play the game,
> As you learnt it at Fletcher's.

Again and again we led Quebec province in the junior
matriculation results. This was galling to the communists
among us, who held we were the same as everyone else,
but to the many more who knew that for all seasons there
was nothing like a Yiddish boy, it was an annual cause for
celebration. Our class at FFHS, Room 41, was one of the few
to boast a true Gentile, an authentic white Protestant. Yugo-
slavs and Bulgarians, who were as foxy as we were, their
potato-filled mothers sitting just as rigid in their corsets at
school concerts, fathers equally prone to natty straw hats and
cursing in the mother tongue, did not count. Our very own
Wasp's name was Whelan, and he was no less than perfect.
Actually blond, with real blue eyes, and a tendency to sit
with his mouth hanging open. A natural hockey player, a
born first-baseman. Envious students came from other class-
rooms to look him over and put questions to him. Whelan, as
was to be expected, was not excessively bright, but he gave
Room 41 a certain tone, some badly needed glamour, and in
order to keep him with us as we progressed from grade to
grade, we wrote essays for him and slipped him answers at
examination time. We were enormously proud of Whelan.

Among our young schoolmasters, most of them returned
war veterans, there were a number of truly dedicated men
as well as some sour and brutish ones, like Shaw, who
strapped twelve of us one afternoon, ten on each hand,
because we wouldn't say who had farted while his back was

turned. The foibles of older teachers were well known to us, because so many aunts, uncles, cousins, and elder brothers had preceded us at FFHS. There was, for instance, one master who initiated first-year students with a standing joke: "Do you know how the Jews make an 's'?"

"No, Sir."

Then he would make an "s" on the blackboard and draw two strokes through it. The dollar sign.

Among us, at FFHS, were future leaders of the community. Progressive parents. Reform-minded aldermen. Anti-fallout enthusiasts. Collectors of early French-Canadian furniture. Boys who would actually grow up to be doctors and lecture on early cancer warnings to ladies' clubs. Girls who would appear in the social pages of the Montreal *Star*, sponsoring concerts in aid of retarded children (regardless of race, color, or creed) and luncheon hour fashion shows, proceeds to the Hebrew University. Lawyers. Notaries. Professors. And marvelously with-it rabbis, who could not only quote Rabbi Akiba but could also get a kick out of a hockey game. But at the time who would have known that such slouchy, aggressive girls, their very brassieres filled with bluff, would grow up to look so serene, such honeys, seeking apotheosis at the Saidye Bronfman Cultural Centre, posing on curving marble stairwells in their bouffant hair styles and strapless gowns? Or that such nervy boys, each one a hustler, would mature into men who were so damn pleased with what this world has to offer, epiphanous, radiating self-confidence at the curling or country club, at ease even with potbellies spilling over their Bermuda shorts? Who would have guessed?

Not me.

Looking back on those raw formative years at FFHS, I must say we were not a promising or engaging bunch. We were scruffy and spiteful, with an eye on the main chance.

So I can forgive everybody but the idiot, personally unknown to me, who compiled our criminally dull English
reader of prose and poetry. Nothing could have been calculated to make us hate literature more unless it was being
ordered, as a punishment, to write *Ode to the West Wind*
twenty-five times. And we suffered that too.

Graduation from FFHS meant jobs for most of us, McGill
for the anointed few, and the end of an all but self-con-
tained world made up of five streets, Clark, St. Urbain,
Waverley, Esplanade, and Jeanne Mance, bounded by the
Main, on one side, and Park Avenue, on the other.

By 1948 the drift to the suburbs had begun in earnest.

Flying into Montreal nineteen years later, in the summer of
1967, our Expo summer, coming from dowdy London, via
decaying New York, I was instantly struck by the city's
affluence. As our jet dipped toward Dorval, I saw what
appeared to be an endless glitter of eccentrically shaped
green inkwells. Suburban swimming pools. For Arty and
Stan, Zelda, Pinky's Squealer, Nate, Fanny, Shloime, and
Mrs. Klinger's rank-one boy; all the urchins who had learned
to do the dead man's float with me in the winding muddy
Shawbridge River, condemned by the health board each
August as a polio threat.

I rode into the city on multidecked highways, which
swooped here, soared there, unwinding into a pot of prosperity, a downtown of high-rise apartments and hotels, the
latter seemingly so new they could have been uncrated the
night before.

Place Ville Marie. The metro. Expo. Île Notre Dame.
Habitat. Place des Arts. This cornucopia certainly wasn't the
city I had grown up in and quit.

Amidst such unnerving strangeness, I desperately sought

reassurance in the familiar, the *Gazette* and the *Star*, turning at once to that zingy, harmlessly inane duo, Fitz and Bruce Taylor, the columnists who after all these testing years are still the unchallenged Keepers of Ourtown's Social Record. Should planets collide, nuclear warfare rage, I could still count on this irrepressible pair to bring me up to date on my old schoolmates, telling me which one, now a mutual funds salesman with a split-level in Hampstead, had just shot a hole-in-one in Miami; how many, as thickened round the middle as I am, had taken to jogging at the "Y"; and if any, prematurely taken by a coronary or ostensibly recuperating from a lung removal operation, would be sorely missed by the sporting crowd, not to say their Pythian lodge brothers.

Fitz and Taylor did not let me down, but I was brought up short by an item which announced a forthcoming radio program, "Keep Off the Grass," wherein local savants, suburban cops, and plainclothes teachers would warn the kids against pot.

Pot.

For the record, pot, like the *Reader's Digest*, is not necessarily habit-forming, but both can lead to hard-core addiction: heroin in one case, abridged bad books in the other. Either way you look at it, a withdrawal from a meaningful life.

In our St. Urbain Street time, however, the forbidden food had been ham or lobster, and when we had objected, protesting it wasn't habit-forming, our grandfathers, faces flaring red, had assured us if you start by eating pig, if you stray so far from tradition, what next? Where will it end? And so now we know. With the children's children smoking pot, making bad trips, discovered stoned in crash pads.

Expo was of course thoroughly exhilarating and my wife and I decided to return to Montreal and try it for a year, not so much new as retreaded Canadians. We arrived in September 1968, picking, as it now turns out, a winter to try men's souls. Dr. Johnson has described this country as "a region of desolate sterility . . . a cold, uncomfortable, uninviting region, from which nothing but fur and fish were to be had." More recently, W. H. Auden has written, "The dominions . . . are for me *tiefste Provinz,* places which have produced no art and are inhabited by the kind of person with whom I have least in common."

Unfair comment without question, but I had only been back a month or so when I read PENSIONER FLUNKS TEST IN MONTREAL'S LOTTERY, thereby missing out on a possible $100,000 jackpot:

> A half-blind disability pensioner yesterday became the first contestant to flunk Mayor Jean Drapeau's voluntary tax non-lottery . . . when he failed to name Paris as the largest French-speaking city. . . .

This, to a sometime satirist, was meaty stuff indeed. A repast unbelievably enhanced when I read on to discover that our cunning, indefatigable mayor, possibly generalizing from the particular of the city council, had commented: "This proves the questions are not easy, and that they are a real test of skill."

O God! O Montreal! Now branded by its mayor as the metropolis wherein recognition of Paris as the world's largest French-speaking city is taken as a measure of intellectual acumen.

And hippies are hounded as plague-bearers.

Possibly the problem is I was raised to manhood in a hairier, more earthy Montreal, the incomparable Mayor Camillien Houde's canton, whose troubles were basically old-fashioned, breaking down into the plebs' too large appetite for barbotte tables and whorehouses. At the time, Montreal endured a puritanical avenger as well as a journalist champion of the permissive society. All-seeing Police Commissioner "Pax" Plante, scourge of harlots, implacable enemy of bookies with something hot on the morning line, raked the debauched streets in a black limousine, a sort of French-Canadian Batman. On the other hand, Al Palmer, with the now-defunct *Herald*, campaigned intrepidly for our right to buy margarine *over the counter*—margarine, once as illicit in Quebec province as marijuana is today. Al Palmer, who was, in his time, the Dr. Tim Leary of artificial foods.

In those days, it should be remembered, no cop would have ventured, as did Detective-Sergeant Roger Lavigueur at a recent policemen's union meeting, to threaten us with a *coup d'état*, saying, "It happens every day in South America. It could happen here too. We, the policemen, may have to take over the government."

In the civilized Forties, before Marcuse, Fanon, Ché, and Mayor Daley, our cops, civic and provincial, never split a head unless it was rock-hard—that is to say, a striker's head. Otherwise they were so good-natured that before raiding a gambling den or brothel they phoned to make sure nobody nice would be there and, on arrival, resolutely padlocked the toilet and picked up a little something for their trouble on the way out.

In the immediate postwar years hippies need not have cadged off unemployment insurance, inflaming Ourtown's overachievers, but instead could have survived and served the straight community as well by voting, as did many an inner-directed St. Urbain Street boy, twenty or more times in any civic, provincial, or federal election. These, remember, were the roseate years when commie traitor Fred Rose, our M.P., went from parliament to prison and was replaced by Maurice Hartt, of whom *Time* wrote:

> Hartt's principal campaign asset is his whiplash tongue, which he has used on many an opponent. Once he so angered

Premier Duplessis in the legislature with an attack on him that the livid Premier called to Liberal Leader Adélard Godbout: "Have you another Jew in this House to speak for you?" Hartt bounded up, pointed to the crucifix behind the Speaker's chair and cried: "Yes, you have—His image has been speaking to you for 2,000 years, but you still don't understand Him."

A time when many a freshly scrubbed young notary was elected to the city council for a dollar a year and, lo and behold, emerged one or two terms later a real-estate millionaire, lucky enough to hold the rocky farmlands where new highways were to be built or schools constructed. This archetypal city councilor, now just possibly a church or synagogue board chairman, certainly a Centennial Medal holder, is the man most likely to inveigh against today's immoral youngsters, kids so deficient in industry that far from voting twenty times they don't go to the polls at all, or respect their parents who grew up when a dollar was a dollar, dammit, and to make one you hustled, leading with the elbows.

To come home in 1968 was to discover that it wasn't where I had left it—it had been bulldozed away—or had become, as is the case with St. Urbain, a Greek preserve.

Today the original Young Israel synagogue, where we used to chin the bar, is no longer there. A bank stands where my old poolroom used to be. Some of the familiar stores have gone. There have been deaths and bankruptcies. But most of the departed have simply packed up and moved with their old customers to the new shopping centers at Van Horne or Rockland, Westmount or Ville St. Laurent.

Up and down the Main you can still pick out many of the old restaurants and steak houses wedged between the sweater factories, poolrooms, cold-water flats, wholesale dry goods stores, and "Your Most Sanitary" barbershops. The places where we used to work in summer as shippers for ten dollars a week are still there. So is Fletcher's Field High, right where it always was. Rabbinical students and boys with sidecurls still pass. These, however, are the latest arrivals from Poland and Rumania and soon their immigrant parents will put pressure on them to study hard and make good. To get out.

But many of our grandparents, the very same people who assured us the Main was only for *bummers* and failures, will not get out. Today, when most of the children have made good, now that the sons and daughters have split-level bungalows and minks and West Indian cruises in winter, many of the grandparents still cling to the Main. Their children cannot in many cases persuade them to leave. So you still see them there, drained and used up by the struggle. They sit on kitchen chairs next to the coke freezer in the cigar store, dozing with a fly swatter held in a mottled hand. You find them rolling their own cigarettes and studying the obituary columns in the *Star* on the steps outside the Jewish Library. The women still peel potatoes under the shade of a winding outside staircase. Old men still watch the comings and goings from the balcony above, a blanket spread over their legs and a little bag of polly seeds on their lap. As in the old days, the sinking house with the crooked floor is right over the store or the wholesaler's, or maybe next door to the scrap yard. Only today, the store and the junkyard are shut down. Signs for Sweet Caporal cigarettes or old election posters have been nailed in over the missing windows. There are spider webs everywhere.

Expo 67

I am an obsessive reader of fringe magazines: DOGS *in Canada* (" 'If people were as nice as their dogs we'd have the finest sport in the world,' observed the Old Timer."); *Police Review*, Weekly Journal of the British Police ("Ex-Supt. Arthur Williams," begins a short story by "Flatfoot," "had served for thirty years in a provincial city Force and was now in retirement. He had never considered himself to be a senti- mentalist but now, each evening, seated comfortably before the television set, puffing gently on his pipe, he invariably found his mind wandering back . . ."). I also take Man- chester *Jewish Life, Men in Vogue, Toronto Life* ("As winter- time became ensconced in Toronto, party began to follow party. . . ."), and many, many more. But in 1967, in the months before I planned to return to Canada for the first time in three years, the magazine that afforded me the most pleasure was *the stage in Canada*, published monthly by the Canadian Theatre Centre in Toronto. The January issue, vintage stuff, featured the report of the Theatre Centre's professional ethics committee, a group that met under the chairmanship of one Malcolm Black. Among the ten articles

in the proposed code of ethics, the ones I found the most
stirring were:

2. *Observe the Golden Rule:* . . . Members ought to treat each
other as they prefer to be treated. Members ought to *observe the
golden rule.*

7. *Enhance the professional images:* Whether or not we of the
Theatre continue to be viewed as "rogues and vagabonds" depends
on us, and our sincere attempts to *enhance our professional
image.*

10. *Use imagination:* As artists, we include imagination as part of
our stock-in-trade. . . . Members are urged, at all times, in all
situations, to *use imagination.*

Canada, Canada. Older than Bertrand Russell. A hundred
years old in 1967. "A nation like no other," begins the Centennial Library brochure, "larger than the entire continent of
Europe, second in size only to Russia. . . . Canada is unique."

IN MONTREAL, I read in *The New York Times,* COMPLETE
ASSURANCE SPEAKS IN 2 LANGUAGES. Mrs. Charles Taschereau
told the *Times* that she found it difficult to keep still. "If I
have nothing else to do," she said, "I might paint a wall."
Mrs. Hartland Molson described my Montreal as a city of
"living within the home," except for hockey games and visiting
friends, while Mrs. Samuel Bronfman said, "I love people,
but my husband is a better judge of them." Such nice, simple
people, the Canadian rich, but I found the new personalities
and events baffling. On arrival, for instance, what should my
attitude be toward Judy LaMarsh, the minister responsible
for culture? Who was Peter Reilly? What was psychedelic TV?
I wished Expo the best, the very best, but where were they
going to find enough fellow-travelers to fill the Expo Theatre
for The Popular Stars of Prague on September 1st? Hungering for more information about home, I devoured the Canadian magazines, especially the intellectual ones, like *The
Canadian Forum.* One month I read: "In 1965, 73,980 Cana-

dians died of heart disease, 63,000 were seriously or totally crippled by arthritis, and 25,637 died of cancer. There were 670 who died of TB, half of them people over 70 years of age." I commit this to memory, my experience of the world has been enriched. Another month I read in the same puzzling magazine: "The 19 Supreme and County Court rooms in Toronto's new courthouse have been panelled in teak from Burma and Siam, mahogany from Africa and Honduras, oak and walnut from the U.S. and English oak. No Canadian panelling was used."

Was this, I wondered, a snippet of dialogue from a new Harold Pinter play? No. It was hard fact. Meant to make me angry, I suppose. After all, why all that snobbish British oak and war-mongering American walnut in our courthouses? Was Canadian wood wormy or something?

The truth was, I had decided, weeks before leaving for Montreal, that I no longer understood the idiom. Doomed to always be a foreigner in England, I was now in danger of finding Canada foreign too. After thirteen almost uninterrupted years abroad, I now realized the move I had made with such certainty at the age of twenty-three had exacted a considerable price. Some foggy, depressing nights it seemed to me that I had come full circle. Many years ago my parents emigrated from Poland to Canada, to Montreal, where I grew up ashamed of their Yiddish accents. Now I had seemingly settled in London, where my own children (spoiled, ungrateful, enjoying an easier childhood than I had, etc. etc.) found my American accent just as embarrassing.

Still, being a Canadian writer abroad offers a writer a number of built-in perks. I have, through the years, been turning over a useful penny in the why-have-you-left-Canada interview, that is to say, once a year I make a fool of myself on TV for a fee.

Most recently a breathless girl from Toronto sat in my

garden, crossed her legs distractingly as the TV cameras turned, smiled cutely, and said, "I've never read anything you've written, but would you say you were part of the brain drain?"

Sure, baby. I also assure her that I'm an Angry Young Man. A black humorist. A white Negro. Anything.

"But why did you leave Canada in the first place?"

I daren't tell her that I had no girlfriends. That having been born dirty-minded I had thought in London maybe, in Paris certainly, the girls . . . Instead, I say, "Well, it was a cultural desert, wasn't it? In London, I could see the Sadler's Wells Ballet, plays by Terence Rattigan. If overcome with a need to see The Popular Stars of Prague, I could hop on a plane and jolly well see them. *In their natural environment.*"

I arrived in Montreal late in June.

"QUEEN LEADS CELEBRATIONS," ran the July 1st headline in the Montreal *Star*. "Canada is 100 years young today and Queen Elizabeth is doing her royal best to make it a real blast." Dominion Day, Prime Minister Pearson declared handsomely, belonged to all of us: "Every one of you, and every Canadian before you, has had some part, however humble and unsung, in building the magnificent structure that we honour and salute today."

Mr. Pearson, once feared to be an intellectual, showed himself a most regular (dare I say all-American?) guy in a recent interview with *Macleans*. Asked who was the greatest man he had ever met, he replied: "If you mean the man—leaving my father out—who made the greatest impression on me personally, it would be Mr. Downey, a teacher in my public school in Peterborough, when I was a boy."

"Can you recall anything that you're now ashamed of?"

"Considering that I've lived 70 years, I have a reasonable immunity from guilt. But I certainly have done some things

I later regretted. I cheated in geography class once when I was in Grade 6 or 7, I think, and I've never forgotten it."

Canadians, notably reticent in the past, flooded the Dominion Day newspapers with self-congratulatory ads. Typical was the full page run by Eaton's, our largest department store chain, which asked, "WHO ARE YOU, CANADA?" Roaring back came the unastonishing answer, ". . . the young giant. The young giant of the North. . . ." Without a doubt, the most imaginative of the Dominion Day ads began:

> A GROWING NATION . . .
>
> A GROWING PROFESSION . . .
>
> A GROWING FIRM . . .

> In just 100 years, our nation has grown to assume a leading position in the world . . . a position of which all Canadians can be justifiably proud as we observe our Centennial.
> Canadian funeral service has grown, too, always keeping in step with changing times . . . And at D.A. Collins Funeral Homes, where we've been serving for 54 out of Canada's 100 years, progress . . .

Canada, ninety-eight years without a flag, went so far as to commission a Toronto ad agency to produce a Centennial song. "What we needed," an executive vice-president of the agency told a reporter, "was a grabber. A stirring flag-waver that would make everybody feel, 'Gee, this is a real good country.'" Bobby Gimby, a radio jingle writer, came up with the grabber, which has been a fantastic success:

CA-NA-DA

(One little two little three Canadians)

WE LOVE THEE

(Now we are twenty million)

CA-NA-DA
(Four little five little six little Provinces)
PROUD AND FREE
(Now we are ten and the Territories—sea to sea)
North, South, East, West
There'll be happy times
Church bells will ring, ring, ring
It's the hundredth anniversary of
Con-fed-er-a-tion
Ev'-ry-bo-dy sing, to-geth-er

CA-NA-DA
(Un petit deux petit trois Canadiens)
NOTRE PAY-EE (Pays)
(Maintenant nous sommes vingt millions)

CA-NA-DA
(Quatre petites cinq petites six petites Provinces)
LON-GUE VIE
(Et nous sommes dix plus les Territoires—Lon-gue vie)
Hur-rah! Vive le Canada!
Three cheers, hip, hip, hooray!
Le Centenaire!
That's the order of the day
Frère Jacques, Frère Jacques
Merrily we roll along
To-geth-er, all the way.

1967 being our big year, there was a tendency to measure all things Canadian, and so the Canadian Authors' Association sent out a questionnaire to writers asking, among other things,

> What contemporary prose writer(s) has the best chance of still being read in 2000 A.D.?.............................
> How many words a year do you write?....................

How many words a year do you sell?. . . . .
As a writer what do you most often wish for: inspiration, ideas,
better research facilities, an agent, a public relations man, more
markets, higher royalties, a grant, more hours to write, etc.
. . . .
NOTE: Please answer only in terms of the Canadian scene in all
questions—whether specified or not.

Enclosed was a copy of *The Canadian Author and Bookman*,
the Association's quarterly, in which I found an ad for *Yarns
of the Yukon*, by Herman G. Swerdloff, with rave reviews
from *Alaska Highway News* and *R.C.M.P. Quarterly*; and a
critical study of Margaret Laurence (*The Stone Angel, A Jest
of God*) that began: "Margaret (Wemyss) Laurence was born
with a pen in her hand and a story in her heart." There was
also a double-page spread of poems by expatriates with the
corporate title HELLO CANADA. One of the poems was "from
homesick Maggie Dominic in New York," who wrote: "This
year, 1966, as prompted by Premier Joseph R. Smallwood,
is Come Home Newfoundlander Year. Being a Newfoundlander and a writer, I was asked to compose a poem, com-
memorating C.H.Y./66 for Newfoundland. . . . I have been
published in the United States, Canada, and most recently
India."

The C.A.A. not only held its 1967 conference at Expo,
but also summoned a Congress of Universal Writers to
"deal definitively with the role of the author (creator of
fiction, interpreter of universal truth, ambassador of good-will,
agitator, reformer, propagandist, inventor of language, etc.
. . .)." The USSR sent Alexander Chakovsky, editor of the
Literary Gazette, and the Reader's Digest (Canada) Ltd.
shipped us James Michener. Already gathered in Montreal
were such Canadian writers as Bluebell Phillips, Phoebe Er-
skine Hyde, Fanny Shulman, Grace Scrimgeour, Una Wardel-
worth, and Madeline Kent de Espinosa. Opening night, there

was a party for Universal Writers, but though it was sponsored by the largest of Canadian distilleries, Seagram's, nothing more potent than coffee was served. At the meeting following the party, a friend reported, the ladies stood up one by one to announce how their branch regional histories were going. It was all very dull, my friend said, until suddenly, one lady rose to announce *she* had just finished a book called *Ripe and Ready*. As things turned out, the lady had not, to quote the *Bookman*, "prostituted her talent by writing sex-dripping prose." *Ripe and Ready* was in fact a history of apples.

"It's just great to be a Canadian this year," as John David Hamilton wrote in the *New Statesman*. "It's as if we suddenly turned on, in the hippie sense, when our hundredth birthday arrived. . . . At any rate, we are in the midst of an earthquake of national pride—for the first time in our history." Yes; and the quake has yielded a mountain of non-books, from the reasonably priced *Life* library-like Canadian Centennial Library (*Great Canadians, Great Canadian Writing, Great Canadian Sports Stories*, etc.), through a Beginning Reader's McGraw-Hill series on the ten provinces, to the overpriced and exceedingly pretentious *To Everything There Is a Season*, a picture book by Roloff Beny (Viking Press, $25). Mr. Beny introduces his book, somewhat grandiosely, with a quotation from Hermann Hesse: "He looked around him as if seeing the world for the first time. . . ." And yet, *To Everything There Is a Season*, like all picture books I've seen on Canada, as well as many an old calendar, manages to contain all the clichés, albeit "poetically" seen. There is, for instance, the photograph of the age-old rocks beaten into egg-shape by the timeless sea; we are given the essential snow-shrouded tree; the ripe and ready apples rotting on the ground; the obligatory field of wild flowers; the autumnal woods; the Quebec churches etc. etc. etc. The truth is that though Mr. Beny is by trade a photographer, it is his prose style that singles his

volume out for special interest. Comparing himself to a contemporary Ulysses, allowing that his collection of photographs
is both "retrospective and prophetic," he writes that his was
a personal odyssey, a voyage of discovery and rediscovery.
Mr. Beny came to Canada via "Olympian heights," risking
"the *son et lumière* of Wagnerian thunderstorms," which is
to say, like most of us, he flew. His findings however were
singular: ". . . the serene stretches of the St. Lawrence recalled the sacred Ganges; the South Saskatchewan . . . was
the Tagus River which loops the fabled city of El Greco—
Toledo . . . Ottawa, its Gothic silhouette reflected in the
river, was Mont Saint Michel . . . and Calgary . . . was
Teheran, which boasts the same cool, dry climate and poplar
trees."

The last time I had been in Montreal, my home town, was
in 1964. "Québec Libre" was freshly painted on many a wall,
and students were fixing stickers that read "Québec Oui
Ottawa Non" on car windows. Militant French-Canadian
Separatism, and not Expo, was the talking point. I had returned to Montreal, as I wrote in *Encounter* at the time, on
Queen Victoria's birthday, a national holiday in Canada. A
thousand policemen were required to put down a French-
Canadian Separatist demonstration. Flags were burned, a
defective bomb was planted on Victoria Bridge, and a
wreath was laid at the *Monument aux Patriots*, which marks
the spot where twelve men were executed after the 1837–38
rebellion. The city was feverish. André Laurendeau, then
editor of *Le Devoir*, developed the popular theory of "Le
Roi Nègre," that is to say, that the real rulers of Quebec
(the English, represented by the Federal Government in
Ottawa) used a French-Canadian chieftain (former, and once
all-powerful, Provincial Premier Duplessis) to govern the
French, just as colonial powers used African puppets to keep
their tribes in order. André Malraux, in town to open a

"France in Canada" exhibition, told the City Council, "France needs you. We will build the next civilization together." Malraux added that he had brought a personal message from General de Gaulle. It was that "Montreal was France's second city. He wanted this message to reach you. . . . You are not aware of the meaning you have for France. There is nowhere in the world where the spirit of France works so movingly as it does in the province of Quebec."

Naturally, this made for an uproar, so that the next day at a hastily summoned press conference Malraux said, "The mere thought that French Canada could become politically or otherwise dependent on France is a dangerous and even ridiculous one."

Since then, as we all know, De Gaulle himself has been and gone, shouting the Separatist slogan "Vive le Québec libre!" from the balcony of Montreal City Hall, and Prime Minister Pearson, rising to the occasion for once, declared that this was "unacceptable" to the Canadian Government. I doubt that De Gaulle's outburst, enjoyable as it was to *all* French Canadians, will make for more than a momentary Separatist resurgence, but it is worth noting that France has not always been so enamored of Quebec, a province which was largely pro-Vichy in sentiment during the war, and whose flag is still the *fleur-de-lis*.

In the summer of 1964, André d'Allemagne, one of the leaders of the RIN (Rassemblement pour l'Indépendance Nationale), told me that in his struggle for an independent state of Quebec he was opposed to violence, but, should his party be outlawed, he might be obliged to turn to it. "Like the *maquis*." D'Allemagne looked to the next Quebec provincial election in 1966 as the big test—and he wasn't the only one.

But, in 1966, the RIN, which claimed 8,500 militant members, failed to win a seat. Quebec, to almost everyone's astonishment, veered to the right again. Jean Lesage's reform Liberal Government, which had worked fairly well with Lester Pearson's Federal Government, also Liberal, was squeezed out, and the Union Nationale, the late Maurice Duplessis's graft-ridden toy for so many years, was returned, with a majority of two, under Daniel Johnson, largely because Lesage was moving too quickly for the backwoods villages and townships.

In the summer of 1967, I returned to Montreal in time for the St. Jean Baptiste parade on June 23. St. Jean Baptiste is the patron saint of Quebec. In 1964, for the first time, he was no longer played by a boy in the annual parade. Instead, he was represented by an adult, and the sheep that had accompanied him in former years was tossed out. That year's St. Jean Baptiste parade was a dull, tepid affair. Minor officials and French-Canadian *vedettes* riding in open cars were followed by a seemingly endless run of unimaginative floats. Certainly the mood a week before De Gaulle's visit was not one to make for double-locks in Westmount Mansions, where Montreal's richest Wasps live. If only three years before, English-speaking Canadians had been running scared, then in 1967, whenever the so-called "Quiet Revolution" came up, it was as a joke. "Have you heard the one about the Pepsi [French Canadian], watching hockey on TV, who lost a hundred dollars on a Toronto goal against Montreal?" "No." "He lost fifty dollars on the goal. And another fifty on the replay." (The replay being the instant TV rerun of the goal just scored.)

In the early Sixties, French Canadians justifiably complained that while it was necessary for them to speak fluent English to qualify for most jobs, English-speaking Canadians were not obliged to know French. English Canada's haste to remedy this imbalance by hiring French Canadians, sometimes indiscriminately, spawned another joke. A man sitting by a pool sees a lady drowning. "Help, help," she cries. The man rushes over to the French-Canadian lifeguard and shouts, "Aren't you going to do anything?" "I can't swim," he says. "What! You're a lifeguard and you can't swim?" "I don't have to. I'm bilingual."

Then newly elected Quebec Premier Daniel Johnson, eager to demonstrate that he was his people's champion, put through a decree that made the use of French obligatory in all inscriptions on packaged foods and tins . . . which led to speculation among Jews about the labels on the next year's matzohs.

Montreal had always seemed to me an unusually handsome and lively city, but in early 1967 the mounting hyperbole in Expo-inspired articles in American and British publications made me apprehensive. A case in point is the London *Sunday Times*, whose color supplement on Canada included a piece with the title, "Montreal: Canada's Answer to Paris, London and New York." In the same issue, Penelope Mortimer, back from a flying trip to Montreal, wrote that she had just been able "to observe the customs of some of the most lively, uninhibited, civilized, humane, and adventurous people in the world today—the Canadians. . . ." I also had serious doubts about Expo itself. If it was ludicrous but somehow touching that Canada, after ninety-eight years and an endlessly embarrassing debate in Ottawa, had voted itself a flag, it seemed exceedingly late in the day to bet $800-million on so unsophisticated an idea as a world's fair dedicated to the theme of "Man and His World" (*Terre des Hommes*). Let me say at once, then, that Expo was, as they say, awfully good fun and in the best possible taste.

Even more impressive to an old Montrealer, perhaps, were the changes that Expo had wrought on the city itself. On earlier visits to Montreal, during the previous twelve years, I had been asked again and again if I could "recognize" the city, and of course I always could. But this time, after an absence of only three years, I was in fact overwhelmed by the difference. Suddenly, all the ambitious building of twelve years, the high-rise apartments, the downtown skyscrapers, the slum clearance projects, the elegant new metro, the Place Ville Marie, the Place des Arts, the new network of express highways, the new hotels, had added up to another city. If, for many years, the choice open to me (and other Canadian writers, painters, and filmmakers living abroad) was whether to suffer home or remain an expatriate, the truth quite simply was that the choice no longer exists. Home had been pulverized, bulldozed, and spilled into the St. Lawrence to create an artificial island: Île Notre Dame. Home, suddenly, was terrifyingly affluent. Montreal was the richest-looking city I'd seen in years.

Many of the new skyscrapers, it's true, were of the familiar biscuit-box variety, but there was also a heartening drive to restore the old quarter, Bonsecours Market, the narrow cobblestone streets that surround it, and the baroque City Hall. The antique market was booming. Montreal was even publishing its very own fervent right-wing magazine, *Canada Month*. In the most recent issue, Irving Layton, the country's best known "most outspoken, exuberant and controversial" poet, had come out for American policy in Vietnam. "I think the Americans are fighting this war, not because they want to overthrow Chinese communism, or for that matter, even the communism of Uncle Ho-Ho"; rather, he felt, America's sole interest was its own territorial security.

I was in Montreal twice in 1967—the first time just a week before Expo opened, and it was then that I first visited the American pavilion, Buckminster Fuller's transparent geodesic sphere, which is still, to my mind, the most fascinating

202 / Notes on an Endangered Species

structure at Expo. The sphere, twenty stories high, 250 feet in diameter, the plastic skin held together by a network of triangulated aluminum tubes, was a delight to the eye seen from any angle, inside or out; and in fact dominated the Expo grounds. The lighthearted stuff on display inside had been severely criticized by the time I visited the sphere a second time, late in June, and the PR man who escorted me explained: "We try to tell all our colleagues in the media that this is not an exhibition. It's only meant to show the spirit symbolic of—well, you know."

Camp, he might have said. There were enormous stills of vintage Hollywood stars (Bogart, Gable, Joan Crawford) and a screen that ran great scenes from past movies, such as the chariot race from *Ben Hur*. On the next floor there was a display of pop art (Dine, Lichtenstein, Johns, Warhol), some pictures running as much as ten stories high. The highest floor was taken up with the inevitable display of spacecraft and paraphernalia. Briefly, it was the softest of all possible sells, radiating self-confidence.

The chunky British pavilion, designed by Sir Basil Spence, was meant to be self-mocking, and so it was, sometimes unintentionally. Embossed in concrete on an outside wall stands "BRITAIN," pointedly without the "GREAT," though the French inscription reads "GRANDE BRETAGNE." Inside, the glossy scenes of contemporary British life suggest what Malcolm Muggeridge has called Sunday Supplement living taken into the third dimension. The pretty hostesses, as I'm sure you've read elsewhere, are mini-skirted and carry Union Jack handbags. If the declared theme is "The Challenge of Change" then, endearingly, it reveals how this challenge has been met. Wall charts of British geniuses list numbered photographs (Dickens, 12; Turner, 82), and before each chart there stands a computer. Theoretically, one should be able to press a number on the computer and come up with a card crammed with information. In practice, at Expo as in contemporary Britain itself, all the computers were marked TEMPORARILY OUT OF ORDER.

With other, larger powers usurping Canada's traditional self-effacing stance, it fell on the host nation to play it straight. Outside the Canadian pavilion there was a decidedly non-joke Mountie on horseback, a sitting duck for camera-laden tourists in Bermuda shorts, who posed their children before him endlessly. Nearby stood Canada's People Tree. "As its name implies, the People Tree symbolizes the people of Canada. A stylized maple soaring to a height of 66 feet . . . it reflects the personal, occupational, and recreational activities of more than 20 million individuals. . . ." Briefly, a multicolored, illuminated magazine cover tree.

At the Tundra, the Canadian pavilion restaurant, it was possible to order buffalo bouchées or whale steak. Robert Fulford of the Toronto *Star* wrote that if the pavilion bar were really to represent Canada it would have to be "a pit of Muzak-drenched darkness . . . or, perhaps one of those sour-smelling enamel rooms in which waiters, wearing change aprons, slop glasses of draught beer all over the tables and patrons." Instead, it was well lit and handsomely designed, with authentic Eskimo murals.

The most truculent of the pavilions was the small one representing embattled Cuba, plastered with photographs of the revolution and headlines that ran to ATOMIC BLACKMAIL, DEATH, LSD, CIA, NAPALM. Outside the Czech pavilion, the most popular at Expo, the queues wound round and round, whole families waiting submissively in the sun for two, sometimes three, hours. Actually, none of the pavilion interiors was so gratifying as the gay Expo site itself, where I spent my most exhilarating hours simply strolling about. The improbable, even zany, pavilions were such a welcome change from the urban landscape we are all accustomed to: there were almost no cars, and the streets were astonishingly clean and quiet. Expo, only ten minutes from downtown Montreal by road or metro, lay on the island of Montreal proper, St. Helen's Island, and the artificially created island of Notre Dame. In the early Forties, when I was a boy in Montreal, St. Helen's Island was the untamed and gritty place to which working-class kids escaped for picnics and swims on sweltering summer days. There was, and still is, an old fort on the island. In 1940, Mayor Camillien Houde, a corrupt but engaging French-Canadian politician of Louisiana dimensions, was briefly interned there for advising young French-Canadians not to register for conscription in a British imperialist war. Houde's companions included communists, also rounded up by the RCMP, and baffled German-Jewish refugees, sent over from England where they had been classified as enemy aliens. Now the island is tricked out with lagoons, fountains, canals, and artificial lakes.

In the months before Expo opened, probably no individual structure was more highly publicized than Habitat 67, Moshe Safdie's prefabricated design for cheap, high-density housing, the novelty being that the roof of one apartment would serve as the garden terrace of another, and that the entire unit, looking rather like a haphazard pile of children's blocks, could be assembled by a crane slipped into place alongside. Without a doubt, this angular concrete block has no place in Montreal, with its long and bitter winters. Habitat 67 projecting out of a green hill in a tropical climate could be something else again.

In any event, I thought Expo was more likely to be remembered for its films rather than any particular building, save Buckminster Fuller's geodesic sphere. Films charged at you everywhere, from multiple and wrap-around screens, bounced off floors, stone walls, mirrors, and what-not. Alas, the pyrotechnics, the dazzling techniques, concealed, for the most part, nothing more than old-fashioned documentaries about life in Ontario, Czechoslovakia, Mod England, etc. The most highly touted and ambitious of these films, the Canadian National Film Board's *Labyrinth*, was also the most popular individual exhibit at Expo, its queues waiting as long as four hours.

Produced by Roman Kroiter, an undoubtedly talented filmmaker, housed in a specially constructed building, *Labyrinth* took more than two years and four and a half million dollars to make. Based on the legend of the Minotaur, *Labyrinth* was actually two films. The first, seen from multi-leveled galleries, was projected on two whopping big screens: one on a wall, the other on a sunken floor bed. At its most successful, it was tricky (child seen on wall screen throws a pebble *which lands with a splash* in a pool on floor screen) or aimed at creating vertigo (suddenly we are looking straight down a missile chute). From here, viewers groped their way through a spook-house-type maze into a multiscreened theatre, wherein we learned that man comes into this world bloody and wailing and leaves in a coffin. Unfortunately, in this case it would seem that it was life that is long and art that's short. En route to the grave, we were instructed that all men are brothers (black, white, and yellow men, popping to life, simultaneously on the multiscreen) and were treated to an occasional brilliant sequence such as the crocodile hunt. But two years in the making, four and a half million dollars spent . . . the return seemed both portentous and inadequate.

Finally, Expo did more for Canada's self-confidence than anything within memory. "By God, we did it! And generally we did it well," Pierre Berton wrote in *Macleans*.

"We're on the map," a friend told me. "They know who we are in New York now."

Hugo McPherson, head of the National Film Board, and a former professor of Canadian and American studies at the University of Western Ontario, said in an interview: "We have our own 'scene' in Canada now. . . . It's no longer fashionable, the way it used to be, for Canadians to knock everything Canadian. Perhaps Expo will be the event we'll all remember as the roadmark. I think it's going to be a vast Canadianizing force, not only in Quebec but all across the country. There's a new feeling of national gaiety and pride at Expo. . . ."

Others went even further, demanding an alarmingly high emotional return from what was after all only a world's fair. A good one, maybe even the most enjoyable one ever. However, within it there lay merely the stuff of a future nostalgic musical, not the myth out of which a nation is forged. Unless it is to be a Good Taste Disneyland.

"Êtes-vous canadien?"

$\mathcal{E}$*arly in April* 1969, *I discovered I was among the year's* Governor-General's Award winners for literature.

"You're accepting it," my Canadian publisher said, astonished.

"Yes."

"You're pleased, you're actually pleased."

"Yes, I am."

Several years earlier, a friend of mine had won the award for a collection of essays. At the reception in Government House, Ottawa, his wife, suddenly distressed, drove him into a corner. "He says he hasn't read it himself, but his maid did and liked it very much."

"No, no," my friend assured her, "his *aide*, he means his *aide*."

Traditionally, the GG, the Queen's very own Canadian second-floor maid, stands behind two major horse races: the Queen's Plate and the Governor-General's Awards (never more than six) for the best books of the year. Though one Queen's Plate winner, the fabulous Northern Dancer, also came first in the Kentucky Derby, so far no Governor-General's Award winner has ever been entered in the final heat for the Nobel. The first Governor-General's Awards were presented by Lord Tweedsmuir in 1937 to Bertram Brooker and T. B. Robertson, who, it's safe to say, are now remembered for nothing else. Among others who have officially signed the Canadian literary skies with their honor there are John Murray Gibson, Franklin S. McDowell, Alan Sullivan, Winifred Bambrick, William Sclater, and R. MacGregor Dawson. I could go on. I could go on and on, seemingly composing a letterhead with names fit to adorn only the most exclusive Montreal or Toronto law office. But, to be fair, in recent years the awards have also been presented to Morley Callaghan and Gabrielle Roy, Hugh MacLennan, Brian Moore, Rejean Ducharme, George Woodcock, Marshall McLuhan, and, posthumously, to Malcolm Lowry.

Until 1959, when the Canada Council took over the administration of the awards, the Governor-General forked out 50 guineas to the horse that won the Queen's Plate, but offered just a handshake (royal only by osmosis since Vincent Massey became the first Canadian-born GG in 1952), and a copy of your book signed in his own hand, to writers. The Canada Council, happily cognizant of the stuff that really excites this country's artistic types, tacked a $1,000 purse to the awards in 1959, raising the ante to $2,500 six years later. What had once been a stigma was now inspiring. It was also made respectable, because the Council saw to it that the judges' panel was literate. A new departure, for in years past the incomparable Canadian Authors' Association adjudicated the awards. "What, who, why, when," asks an editorial in the Association's *Author and Bookman*, "is a Canadian writer?"

> If a writer wants to make big money he will probably stop writing about Canada and almost certainly leave Canada. If a writer wants 'instant fame' he will very likely have to prostitute his talent by such things as writing sex-dripping prose or taking a deliberately shocking stand on a touchy subject.

This year's awards created a small uproar. THE ESTABLISH-
MENT BEWARE!, ran the headline in the Toronto *Globe and
Mail*, THESE AWARDS ARE WITH IT. Winners for 1968 were
Hubert Aquin, for his novel *Trou de mémoires*, Fernand
Dumont, for his sociological work *Le Lieu de l'homme*, and
Marie-Claire Blais, for her novel *Les Manuscrits de Pauline
Archange*. English-language writers were Leonard Cohen, for
his *Selected Poems*; Alice Munro, for her first book of short
stories, *Dance of the Happy Shades*; and me, for *Cocksure*,
a novel, and *Hunting Tigers Under Glass*, a collection of
essays.

Well now, the truth is we were a scurvy lot. Cohen, who
enjoys an immense campus following in Canada and the U.S.,
is a self-declared pot smoker. Hubert Aquin, a former vice-
president of the militantly separatist RIN party, was once
arrested and charged with car theft and being in possession of
a revolver. My novel, *Cocksure*, had been banned by the rest
of the white Commonwealth, not to mention W. H. Smith
in the mother country. Aquin, as was to be expected, turned
down the award instantly, the GG being anathema to him.
Fernand Dumont accepted the award, but two weeks later
donated his prize money to the separatist Parti Québecois.
Cohen, pondering the inner significance of the award in his
hotel in the Village, wavered. He told a Toronto *Star* reporter
he wasn't sure whether he would accept the award, it would
depend on how he felt when he got up that morning. In the
end, he didn't wait that long, but instead issued a statement
saying there was much in him that would like to accept the
award, but the poems absolutely forbid it.

Another reporter caught up with Cohen in Toronto and
asked him, yes, yes, but what, exactly, did he mean?

"Well, I mean they're personal and private poems. With any of
my other books I would have been happy to accept, but this one
is different. I've been writing these poems since I was 15, and

they're very private, their meaning would be changed. And there's another reason. I can't see myself standing up there and accepting the award while there's so much unhappiness in the world, so much violence, while so many of my friends are in jail."

I accepted the award at once, but with mixed feelings. As a writer I was pleased and richer, but as a father of five, mortified. When *Cocksure* was published in Canada, the reviewer in the Montreal *Star* revealed that I had churned out an obvious potboiler with all the lavatory words. The man who pronounces on books in the New Brunswick *Daily Gleaner* put me down for a very filthy fellow and warned parents in Montreal that I would be teaching their children at Sir George Williams University, where I was to be writer-in-residence for a year. Others denounced me as a pornographer. And now the ultimate symbol of rectitude in our country, the GG himself, would actually reward me for being obscene. For the establishment's sake, I couldn't help but be ashamed.

The Governor-General, I was assured, had read and loathed my novel, but unlike Aquin or Cohen, he did turn up for prize-giving day. Which is not to say he didn't protest. "The Governor-General is a patron of all the arts, but has little time to master any," he said. "But I do have my views, literary as well as political, even though, as in the Speech from the Throne, I have to refrain from expressing them."

Many Canadians feel the Governor-General is an anomaly; his office at best tiresome, at worst divisive. Not so old Johnny Diefenbaker, who is fond of complaining that Prime Minister Trudeau is an anti-monarchist. Diefenbaker says that before Trudeau became PM, he was asked how he would have voted on a resolution calling for the abolition of the monarchy, and replied: "If I had been completely logical, I would have abstained because I . . . you know I don't give a damn." Trudeau has denied this in the House, saying, "I believe the monarchy is an important symbol to many people. I think more energy would be lost in Canada by debating this subject than would be gained by our institutions."

My own earliest recollection of the monarchy goes back to the war years, when we used to purchase calendars with toothy photographs of Elizabeth and Margaret in their Brownie uniforms. On my way to school every morning I passed another monarchical symbol, the armory of the Canadian Grenadier Guards, and outside, under a funny fur hat, there always stood some tall unblinking *goy*. "If they were ordered to do it," I was told, "they'd march over a cliff. There's discipline for you."

I have, in my time, lived under seven Governors-General. Only one of them, Lord Tweedsmuir, was abhorrent to me, because under the name of John Buchan he wrote thrillers choked with anti-Semitic nonsense.

Our present Governor-General, however, is hardly the sort to arouse strong feelings. Daniel Roland Michener is an upright, compact little man with curly grey hair and a natty moustache; he has, in this age of rock, the manner of the *maître d'hôtel* in a palm court restaurant. Mrs. Michener, a more obdurate figure, is a case of life improving on the art of Grant Wood. She was born to chaperone the dance in the small town high school gym.

All of us assembled in the reception room at Government House on May 13 rose respectfully when the Micheners, preceded by uniformed aides, drifted in, their smiles frozen; but I, for one, would have found Mr. Michener more credible proffering that large black menu than mounting the dais with such confidence. Behind the Governor-General and his lady, bolstering their acquired royalty as it were, hung enormous portraits of Queen Elizabeth and Prince Philip. The portraits were resoundingly awful, not so much poor likenesses as badly proportioned grotesqueries. Roland Michener, rising to address us, seemed distracted, his manner that of a man who had just come from being photographed accepting a gift of snowshoes from an Eskimo child and must push on to award a Brotherhood plaque to a western mayor in a ten gallon hat, rimless glasses, and high-heeled boots.

The speech Mr. Michener read to us from small cards made for some nervous smiles and at least one giggle from the assembled literati. Observing that all but one of the six award winners were from Quebec, he noted that this might not be a coincidence. "Politics in Quebec today are tense . . . social order is in the process of rapid change and upheaval. This is the atmosphere which stirs people to write more and sometimes better, and to produce exciting paintings, sculpture, theatre, and films."

Alas, the writings of Cohen and Marie-Claire Blais are equally nonpolitical. They have been living in the United States for years, and I am normally rooted in London.

Finally, the award winners were summoned to the Governor-General one by one to accept leather-bound copies of their work signed by Mr. Michener. When my turn came, the Governor-General asked me, "*Êtes-vous canadien?*"

Startled, I said, "*Oui.*"

He then went on to congratulate me fulsomely in French. *Is it possible,* I thought, appalled, *that the Governor-General is a covert Separatist?* If not, why, when I answered yes to his question, had he assumed I was necessarily French-speaking? The mind boggled. In any event, once he was done, I said, "*Merci.*" I did not correct the Governor-General. In my case, it was *noblesse oblige.*

A Note on the Type

This book was set in Electra, a type face designed by William Addison Dwiggins for the Mergenthaler Linotype Company and first made available in 1935. Electra cannot be classified as either "modern" or "old-style." It is not based on any historical model, and hence does not echo any particular period or style of type design. It avoids the extreme contrast between thick and thin elements that marks most modern faces, and is without eccentricities that catch the eye and interfere with reading. In general, Electra is a simple, readable type face that attempts to give a feeling of fluidity, power, and speed.

W. A. Dwiggins (1880–1956) began an association with the Mergenthaler Linotype Company in 1929 and over the next twenty-seven years designed a number of book types, the most interesting of which are the Metro Series, Electra, Caledonia, Eldorado and Falcon.

Composed, printed and bound by
The Book Press, Brattleboro, Vt.
Typography and binding design by
VIRGINIA TAN